CALIFORNIA DEMON

CALIFORNIA DEMON BOOK 1

DEBRA DUNBAR

I squatted down behind the burned-out truck and wished I was somewhere else. Aruba. Jamaica. Cabo. Hell, I'd go for Detroit at this point. The air shimmered with the heat. The smell of melted tar and rancid garbage filled my nose. A bead of sweat trickled down the back of my neck and I resisted the urge to scratch, unwilling to break my focus even though I was ready to give up on this particular job.

A jogger turned down the street and ran past where I was hidden. A jogger. I rolled my eyes marveling at the foolishness of people. That someone would care so much about their fitness routine that they'd go out for a run in what residents now called New Hell was the epitome of stupid, even though his Lycra shorts and tank top were accessorized by a shoulder holster and pistol. Jogging with an open carry. This is what the world had come to. Idiot should have just bought a treadmill.

A Buick sedan that looked like it came out of a '70s movie set came careening the opposite way down the street, swerving and nearly hitting the jogger as the passenger yelled something rude out the window. The jogger jumped out of the way, pulling the pistol from his shoulder holster and swearing as he turned and popped a shot off at the car.

The Buick hit the brakes then slammed into reverse. The jogger widened his stance, shooting into the open space where the vehicle's back window had once been. The man leaning out the passenger side window returned fire. The jogger danced around, still shooting. A few stray bullets hit the burned-out truck, pinging against the hood and knocking a spray of mortar from the brick wall behind me into my hair.

This was the hit I'd been tipped off about? This? I'd expected a drug-deal setup, not an armed jogger getting shot by two yahoos in an ancient Buick.

The car swerved, then abruptly sped up. With a yelp, the jogger sprinted across the street toward a metal dumpster, still firing. The Buick's passenger slumped from the window, dropping his gun. The jogger tried to dive for cover behind the dumpster, coming up short and hitting the ground just in time for the Buick to run him over with a sickening crunch. The back of the sedan slammed into the corner of the dumpster, sliding sideways and coming to a rest against a graffiti covered wall.

I stayed put, biding my time. When no one got out of the Buick, I made my move. Sprinting forward, I scooped the pistol off the pavement and darted behind the damaged dumpster.

The pistol I'd just grabbed was a Glock 43. Nice. Small. Perfect for concealed carry. Glocks could take a beating, so I was sure being bounced onto the street hadn't done any significant damage. I dropped the magazine and checked it as well as the chamber. There were still a few bullets left, so I snapped the magazine back in, then stuffed the pistol into my pocket.

No one had emerged from the car, or come racing down the street, so I tentatively made my way forward. The jogger was flat as roadkill on the 405. I could tell by his scant attire that he didn't have anything of value besides the one pistol and maybe a few bucks in his pocket, so I turned my attention instead to the occupants of the Buick.

From the condition of his skull, the driver was clearly dead. I slunk around the front of the car and checked the passenger, who was also dead. Then I eased my own pistol out of my shoulder harness and peered into the backseat.

Empty. Well, empty of bodies or living beings, that was.

I glanced around to make sure no one else was coming, then stuck my weapon back in the harness and got to work. Five minutes later the two bodies were out of the car and dumped in the road. I'd scored another 9mm, a bent spare magazine off the squished jogger that I tossed aside, and a .45 off the driver, but the real haul was what I'd seen in the backseat—five cases full of ammo.

In New Hell, guns were everywhere. Bullets were the commodity everyone paid top dollar for. The backseat of the Buick had the equivalent of what I'd make in three months scavenging.

Looking up and down the street to make sure I was still alone, I broke open the case full of nine millimeter bullets and stuffed as many boxes as I could into the pockets of my cargo pants and the small backpack I carried with me. I could hardly move with the weight, and had barely made a dent in the contents of the back seat. Fuck. I didn't want to leave this behind, which meant I'd need to leave my motorcycle behind and take the ancient Buick instead,

Okay. Decision made. If I was going to take this piece of shit and drive it to the pawnshop, then I might as well check the trunk. For all I knew there was an entire family of dead bodies back there.

I waddled around behind the car and popped the trunk. Holy shit. I'd assumed the low-rider state of the sedan was from either bad springs or dead bodies, not a fucking dozen additional cases of bullets.

There was a fortune in ammo in this crappy old car. A *fortune*. I caught my breath realizing that after I sold this, I might finally have enough to get us out of here.

I shut the trunk and wiped my sweaty hands on my shirt, suddenly afraid that this bounty would be snatched away from me. A pistol and the guns I'd stolen off the dead guys wouldn't mean shit if a gang waltzed into the street right now and pointed their weapons at my head. I only had two hands, and I wasn't the best shot with my left. I'd pick off one or two if I was lucky, but in the end I'd be dead on the street and some fucking ganger would be driving off with my salvage haul.

I needed to take this Buick and drive like Satan herself was after me.

With another quick, panicked look around for any passerby who might decide to get in on this windfall, I ran to the driver's side door. Eyeing the disgusting combination of blood and brain matter all over the dash and steering wheel, I steeled myself for what was going to be a truly gross drive. If I could get this thing started, that is.

The sound of footsteps from across the street sent me into panic mode. Instincts took over and I pulled my pistol from the harness and spun around, squatting behind the sedan. A woman across the street dressed in police-issue combat attire was doing the same behind the burned-out truck. There was a pistol in each of her hands, and the one in her right had a white barrel, meaning that it was modified to negate any magical ability I might have, or any spell I might have purchased.

"Drop the gun," she shouted, the shimmer of a magical shield like a blue mist around her.

Anti-magic guns shot the equivalent of paint balls. They disarmed demons, elves, shifters, and any magical spell in progress, but beyond that they did little more than ruin your clothes and bruise your skin. She had a big fucking pistol, so I was assuming the bruise would be stupendous, and I'd be breathless long enough for her to nail me with the more conventional pistol in her other hand—the one that fired flesh-and-bone destroying bullets.

There was one of her and one of me, but no doubt her partner was nearby. And either way, I wasn't going up against a cop. They might not have all that much power in our new world, but I didn't want to risk my salvager's license on a backstreet dustup.

I lifted my hands, dropped the magazine from the pistol and set both it and the weapon on the hood of the Buick.

"Just picking up scraps," I called over to her.

She straightened a bit at that, but motioned with the one of her pistols for me to move out from behind the sedan. I complied, walking slowly because I had thirty pounds of ammo in the pockets of my cargo pants.

"Salvage number?"

Fuck. So much for selling all this shit without paying taxes. I'd be lucky if I walked away with grocery money now. I'd be lucky if she just took a bribe and let me walk away with anything.

"Eight six four, nine two four, eight six one five one."

She repeated the numbers into the comm on her shoulder, then lowered her pistols a fraction as a voice on the other end confirmed my name and status.

"Leave the car and get going," she told me with wave of a gun.

I ground my teeth in frustration. So much for my windfall. I hated to leave the biggest haul I'd ever seen behind, but I wasn't going to risk getting pulverized by this woman. Plus, I could hear sirens in the distance, quickly getting closer.

"Can I take my gun?" I motioned toward the pistol on the hood of the Buick.

She nodded, and I scooped it up, snapping the magazine back in and sticking it in my holster. It wasn't worth much, but I kinda liked this gun. Holding my breath, I grabbed my bulging backpack from the front seat of the car and tried to casually walk away.

"Hey Alvaro," the cop shouted after me. I froze and glanced over my shoulder at her. "Leave the backpack."

Fuck. I set the backpack on the hood of the car, hoping she wouldn't make me empty my pockets too.

"Make sure you fence those bullets in your pockets under your account," the cop called out. "I'll be checking later."

Fucking taxes. And who was she to get all snotty about my being legal when she was probably going to skim most, if not all, of the ammo in the Buick for her own personal gain? But there was nothing I could do about it. Well, there was plenty I could do about it, but the chances of my coming out of that fight alive were slim to none. I grumbled under my breath and continued down the street.

"Scene's clear," I heard her say into her transmitter. "No one here but a Vulture, and I sent her on her way. No, there's nothing here. Only three dead bodies and a worthless car."

Just as I suspected. She and her partner were going to take the whole lot. I clenched my jaw and forced myself to keep walking, thankful that I'd at least gotten away with the pistols and what was in my pockets.

* * *

BEAR STATE PAWNBROKERS was always my go-to when I had salvage to fence. It had gotten to the point where the place felt like a second home to me. I parked my bike on the slice of dirt between the sidewalk and the road, then smoothed back the snarled hair that had blown free of my ponytail before taking off my bug-encrusted sunglasses. Someone had stolen my helmet a few days back so I'd been driving around without one. Hopefully I'd come across a helmet I could steal myself, because driving on the freeway without one was a total bitch.

I walked to the entrance. Stepping through the heavy glass door with the metal grate, I inhaled the familiar musty odor of antiques mixed with the smell of lubricating oil and tobacco. Little round cameras lined the ceiling, recording the store from every possible angle. I made my way past bicycles and motorized scooters, shelves of used drills and circular saws, and the glass cases packed with jewelry desperate people had sold for pennies on the hundred dollars.

The man behind the counter was brown as a walnut and just as round. His face was heavily lined, but his dark eyes were sharp. The limp he walked with was deceptive. Bags could move with the speed of a high school track star when he needed to, and the shotgun he kept behind his counter wasn't just for show.

"Eden!" The man smiled and spread his arms wide, as if he were going to hug me across the three-foot counter. "What you got for me today?"

"Not as much as I was hoping to have." I set the guns on the counter, pulling the magazines out and clearing them first. Then I started removing boxes of bullets from the pockets of my cargo pants, separating them from the guns.

Bags chuckled. "How much do those pants of yours hold? Are they magic?"

"I wish." If they were, then I would have gotten away with the entire contents of that Buick.

"Nice." Bags surveyed my haul while I waited. After a few minutes of hemming and hawing, he threw out a number.

It was a fair number—Bags was always honest with me—but I needed more. The last year had been tough, and I didn't want to risk us staying any longer than we had to, so I countered, and we did a our typical back and forth, complete with lots of hand-waving and dramatic exclamations about how one of us was going to starve, and how this deal would bring the other to financial ruin. Finally, we settled on a number that we both could live with.

Then I recited my account number and watched as Bags's porcupine-like eyebrows drifted toward the top of his bald head.

"Sure you wanna make this legit?"

It wasn't a big haul. Normally I'd keep this one under the table, but...

"A cop saw me," I explained. "She's got my salvage number."

Bags winced and scratched his chin. "Those tax guys scare me more than the cops."

"Me too." The cops might have some magic on their side, but they worked for humans. Tax collectors didn't.

"Won't be much left once I deduct their cut," Bags warned me.

It was more than a warning. This was my last chance to fudge what I'd brought in and keep some of it under the table. Or keep all of it under the table.

I *needed* this money. I needed *all* of this money. I was so close to getting us the fuck out of here, away from this city with its demons and gangs and back into the States where there were gangs, but there weren't demons. At least, I didn't think there were.

It wasn't a huge haul. If the cop filed it, the tax collectors wouldn't prioritize such a modest sum. I planned to be gone before they came calling, and if we weren't, the most I'd probably suffer for this infraction would be a fine and a beating.

"Keep it off the books," I told Bags, feeling my stomach twist as I voiced the words. That cop didn't know exactly how much I'd stashed in my pockets. Plus, she was probably too busy diverting the profits from all that ammo away from the city's coffers and into her own to bother checking up on my measly haul.

It wasn't just that cop, though. I was trusting that no one had been watching me, that no one had followed me, that this place wasn't magically bugged and that all the people who might know what I was doing wouldn't sell me out.

A fine and a beating. Probably a bad beating, but I'd survive. It was worth the risk. I was so close to having enough money to get us the fuck out of here. So close.

Bags hesitated just long enough for me to have the option of changing my mind, then tore up the ticket that showed a sale by Eden Alvaro, registered Vulture. I then accepted more cash than the pawn broker would normally have given me had this been an above-board deal.

The man wasn't being altruistic. Those bullets he'd bought without any paperwork wouldn't need to be taxed as he sold them. I profited. He profited. Now we both needed to make sure neither of us got caught.

Bags had a huge storeroom downstairs with all sorts of contraband stuff. I knew this because I'd bought things from him on occasion—things that weren't readily available in New Hell at any price. Bags could have gouged me big time, but he hadn't because he knew his life depended on me keeping my mouth shut, and a reasonable profit was a good trade-off for not pissing a business associate off to the point they squealed.

The boxes of bullets quickly vanished to some secret place under the counter.

"Wanna sell the guns?" he asked.

"Think I'm gonna keep the Glock 43, but I'll sell the 17 and the Sig P220"

Bags grunted. "Really? The 17 is the gold standard of Glocks. And if you want something to stay dead, a .45 is better than a 9."

"I've already got two 17s, and I'm not accurate enough with a .45. It's got too much kick." If bullets grew on trees, I'd keep the Sig Sauer and pick up one of the supersized magazines that were available now that nothing was illegal. That way I could just keep shooting until I managed to actually hit my target.

But bullets were a premium, and I didn't trust my accuracy with anything larger than a 9mm.

"You want cash or trade?" Bags asked, knowing my answer.

"What do you have in the pharmacy?"

"Amoxicillin. Warfarin." He grinned. "Nordette."

I snorted. Like I needed birth control pills. "I'll take as much Warfarin as I can get and the rest in Amoxicillin"

He nodded, then vanished into the back. I heard his heavy footsteps descend, then a few minutes later coming back. He handed over two prescription bottles. The antibiotic just had the brand and dosage, but the blood thinner was labeled for some guy named Howard Fillistino.

I didn't bother wondering whether Howard Fillistino was dead or trading his medicines in for cash. None of that mattered in this new world we were living in.

"Thanks Bags. Got any tips? I could use another good haul this week—preferably in the next day or two."

There was a symbiotic relationship between Vultures and pawnbrokers. Bags's biggest customers were the gangs and the police. When he had a big buy, trouble was coming. And trouble meant an opportunity to pick over the corpses for salvage.

"The Southside Militia is planning to make a move on Gray Dogs, but I don't know precisely when."

I pursed my lips. That *would* be a bloodbath. Militias in New Hell were like privateers. Any group could band together, apply to the state's Governor for a charter, and be granted license to take out the riffraff. They kept what they found, only having to pay tax on what they sold. And all they needed to do for this license-to-kill-and-steal was to abide by some very loose, vague rules—rules that militias rarely followed.

"It's gonna be a party," Bags warned.

"Oh, I'll bet." Every licensed Vulture in town as well as casual looters would be there, ready to jump in and pick up the pieces. We'd not only be fighting each other for the best scraps, we'd be fighting whoever was left standing. The militias weren't known for leaving anything of value behind, and neither were the gangs. The best-case scenario would be if everyone died, or was so badly injured that a quick shot could take them out.

And even that best-case scenario still left me scrapping with several dozen very motivated individuals.

If I were cautious, I'd skip the whole thing. I had money in my pocket. There was no sense in being greedy and getting killed. I'd gotten really lucky and scored today, but this sort of thing didn't always happen. Most of my takes were small stuff here and there that barely put food on the table. What I had in my pocket and what we'd managed to save so far wasn't quite enough. Any extra money I could manage to snag up before we ran for the border would help us make a new life.

"Think they'll hit on accounting day?" I asked.

"That's what you, me, and everyone else in this city thinks," Bags replied.

If I was going to start admitting my sins, greed wouldn't be one of them. Caution had kept my blood on the inside of my body so far this year, and for that I was grateful. I needed to remember that before I did something reckless and put myself and the people I cared about in danger.

But…

I'd go, wait, and watch. If I was sharp, patient, and cautious, opportunity might present itself.

And I sure could use another bit of luck like I'd had today.

CHAPTER 2

I parked my bike in the driveway beside the sun-bleached red Nissan Sentra and walked up the cracked sidewalk to a small one-story house. I had keys, but I knocked on the door. It was a ritual. It was practice. It was my way of keeping the girls on their toes.

An eerie silence greeted me. The curtain beside the door twitched and I saw the nose of a pistol barrel. Looking up at the peephole, I lifted the grocery bags and smiled.

The knob rattled and the door opened a bit, still restricted by two chains. Dark eyes in a pale face peered out at me.

"It's me," I announced. "And my favorite color is bacon."

I heard a giggle. The door closed, chains rattled, then the door opened again—this time wide enough for me to enter.

"It's Eden," Nevarra called out, lowering the pistol and setting it on the table before coming forward to wrap her arms around me.

"Careful. I've got eggs," I told her as I shifted the bags to embrace her one-handed, then reaching out another hand to pull Sadie in for a group hug.

For a solid thirty seconds I did nothing but hold the two girls close. Feelings that had been absolutely unfamiliar ten years ago flooded through me. Living here had changed me, and I still wasn't all that sure those changes were for the better.

Nevarra pulled away first. "Aunt Bea's making stew." She took one of the bags from me.

I was glad Bea was home. After the demons came, her company had closed and left California. She'd managed last year to find work doing the books at a trash collection company. It paid less than half of her former job and often required unpaid overtime, but it was better than nothing.

"Did you bring candy?" Sadie asked into my shirt.

I set the other bag on the floor and extracted a small plastic bag of gummies. "You need to share them, okay?"

Sadie squealed and danced in excitement, snatching the gummies from my hand. Candy was almost as expensive as meat, but I always found something to bring the girls. They'd had enough shit in their life. Every little bit of sweet helped counteract that.

If all went well, their future would be full of sweets.

I picked up the bag and took the other back from Nevarra. "You guys go in your room and divide the gummies. I need to talk to Aunt Bea in private."

Sadie took off, clutching the bag of candy. Nevarra shot me a worried glance before following her. It was hard to believe that only four years separated them in age. Nevarra seemed so much older, always cautious, always wary of a fist that might come out of nowhere, always expecting bad news. Sadie had suffered the same in her ten years of life, but somehow none of it had left a mark on her. She was perpetually happy, always trusting, instantly forgetting about the blows and focused on what little joy life gave her.

I watched Nevarra leave and wished she was as innocent

and free as her foster sister. Maybe once they were out of New Hell, once they were safe in a world where they could go to school again, and walk to the neighborhood park without fear of being accidentally shot or worse, she'd recover some of her childhood.

Aunt Bea was in the kitchen, standing over a huge pot, sliding sliced peppers into the soup.

"I've got cabbage if you want to throw some in," I told her.

She leaned over to plant a kiss on my cheek, before giving the soup a quick stir. Her real name was Barbara, but some foster kids long before me had christened her Aunt Bea after the matriarchal figure in an old television show. I had no idea what the TV Aunt Bea looked like, but mine was tall and soft with a short cap of iron-gray curls and kind, dark brown eyes. Everything about her was generous—her figure, her wide mouth, her sunny nature. Over a decade of mothering the most damaged and difficult kids in the system hadn't changed her generosity one bit.

"How fresh is that cabbage?" she asked.

"Fresh. It'll last if you want to wait."

She pursed her lips and nodded. "We'll save that cabbage then. Cook it up later this week when the soup runs out."

I hoped we'd be gone in the next few days, but raw cabbage on the road would serve us as well as fried. Leaning over, I sniffed the soup. It had chicken, carrots, peas, potatoes, tomatoes, and peppers, with a spicy aroma that told me Bea had thrown some hots in the pot.

"Chicken?" I asked her, wondering where she'd gotten the meat.

"I traded Linda some of those apples you brought in for a breast and a few thighs. She's going to give me a couple of hatchlings in exchange for the soap I've been making and a little sewing. Her son's pants are looking like shorts lately." Bea chuckled.

I did my part through salvage, and Bea supplemented her paycheck through trade. It paid the bills and allowed us to save a little here and there. The soaps Bea was trading to Linda were homemade; she'd once sold them to a local shop as a side gig and a hobby. Now, her stock of soaps and her mending and sewing skills were valuable—easily swapped for things I found it difficult to buy at the few local markets that remained open.

I held up the grocery bags. "Where do you want me to put these?"

"Ooo, what else is in there?" She set the ladle down and we both unpacked the groceries, lining the food up on the counter. Cabbage. Eggs. Milk. Bread. Six oranges and two limes. Two pounds of cheese. A package of bologna and one of pimento loaf.

"Is the electricity still holding on?" I asked. "I wasn't sure about the fridge, but I didn't want to pass up milk and luncheon meat." The cheese and eggs would keep unrefrigerated, but we'd still need to use some of these groceries in a few days or risk them spoiling—sooner if the electricity was off.

"Rolling blackouts, but we've had enough electricity to keep the fridge cool," Bea told me. "It's the water I worry most about."

I grimaced. Lately the water wasn't on more than once or twice a week. No water didn't just mean a risk of dehydration, it meant looming sanitation problems in the Valley. No water to wash dishes, hands, bodies, clothes. And if people were forced to drink whatever they found, disease would spread like butter on hot toast.

Aunt Bea looked at the groceries, then eyed me. "You okay? I don't want you taking unnecessary chances for us, you hear?"

She knew what food cost these days, and what sort of

score I would have needed in order to bring this kind of money in—especially with the exorbitant tax rate. Big hauls brought risk, and Aunt Bea still saw me as a skinny, angry teen who ran straight into trouble like I had a death wish.

"Yeah, I'm fine. And I brought home more than the food." I pulled out a wad of money and set it on the counter between the oranges and the cheese.

Bea's hands shook as she picked it up and leafed through it. "Is…is it enough? I've got what I saved before the banks closed plus the extra we've been putting away each week. If we put it all together…?"

Getting to the Nevada border would mean gas money and bribes—and possibly more if Bea's old car broke down. But we'd also need cash to get past the border wall, bribe the guards, get new identification, and get ourselves settled somewhere while we looked for jobs. The farther east we could go, the better. The towns close to the states the demons had seized were filled with people desperately trying to carve out a new life. The competition for housing and jobs as well as the crime rate wouldn't be much better than it was here, and I wanted better for my family—much better.

"Yeah, we'll have enough," I lied. It would have to be enough. But to be on the safe side, I needed to do one more job, have one more decent take, then we'd leave. This plus what we'd saved was hopefully enough for transportation and to bribe us across the border—maybe even get us some papers and a place to stay for a week if we were lucky—but extra money would give us clothes, food, and more of a cushion so we could look for jobs while we adjusted.

I tried to have some faith in our future, but I couldn't. I'd never been much of one for faith, especially after the demons had come. But the one thing I did have faith in was family. Bea. Nevarra. Sadie. If we stuck together, we'd make it. We had to make it. I'd do anything for them. We were so close to freedom. So close. And I wouldn't allow my fears to ruin this.

Bea planted another kiss on my cheek. "I'll hide the money. You stir this soup. Make sure it doesn't boil over, now."

She hustled out of the kitchen while I did as I was told, putting the groceries away in between soup duty. *That* made me relax. It felt so familiar to do this. When I'd been placed with Bea, Nevarra and Sadie hadn't entered the system yet. There'd been a boy here, then. Drew. He'd aged out four years after Aunt Bea had taken me in, and although the woman always had an open-door policy to all her kids, Drew had taken off the day of his eighteenth birthday and never returned.

He hadn't been the first boy I'd ever loved, but I'd fallen for him hard. We'd been an item off and on pretty much since I'd been placed here. Then he'd left. He'd left not just me, but *us*. It still hurt. His leaving churned like acid in my stomach even six years after he'd walked out. Thinking of him stirred up all the old fears of abandonment that I'd never really buried.

Bea shuffled back into the room. "When are you thinking of leaving? A week from now? Two? That would give us time to get things sorted with the house and my job."

A week. I could pull together more money if we stayed for another week or two instead of leaving right away. This was something else I feared. What if we didn't have enough money? If we got robbed along the way? Or lost? Or couldn't find jobs in the States and found ourselves homeless and rooting through dumpsters for food? A week or two would give us a bit of a cushion.

But if that cop checked today's pawn and reported me, the tax collectors would be knocking on my door in a week or two. That cushion would be eaten up by the fine, and I'd likely be dealing with broken bones and bruises as I tried to get my family to the border.

That made the decision for me.

"I'd like for us to leave late tomorrow, maybe between midnight and dawn the next day."

Bea eyed me over her shoulder. "That's pretty quick. What trouble did you get yourself into, Eden?"

"Nothing," I lied. "I just want us out of here as soon as possible. We've got enough money. There's no sense in lingering."

Bea watched me for a moment, those keen, dark eyes of hers seeing right through me, just as they'd always done. "I don't like you taking risks, Eden. If we need to stay a few more weeks or months or years, it's fine. We'll manage just fine. We *won't* manage just fine if you go and get yourself shot or stabbed or hauled into jail."

I never could lie to Bea and get away with it. "What's done is done. It's nothing that would get me shot or stabbed or hauled into jail. Worst case I get fined, and I'd rather us leave now before that fine makes a dent in our savings."

Bea made a disgruntled sound and turned back to the soup. "Okay, we'll leave tomorrow night."

My shoulders relaxed at her words. The sooner we got going, the better. "I've got one more job I want to do tomorrow. Be ready, because when I get back, we're going to be moving fast."

She nodded. "Just as well. I don't like having this much money here for long."

Me either.

"Bags isn't the kind to double cross, and I was careful that no one followed me." I pulled a bag from my pants pocket. "I got this as well. Some antibiotics, just in case, and your blood thinner."

"I'd have been fine without it," she protested, taking the bag.

"It didn't cost all that much, and I'd rather you have your medicine."

Bea had been on the Warfarin since before I'd come here. Drew had told me that without it, she was at a high risk for a stroke. Ever since the demons had come and health insurance had vanished as had regular access to pharmaceutical supplies, I'd made sure Bea had the drug. It wasn't just my fear that she might die without it; it was the thought that Sadie and Nevarra might see it happen. There were no ambulances beyond the private companies, the hospital had an eight hour wait on a good day, and only the rich had quick access to doctors, so if Bea were to have a stroke, the girls would be able to do nothing but watch their foster mom die.

Then they'd be alone with no one but me to protect them. And I wasn't fit to be anyone's guardian.

Bea left the soup to envelop me in a huge hug. I sank into her soft, pillowy body and closed my eyes. When I was younger, I'd thought that Bea's hug could protect me from everything. I knew better now.

She squeezed tight, then pulled away, wiping her eyes. "We're gonna be fine, Eden. We'll head south once we're across the border and go to Phoenix, or maybe Dallas if we have enough to get that far. No matter what happens, we've got each other. We'll be okay."

"We'll be okay," I agreed, even though that tight dread was wrapping itself around my chest once more.

She patted my shoulder. "Go out back. I'll send the girls out to play. Dinner should be ready in about an hour."

The girls weren't usually allowed outside of the house without an adult. I was gone sometimes overnight with my job, and Bea worked nine-to-five. Schools hadn't been open for the last two years so Nevarra and Sadie locked the doors and stayed inside, supposedly studying with old textbooks. They were bored out of their skulls, and I doubted those textbooks had been opened in months. Bea had asked a neighbor teenage boy to pop over a few times during the day and keep an eye on the girls for her, which annoyed Nevarra to no end. She'd just turned fourteen and was furious that Bea had assigned her a babysitter, especially one that was only a year older than she was.

She had a point. Nevarra was getting confident enough with a gun that she would probably be safe enough to run to the store in an emergency, but it was still dangerous. Gunfire happened at random moments each day, but my worst fear wasn't that the girls would be a casualty of a shootout. There weren't all that many kids left in the Valley. Quite a few families had fled or been killed when the demons arrived. Any children who hadn't been lucky enough to escape with their families were hidden away, lest they be snatched up and sold either to the demons—or pedos.

I left the kitchen, hearing the screen door slap against the threshold as I went outside. What little grass remained in the yard was overgrown in dry, wiry patches. A sun-bleached plastic play house sat under a twisted dead tree. There were a dozen different sized balls against the rickety stockade fence. At the bottom of the porch stairs sat a wagon filled with Legos. I smiled and sat down on the bottom step, picking up the blocks and putting them together into a makeshift house. I'd just started on the roof when I heard the door and light footsteps on the stairs.

"I heard you and Aunt Bea talking."

Of course she had. Nevarra always snuck around and listened in. It had probably saved her life in the past, and had become a habit she couldn't break even with the safety of Bea's care.

"We're leaving tomorrow, hopefully around midnight," I told her. "Or early the next morning at the very latest."

She edged past to stand in front of me so she could see my eyes. I met her gaze, showing her that I was being truthful. Then I reached out and touched her springy black curls, tucking one behind a brown ear.

"We're going to be okay," I promised. I'd do anything to get my little family out of here. *Anything.*

"You're coming with us, Eden, right?" Nevarra bit her lip.

"Absolutely." There was a part of me that felt like I didn't deserve to leave this hellhole, part of me that felt like staying here might be penance for all the shit I'd done in my life.

Bea would have told me that was bull, that I was just as deserving of happiness as anyone else.

"Good." Nevarra sighed. "I feel safe with you, Eden."

The door slapped again. This time the footsteps raced with an eagerness that made me smile.

"Can we play with the balls, Eden? Can we?"

I stood and turned in one motion, scooping Sadie up in my arms and setting her down next to Nevarra. "Until dinner. If anyone manages to hit me, I'll buy them chocolate."

Sadie shrieked, and even Nevarra grinned. In a flash they were off, running to gather the balls from the fence. For the next hour the girls tried to pelt me with the balls and I attempted to deflect them before they got to me with only a wave of my hand. The girls were fast and had gotten good at strategizing, and I found myself spinning around, having to actually dodge a few of the balls that came at me too fast to magically redirect. Bea and the girls were the only ones who knew I could do this minor kind of telekinesis. I kept these skills carefully hidden from the rest of the world.

I kept my other magical abilities hidden even from Bea and the girls. Early in my childhood, I'd sensed that normal humans couldn't do these things. Now I knew better. Some humans could do magic. Some could turn into animals. Some humans weren't even human. Still, something made me hide my abilities. Even in this new world, I didn't want to be a freak.

I kept playing with the girls and by the time Bea called us for dinner, we were all sweating and laughing. Sadie launched one last ball at me, taking me unaware and hitting me as I climbed the stairs to the kitchen.

"Yay! Gotcha! Now you have to buy me chocolate. I want M&Ms. The ones with the peanut butter in them."

Nevarra scowled. "The game was over. That doesn't count."

It didn't, but I was in a good mood. All the adrenaline of the game, plus being here with the people I loved had sent my spirits to the sky.

"Peanut butter M&Ms it is," I promised, thinking that I'd put aside a little of the money I got tomorrow and get the girls a special treat. Once we were across the border, I'd get them chocolate every night. And all the candy they wanted.

"I'll share." Sadie put her arm around Nevarra. The elder girl's face softened, and she returned the embrace.

One more night, I thought. We'd eat soup. I'd stay here tonight with Bea and the girls. Tomorrow I'd be at the raid, waiting to salvage what I could. Then I'd cash it all out with Bags, come collect my family and the money, and we'd run for the border.

Then we'd be safe.

CHAPTER 3

We ate soup and bread, and talked about all the things we'd do once we were out of Los Angeles. Nevarra wiped the bowls with a rag she'd dipped in a bucket of water, then lined them up on the counter, the rag folded beside them. Out of habit, she turned the faucet and squealed in surprise when water spurted out.

"Hurry." Bea clapped her hands together. "Draw water for a bath, and don't forget to wash your clothes before you drain it out. I'll do the dishes."

The girls raced to the bathroom, and I helped Bea gather all the dishes from the last week. She washed, I rinsed. And when we'd drained the dirty water, we refilled the sinks with fresh. Yes, we planned on leaving tomorrow night, but it was always good to have water in case we were delayed. And if we did leave as planned, we could scoop this into all the plastic bottles we'd saved and take it for our trip to the border.

The sun was setting as the girls came back, dressed in clean pajamas and carrying laundry baskets full of wet clothes. I motioned for Bea to sit, then took the baskets outside, hanging the clothes on the line. A light breeze caressed my face and sent the lighter weight garments to swaying. Quite a few were pushing the limits of what the girls could squeeze into, and I made a mental note to look for children's clothing as I scavenged. Or teen clothing. Nevarra had just turned fourteen. She'd be wanting something more mature than the striped T-shirts and elastic-waist jeans I was hanging up. I fantasized for a moment about finding the girls nicer clothes.

Soon. Soon we'd have that and more.

I came back in with the empty laundry baskets to find Bea reading to the girls. The lights flickered and went out, and Bea sighed.

"Time for bed." The woman stood and pulled a flashlight off one of the kitchen shelves, handing it to Sadie. "Keep it by you in case you need to get up in the night."

Sadie nodded and turned to me.

"I'll take them," I told Bea. I was still in that dreamlike state of peace from the domestic chores, my full belly, and the nearness of those I loved.

The girls led the way, chattering excitedly about what they would do once we were across the border. Sadie wanted friends, school, and a puppy. Nevarra was going to pretend she was older so she could get a job.

I didn't say it aloud, but *that* was so not going to happen. She was going to school. Sadie too. And they were going to college, even if I had to pimp myself on a street corner to pay for it.

"Can you do my hair, Eden?" Nevarra ask, sitting on the edge of her bed.

"Of course." I unwound the towel from the girl's damp hair, and gently finger combed it. She handed me a jar of shea butter, and I began smoothing it through her thick curls a section at a time, braiding and pinning the finished parts up as we all chatted. Nevarra leaned back against me with a sigh; Sadie stayed at my side with her head on my thigh. When I was done, I put a cap around Nevarra's hair and turned to Sadie.

"Want me to do your hair too?"

She laughed. "Mine's easy."

"Doesn't mean your hair deserves any less attention," I insisted.

Sadie got up and took Nevarra's place. I combed her long golden-brown hair, twisting sections up onto the top of her head and securing them in place with some small scrunchies.

"There. When it's dry, you can take it down and it'll be curly," I told her.

"As curly as Nevarra's?" She reached up a hand to carefully pat the twists.

"You'd need to be a whole lot browner for hair this curly," Nevarra teased.

"It'll be curlier than mine, but not as curly as Nevarra's," I told her. "Now off to bed with the pair of you. You'll need to pack your things and help Aunt Bea get ready tomorrow. We've got an exciting few days ahead of us."

The girls climbed into their own beds, and I tucked them in as if they were still babies.

"I ran more water in the tub," Sadie told me with a smile as she snuggled into her blankets. "So you and Aunt Bea can take a bath later."

"Thank you, peanut." I leaned down and kissed her cheek, feeling a painful twinge in my chest as I stood and looked at the girls.

"I love you," I whispered.

"Love you too, Eden," they both replied.

I tiptoed down the hallway, through the living room and into the kitchen. Bea was out back, sitting on the porch with the pistol in her lap. I joined her, watching the moon rise over the mountains. Off in the distance, a smattering of lights came on. Judging from the houses around us, we still didn't have electricity. Not that Bea liked to use it at night anyway. Ever since the demons had come, she'd claimed it was better if the house looked vacant at night.

Bea handed the gun over. It was the other Glock 17—the one I'd stolen and hid in my room when I'd still been in high school. Bea'd never liked guns in the house, but I was glad I'd had it that day almost two years ago when life in Los Angeles and the surrounding areas had turned into a nightmare.

"I kept a box of bullets from my salvage today," I told her. "And picked up another 9mm."

"Best keep those bullets for yourself," Bea said. "I've got a full magazine in this one. If that doesn't do the job, more bullets aren't gonna help us."

I shivered at the thought, but she was right. Tomorrow there was a good chance I'd need to defend myself. Pulling the 43 out of my pocket, I wished I'd used some of my money to buy an extra magazine from Bags. This one only held six rounds, and in a fight I wouldn't have time to reload. But I had the other 17, and Bea was right. If that wasn't enough, I shouldn't be sticking around and continuing to shoot.

"What's the first thing you wanna do once we're out of here?" Bea asked.

I thought for a moment. "Eat a steak. Rib eye, or maybe a T-bone. Rare. Biggest steak I can get. And a baked potato with crispy skin, loads of butter and sour cream."

"Crusty French bread," Bea added. "Grilled asparagus."

"Chocolate mousse after dinner." I grinned. "Extra chocolate mousse for the girls."

Bea laughed. "Better get three for Sadie. That girl likes her chocolate."

"Who doesn't?" I smiled at the thought of Sadie digging a

spoon into a giant bowl of chocolate mousse. "What about you? What's the first thing you want to do?"

"Buy new clothes. New underwear. New shirts. Maybe a dress or two. And lots of clothes for the three of you as well." Bea patted my arm. "You need some dresses, Eden."

I certainly didn't need dresses in New Hell, but it was nice to think there might be an occasion in my future where I'd want to wear a dress. I remembered before the demons came, when I actually went out on dates and to clubs with friends.

"Makeup," I chimed in. I couldn't remember the last time I'd worn makeup. It would be nice to spend time on my appearance, to style my hair, do a smoky eye, find the brightest red lipstick I could lay my hands on.

"And a hot shower." Bea sighed. "I think I'm going to spend an hour in the shower my first night out of here. Soap this place right out of my hair and skin."

Amen.

"Sadie ran fresh bath water for us," I told her. "It's not a hot shower, but it's better than nothing. You go on up. I'm filthy. You'd probably be dirtier coming out than going in if I go first."

Bea stood. "I won't say no to that. Think I'll head to bed afterward. We've got a busy day tomorrow getting ready."

I wished her goodnight, then sat on the back porch, listening to the occasional car going down the block, hearing the frequent gunfire in the distance. After a few hours I went in. The girls were sound asleep when I checked on them. Bea's door was closed. I went into my room and grabbed some clean clothes out of the dresser. Then I took a bath, the cold water feeling downright luxurious as I washed days of filth from my skin and hair. I'm sure the water was a murky gray by the time I got out, but I still washed my clothes, draping them over the shower rod to dry.

Then I bundled my hair up in a towel, put on my clean

clothes, went into the girls' room, and laid down on the floor between their beds, snagging a spare blanket to ward off the evening chill. There, I had the best night's sleep I'd had in weeks, dozing off to the sound of soft breathing, knowing everyone I loved was safe and nearby.

29

CHAPTER 4

$\mathcal{I}$ was up before dawn, making my way through the house in stocking feet so I wouldn't wake anyone else up. In the kitchen I eyed the coffeemaker sadly and tried the electric just in case.

Nothing. There would be no coffee this morning. I missed the days when that enticing aroma would reliably fill the house every sunrise. I'd give my eye teeth for a cup of dark roast right now. Instead I stuck some pimento loaf in between two slices of bread, drank a glass of milk, and packed myself a lunch of bread, cheese, and an orange, then filled a bottle with water from the sink, grateful that at least the water was still running.

Accounting day was truly a day-long affair. I had no idea when the militia intended to make their move, so I could be sitting around for a very long time. Hence the bottle of water and the snack.

Every Thursday the leader of the Gray Dogs and his top mongrels congregated to dole out cash, bullets, and other payment to their members as well as to collect the take on their various enterprises. It was the perfect time to hit them if the goal was to hit as many of the gang members as possible and grab the majority of their assets.

I had no beef with either group. The Gray Dogs and I had crossed paths a few times in the last year. If I was scavenging in any of their locations and they came on the scene, I always relinquished what belonged to them. In return, they let me take the rest, except for a few key items, without argument. They also were generous about providing me with a finder's fee if I brought them any Gray Dog property I scavenged off someone else.

The militia wasn't quite as amiable, but they weren't total assholes either. They pretty much confiscated everything I'd salvaged if they came across me doing a job, but they didn't smack me around over it. They didn't offer any finder's fee, so if I scavenged any militia weaponry, then I hauled it in to Bags for him to file the marks off and resell.

Over the last year the Gray Dogs had grown in membership and territory, expanding from their base in Van Nuys to Reseda and Encino. The militia wasn't having any issues over this expansion that I was aware of, but there were occasional scuffles over the shared border along Sherman Oaks. The Dogs were a gang. They sold drugs, ran protection rackets, had a few gambling spots, and that was about it. If you ran a business in any of their neighborhoods and you wanted your customers un-harassed and your goods to remain on your property, you paid them a monthly fee and they left you alone. They didn't bother the residents, because anything they had worth stealing had probably been stolen long ago. The only dustups came when a rival gang tried to move in, someone in the Dogs attempted a coup, or one of the members got into it with another.

The militias liked to think they were some sort of civilian police force, but honestly the line between the two groups was pretty thin. Most of them didn't sell drugs, although if they came across a stash, they'd happily unload it. Militias made their money performing security, which was a more socially acceptable word for the protection racket the gangs ran.

Businesses and residents paid a monthly fee for security, and in return they were supposed to get a quick response to a crime in progress. With budget cuts and a shrinking police force, the chances of a cop responding to your 911 call in under a half hour was nil. The militias were supposed to be right there, in your neighborhood, patrolling with weapons at the ready, to serve and protect.

The reality was they picked and chose who they served and protected based on what sort of reward they might get. They might show up if the neighbor was beating the crap out of his wife, or they might not. The Southside Militia spent more time collecting their security payments, knocking down beers, and shooting cans down at the old recycling center than helping with any crime.

I got the feeling today's rumble was because the Gray Dogs had gotten to the size where the Southside Militia saw an opportunity. Their opportunity was my opportunity. The aftermath of the fight between the two groups would spell some truly awesome scavenging opportunities. I was absolutely going to be there, even if it meant waiting all day for the action to occur.

I grabbed an old backpack out of the closet to replace the one I'd had to leave behind yesterday, stashed my food and drink in the outside pockets, then slid it on. Shoulder harness, check. Fully loaded magazines, check. Extra bullets, check. The 17 in the harness and the 43 in my pocket, check. Quietly locking the door behind me, I went around the side of the house and started my bike.

It took a while. The thing was as old as I was, but Drew had told me when I'd bought the 1989 Yamaha Fazer that the engine was damned near bulletproof. The downpipes had rusted to nothing. The rear brakes sometimes seized up. The gearbox liked to pop out of second. If I couldn't start it in three tries, the carburetor flooded and I needed to let it sit. But all in all, it was a good bike, and best of all nobody would ever bother to steal it.

My bike roared to life. I was glad the old girl had started this morning, otherwise I would have needed to hitch a ride. Hitching wasn't quite as dangerous as it sounded, but plenty of people were reluctant to give a woman a ride when she had a pistol in plain view.

It was twenty minutes to half an hour from our home in Sun Valley to Encino by highway. Yes, there was a more direct route weaving through the city streets, but that would have taken longer and some of those streets were no longer passable. The freeways weren't all that great either, but at least there had been an effort to clear debris and fill in the sections that demons had blown up.

In typical Southern California fashion, I had to go a couple miles north to catch the 405 and go south. Even though the sun was barely coming up, traffic heading south was insane. LA was half the population it had been two years ago, but that still meant it was a huge city—a huge sprawling city. Lots of businesses had closed, but others hung in there, and those businesses offered employment to all these poor folks inching down the freeway by my side.

Six miles later I saw that the problem wasn't a sudden increase in commuting, it was a tractor trailer twisted up like a pretzel and blocking several southbound lanes. I squeezed over onto the shoulder with the rest of the vehicles, and eyed the truck as I went by. The cab had been stretched out like a piece of taffy and the trailer portion was twisted around on itself then folded in half. The sides of the trailer had split open and the metal had been peeled back. Boxes littered the median.

I had no idea what the fuck had happened. Demons probably. Or maybe one of those dragons had come back. All I knew was that I was glad I hadn't been the one driving that truck when whatever supernatural creature had decided to make the two-ton metal box into a chew toy.

Traffic opened up after that, and I picked up speed, exiting on 101 west, then hopping off the ramp. Farther south were parks and the numerous country clubs where the old money residents played. The Santa Monica Mountains stood between the neighborhood and the even ritzier neighborhoods of Bel Air and Brentwood, but unlike those neighborhoods, Encino hadn't survived the demon wars completely intact. Ventura Boulevard still sported shopping and dining, but over half the businesses were shuttered. The quiet streets with their well-manicured houses were gone. The place looked like a war zone with torn up asphalt, blasted cars no one had bothered to move, and holes where buildings had once stood. For every house or business that had been repaired, six stood abandoned and empty shells.

The Gray Dogs had repurposed a country club for their headquarters, but accounting day was always at a location more convenient to the freeway.

I parked my bike a few blocks away from where I thought today's activities might be going down. As I walked down the street, a guy delivering produce offered me a ride as well as a quickie in the bed with the crates of romaine and swiss chard. I declined, instead walking the five blocks and trying to look inconspicuous while observing both foot and vehicular traffic.

Even in the few remaining good neighborhoods, my rule was to stay on the other side of the street, to assume any passing stranger was going to knife you and rob you of everything you had—including your shoes. Trust no one, and always carry a gun.

Which meant I got some hard looks from the men and women emerging from their houses and heading to whatever job they'd managed to hold on to. I watched them as well, not so much because I was afraid a waitress or cleaning guy was going to stick me, but because I was looking for patterns.

Who was heading where? People would be coming in from all over the Valley for accounting day. Bags's intel was usually right, but on occasion even he was wrong. Sitting outside a shuttered grocery store or an old school all day only to find out the action had been six blocks away would totally suck. If I could make a few of the people heading in to drop their cash or pick up their wages, I could discreetly tail them to where today's activities would be going down. Then I could sit and wait for the fallout like the Vulture I was.

I let my intuition lead the way, watching and thinking I was headed in the right direction as I saw a group of three motorcycles with burly men pass me by. Four blocks in I noticed a tall, thin woman with a short crop of dark hair in twists come around a corner. She had a long angular face and a sharp square chin. A line of small earrings worked their way up her ear in silver, turquoise, and coral.

She grinned when she saw me and jogged over. "Eden! Here for the pickings, I see."

"Hopefully. What are you doing in the Valley?" We Vultures didn't have assigned territories, but people did tend to get growly when others encroached on their neighborhoods. Telaney used to work the Valley, but she'd grabbed a house in Silver Lake a few months back and had eventually started scoping out salvage opportunities closer to home.

"I miss my old stomping grounds. Besides, I heard there might be a shoot-out. You know I can't resist a good shoot-out."

I rolled my eyes. Telaney Miller was my age. She was honest, loyal, and wouldn't hesitate to shoot if someone looked like they were going to draw on her. She was someone you wanted at your back in a fight, so I had no problem sharing any salvage with her.

"They working out of the old Goodwill today, or the Jiffy Lube?" I asked.

Telaney shrugged. "I heard either the Goodwill or that ratty gas station on Corbin."

I recognized another Vulture coming toward us. "Isn't that Poodle?"

Telaney squinted. "Looks like her."

The woman nodded our way and we nodded back—acknowledgement and wordless agreement that we'd stay out of each other's way and not pull any shit. Poodle turned down a side road. She seemed to know where she was going, so we followed, keeping her in sight.

Another four blocks and we were there. I knew we were there because of the cars and trucks lined up and down the street as well as the three motorcycles I'd seen parked in front of an old gas station across the street. Armed guards stood outside the gas station service bays, smoking and laughing, with semi-automatic rifles slung over their shoulders. A few of those rifles had white muzzles. The Gray Dogs were prepared for trouble—even trouble of the magical kind.

I counted eight Vultures milling about the perimeter, and assumed that more would be coming once they figured out the location. The guards eyed us, not particularly alarmed. We were here to scavenge, not attack, and our presence here wasn't any sort of portent. Gatherings like this always had the potential for a fight, and if there was potential, we Vultures would gather. Just in case.

Telaney elbowed me. "Told ya."

Gas station. She'd been right. I was glad I hadn't wasted time hanging around the Goodwill or the Jiffy Lube.

"I'm heading down behind that Tahoe." Telaney pointed at the SUV.

It was a good spot. Lots of cover in case bullets started to fly, and with some shade.

"I'll be across the street in front of the Panda Express." I could always dive behind a parked car if the shooting turned that direction, and it was closer to the entrance where gang members were already beginning to go in and out. The sun would be beating down on me, and unfortunately the Panda Express was no longer in business, but I'd be ideally positioned to swoop in and claim any fallen once the shooting stopped.

Telaney gave me a fist bump and headed to her spot while I headed across the street and leaned against a signpost.

Two hours later a few more Vultures had arrived; a few others had given up and left. I wasn't giving up. I'd seen the Gray Dog members wander in to make their weekly reckoning then leave. The Southside Militia wasn't stupid. They'd wait until most, if not all, of the money was in and the accounting was finished before striking. This wasn't about licensed vigilante law enforcement for the militia, it was about licensed theft. This risk in taking on a big gang like the Gray Dogs was huge, so they'd wait to strike until the payoff was equally huge.

The gang members continued to trickle in and out after the sun reached its zenith and began to descend. I ate my cheese and my orange and drank most of my water. A few hours later, I was eyeing the boarded up Panda Express, thinking that I'd give my right arm for some Beijing Beef right now. By five o'clock, there were only four of us left watching—two guys I recognized from larger scavenger jobs in the Valley, Telaney, and me. Others had headed off to try their luck somewhere else rather than wait on a big payoff that might not even occur.

It was six thirty when I noticed three repurposed SWAT trucks tear down the street and squeal into the gas station parking lot, knocking over two motorcycles as they came to a halt. The guards snapped up their rifles and opened fire, but so did the Southside Militia from behind the heavily armored doors of their vehicles.

My muscles had started to cramp from the lack of activity, but they quickly loosened with the adrenaline that poured through me. I jumped up and to the side behind a parked car, hoping I didn't catch a stray bullet as I waited the whole thing out.

The militia quickly took out the four guards and poured from their vehicles just as the Gray Dogs began to shoot from the gas station. Windows shattered, and bits of concrete sprayed from the building in the firefight. I noticed the militia were quickly surrounding the structure and felt a bit sorry for the Gray Dogs. They were outnumbered and trapped—which sucked. If the militia won this fight, they wouldn't leave much for us to pick over.

A few pipe bombs thrown through the windows would have taken the gang out, but I knew the militia didn't want to destroy all the cash and other goodies they were hoping to grab. The Gray Dogs didn't have any such qualms. Incendiary devices flew from the windows, setting vehicles and a good number of the militia themselves on fire. In the resulting chaos, gang members fled out the back door under a cover of gunfire. Those who weren't shooting were carrying bulky duffle bags and shouting, "Go, go!" I expected the militia to spray them down in a hail of bullets, and was momentarily perplexed to see them running—some for the armored vehicles, and others taking off down the street at top speed.

Fuck. The gas tanks.

I scrambled to my feet and hauled ass, barely making it a block before the whole thing blew. Dropping to the ground, I rolled under a nearby box truck and watched debris bounce along the road. My ears were ringing too much to hear the concrete and rebar raining down on the truck I'd taken shelter under, but I could see and feel it bounce from the impact.

Once things stopped flying past me, I counted to one hundred before I peeked out from under the truck. Flaming shit and bits of building and vehicles were all over the place, some of them still on fire. I scooted out from under the truck and made my way back, just in case something worth scavenging had survived the blast.

The gas station was a blackened hole in the ground with bits of steel jutting upward. Mangled vehicles were scattered around the streets. One of the SWAT vehicles was leaning sideways against an abandoned dry-cleaning shop with a scorched front and blasted out windows.

There were bodies less than half a block out—some wearing Gray Dog colors and others with Southside Militia jackets. I was a Vulture, so I held my breath against the stench of burning flesh, turned them over, and searched them for anything worth selling. As I worked, a few other salvagers came out of the woodwork, giving me a nod as they did the same. I grabbed a couple pistols with some spare, fully loaded magazines, although I wasn't sure if any damage they'd suffered would be repairable. Bags might give me a couple bucks for them, and right now every dollar counted.

I saw Telaney eyeing up the SWAT van leaning against the old dry cleaner and made my way over to her.

"Give me a lift," she said.

I hoisted her up through where the door had been blown off the vehicle, hearing her curse as she cut her hand on a jagged piece of metal. A few seconds later she was handing out two long guns, and something that looked like a radio transmitter. I grabbed them, set them on the ground, then gave her a hand as she climbed back out.

"Fucker bit me." She examined the cut on her hand. "Now I'll have to waste money on antibiotics and bandages."

I grunted in agreement, then eyed the stash at our feet. "How about I grab this Browning, and the rest is yours."

It was a generous offer. I knew she'd crammed some stuff into her pockets while she'd been in the van. She knew that I could have taken off with both guns and the electronics unit while she'd been struggling to climb out.

"Deal." She grabbed the second gun and the box. "Think this is all I can carry anyway. You might want to check around back where the junked cars are. I don't think anyone's gone through that yet."

I thanked her, grabbed the rifle and heading around the hole where the gas station had been. One of the male salvagers was ripping some copper off some twisted heap that might have been a water tank, and the one with the red bandana on his head was digging through a dead guy's pocket. I checked the junked cars, but didn't find any other guns, bodies, or duffle bags of cash. It was starting to head toward dusk, so I decided to call it a day and see what all this crap I'd scraped up off the streets was worth.

What a disappointment! I'd spent the entire day waiting here in hopes of some good pickings, and would be lucky if what I'd found would get me ten bucks. Heading back toward my bike, I fumed. Ten bucks was better than nothing, but it wasn't worth sitting outside an old gas station all day long. We should have just left this morning. I could have scavenged along the way to the border. I could have stolen some stuff if we needed more money. A whole day and *this* was all I'd gotten?

I was grumpy. I was tired. I was filthy. And I flooded my bike trying to start it and had to wait twenty more minutes before I could get it going.

It was a long drive to Bags's. It would be a longer drive to the border, though. As tired as I was, I'd need to just deal with it, because as soon as I made it home, we were leaving.

And we weren't coming back.

CHAPTER 5

I knew something was wrong before I reached the pawnshop door. Something just felt off, and I reached over to touch my gun, flipping the snap that held it in the shoulder harness. Opening the door, I saw shelves knocked over, merchandise strewn across the floor, the row of bikes tangled and in a heap to the side. The shop had always been a jumble of assorted items, but there had been a strange order and neatness to their seemingly haphazard arrangement. No more.

I eased my pistol from the harness, but before I could call for Bags, I heard someone sweeping.

I never knew there could be sadness in the noise of a broom swishing across a concrete floor, but something in that sound broke my heart.

"Bags?" I kept my voice soft and put my pistol back in the harness.

The sweeping stopped. "Back here, Eden."

His voice was garbled, as if it pained him to talk. I wove my way around the scattered tools, broken televisions, and the smashed jewelry counters to where Bags stood, sweeping up the glass. The side of his face was so swollen that I couldn't see his left eye. His nose was crooked and dried blood splattered along his mouth, chin, and bare chest. A huge red welt ran diagonally across his ribs and round belly, and the hand that held the broom had two fingers in makeshift splints.

Bags was a business associate. Before today, I wouldn't have called him a friend. I certainly wouldn't have called him family. I was wrong. As I took in his injuries, something hot and angry filled me.

Over the last two years, Bags had become more than a business associate. He'd become *more*. All my life people had accused me of being cold, of being unfeeling, of lacking empathy. I'd been called amoral and hauled to psychologists and priests. It had taken Bea to show me that I *did* care, that I *could* love. But only a few—only those who I could trust to love me back.

Somehow Bags had become one of those few, and I'd only just now realized it.

"What happened?" My mind filled with visions of a gang robbery, of a demon on a spree—anything but what he next told me.

"Tax collectors."

Why the hell had the tax collectors come for Bags like this? Yeah, he skimmed just as much as any other pawnbroker, but this seemed completely overkill for such a minor fudging of the books. I thought back on yesterday, on the deal I'd closed under the table.

It *couldn't* be. Even if the cop had checked last night and notified the tax collectors about my infraction, they wouldn't have acted this quickly, or this violently—not over what to them would have been a minor amount.

"They came asking for you, wanting to know if you'd sold anything in the last twenty-four hours."

I felt guilty. I shouldn't have felt guilty because Bags was a grown man and he'd been more than willing to keep the sale off the books, but I did. "They did *this* over a few boxes of bullets and three guns?"

"They think you salvaged more than a few boxes of bullets and two guns yesterday." Bags leaned on the broom and shifted his weight off one leg. "They think you took seventeen *cases* of bullets and over a dozen guns."

That motherfucking cop. She and her partner had taken all the rest of the salvage from that hit gone wrong, then typed up the report to say I'd scooped it up. No wonder the tax collectors had come down fast and hard.

"I only took what I sold you. I swear to you, Bags, I didn't take the rest—I *couldn't*. That cop who caught me and got my salvage number? She wouldn't let me take any more than I could carry. She even made me leave my backpack behind, the bitch."

Bags sighed. "I'm sorry, Eden. She hosed you good on this one. You need to lay low for now. They'll tag your salvage license, and they'll be looking out for you. Until you find this cop and retrieve the stash or the cash to turn in, you've got a target on your back."

With a quick electronic report, this cop had signed my death warrant. It was a good thing we were leaving town tonight.

Bags set the broom aside. "What have you got for me?"

I shook my head. "You can't. They tagged my license. I can't fence anything anymore."

He snorted. "Fuck that. Those bastards come in here, trash my store, and beat on me? Now, what have you got for me?"

I handed him the rifle, the two damaged guns, and emptied my pockets and backpack of the miscellaneous stuff I'd managed to pick out of the gas station rubble and off the dead. The rifle was in decent shape, but the money he gave me for the battered pistols was far more than they were worth.

"This is too much, Bags," I protested.

"No, this is just enough." His voice was soft, but stern—the type of voice you didn't argue with. "You need a place to stay? I got a mattress in the back. They'll be looking for you. Probably already trashed your house searching for the bullets or the cash. It'd be safer for you to hole up here for a bit."

My entire body went cold. *Trashed my house.* I'd used Bea's address on my license. At the time it made sense. None of my little hidey-holes were a valid address for the form, and I didn't have an apartment of my own or anything. Bea's house was my home. Of course, I'd put that address in the application.

Trashed my house.

Bea and the girls were there. Oh God, Bea and the girls.

I slapped some of the cash Bags had just given me on the counter. "I need extra magazines for my two Glocks."

With a quick motion, he put four loaded magazines on the counter and shoved them toward me along with the cash. "Just take them. Is everything okay? Eden, what's wrong?"

I crammed the magazines and cash into the pockets of my cargo pants, and spun around. "My family," I said as I ran for the door. "My family lives there."

I drove as fast as I could to my home, forcing myself to slow down when I saw the front door was off its hinges and laying in a splintered mess in the front yard. Fear threatened to take me apart, but now wasn't the time to let emotion overcome cold, hard, thinking.

Parking my bike where I could get out fast if I needed to, I pulled the pistol from my pocket, walked to the side of the entrance and listened. Hearing nothing, I carefully made my way into the living room.

Everything had been broken, shot, and smashed. The walls were full of bullet holes and places where the drywall had been bashed in and ripped out. The sofa and chairs were in pieces with stuffing ripped from the cushions. End tables were broken, all the artwork Bea had collected through the years from her foster kids had been knocked over, stepped on, and crushed. I made my way down the hall, zigzagging so I wouldn't hit the parts in the floor that squeaked.

In the bathroom Aunt Bea was propped beside the tub. Both eyes were blackened, and blood stained her mouth and down the front of her shirt. One hand was very still on her lap. She slumped when she saw me, leaning her head gingerly back to rest against the wall.

"They're gone," she said in a pained whisper. "Thought you was them coming back."

I pocketed my gun and dropped to my knees beside her, wincing as I saw the abrasions on her face.

"They were looking for you," she said, her voice a bit stronger. "I lied and told them you haven't lived here since you were eighteen, that I had no idea where you were, but they didn't care. They wanted money. I told them where it was, but then they kept insisting it wasn't enough. Said there should have been more money or cases of bullets."

"Someone set me up," I told her. "Where are the girls?"

"Told them to hide and stay safe. Was trying to get myself up to go check on them, tell them the coast was clear."

"Stay here." I went to pat her shoulder and decided that wouldn't be a good idea. "I'll get the girls and be right back to help you."

I ran down the hall, heading straight for the kitchen only to stop and stare at the room in shock. The coffee can with our food money was empty and on the floor, the table knocked over on its side. What had me terrified, though, was that the intruders had shot up the cupboards.

With a steadying breath, I walked over to the under-sink cabinet.

"Sadie? It's me, Eden." Only silence answered me. I reached for the handle. "My favorite color is bacon. Sadie, please be okay. Please be okay."

I opened the door and knelt down to peer inside, nearly passing out from relief when a pair of big brown eyes met mine. She was alive. And she had the Glock 17 pistol in her lap. Nevarra must have given it to her to defend herself if needed.

"It hurts Eden. It hurts."

She started to cry. That's when I noticed she was covered in blood. Oh, God. Had she been shot? It would have been a miracle if she hadn't with all the bullets those assholes had fired into the cupboards. Reaching in, I smoothed the hair away from her face, seeing several cuts—no doubt from flying splinters of wood when they'd shot the cabinet she was hiding in.

"What hurts sweetie?"

"My arm," she sobbed. "My leg."

I looked at her arm, trying to gently peel the blood-soaked fabric from her shoulder.

"Can you move your arm?" It looked like a graze to me, but it was so dark under the sink I couldn't really tell.

She nodded. "But it hurts."

I was guessing that meant no broken or splintered bone, and the muscle wasn't too damaged. Looking at her legs, I realized the majority of the blood was coming from her left calf. The smart girl had taken one of the rags from under the sink and tied it just above the wound. I didn't think it was tight enough for a tourniquet, but at least she'd remembered the first aid techniques Bea had taught us.

"Do you think you can crawl out from under the sink?" I asked.

She shook her head. "I can't. It hurts too much to move."

I had to get her out of there and into the light so I could see her injuries better. Removing the pistol from her lap, I set it on the counter by the sink, then knelt down again.

"I'm sorry, sweetie." Without any other warning I reached in and wrapped my arms around her chest, dragging her out onto the kitchen floor. Sadie screamed, the sound mingling with her choked sobs before she went limp against me.

I worked fast, yanking my pocket knife open and slicing through her shirt and pants. The shoulder wound was thankfully a graze, but the leg injury was an in-and-out bullet wound. I looked around for the cleanest rags I could find, soaked one in the bucket of water we'd poured last night and tried to clean both wounds as best as I could before packing the leg injury with some gauze from an ancient first aid kit and wrapping both wounds with bandages and rags.

That done, I went to find Nevarra. Sadie's spot was always under the kitchen sink, but Nevarra liked to hide out back under the porch.

"Nevarra it's me, Eden. There's a penguin in the back-yard." I called out her safe-phrase from the top of the steps. Nevarra had given Sadie the gun, but there was no guarantee that the girl didn't have some sort of weapon. I didn't want to end up with a knife shoved into my foot from between the stair risers.

I didn't hear a response, but I went ahead and made my way down the stairs. The backyard wasn't trashed like the house was, and I didn't see any bullet holes. The back gate swung open, and that did give me pause. Had Nevarra fled when she'd heard the shots? No, I couldn't see her ever running and leaving Bea and Sadie to face the intruders alone.

Nevarra wasn't under the stairs, but one of her shoes was as well as a torn piece of her top. There was blood on the jagged edge of the skirtboard. Fear and rage tore through me, because I knew exactly what had happened. They hadn't found Sadie. She'd been shot by stray bullets, but they'd never realized she was under the sink. They hadn't found Sadie, but they'd found Nevarra.

And she'd fought like the scrappy wildcat she was, making them drag her out by her top as she gripped the wood skirtboard and hooked her feet around whatever she could grip. But in the end they'd taken her.

I sat down on the bottom step and let the fear wash over me. Sadie was shot and suffering from blood loss. Nevarra was gone and facing horrors I didn't even want to think of. Aunt Bea had been beaten and most likely had a concussion as well as a broken arm or dislocated shoulder. They'd taken all our money, and what I had in my pocket wouldn't be enough for ransom *or* doctors, let alone both. I barely had enough money for our weekly food budget. And Nevarra…

I got to my feet. This was no time for panic. First I needed to take Sadie to her bed, make Bea comfortable on Nevarra's bed, get them water, clean bandages, whatever was left in that first aid kit, and the bottle of antibiotics.

I needed help. The clock was already ticking on my chance to find Nevarra before she was sold. There weren't many places a person could turn to in New Hell for help. The police, at least the ones who weren't on the take, were overwhelmed. I didn't have any money to pay any of the militias. Bags was already in enough trouble as it was.

Sadie was stirring when I came back into the kitchen, her face softening with relief when she saw me.

"What happened?" I asked as I knelt and checked her bandages. It hadn't been more than a few minutes, but already blood was seeping through the gauze on her calf.

"Two trucks with men pulled up fast and stopped in front of the house." She took a shallow breath, fixing her brown eyes on mine. "Aunt Bea shouted for us to hide, and we ran, just like we'd practiced. Nevarra gave me the gun and told me not to be afraid, to shoot whoever opened the cabinet door. I'd hardly heard the back door shut when there was all this crashing and yelling from the front. I heard Aunt Bea, but couldn't make out what she was saying. The men were loud, but I stayed very quiet and had the gun ready. I was going to shoot them, Eden. I know I'm not brave like you and Nevarra, but I was going to shoot them."

I smoothed her hair, still curly from last night's scrunchies. "You're very brave, Peanut. Very brave."

"There was shooting and the men laughing." Her lips trembled. "They were in the kitchen and shooting. I closed my eyes tight because of the splinters, and it felt like being burned with a million cigarettes, but I didn't scream, Eden. I didn't make a sound."

"So brave," I murmured, choking back a mix of sorrow and fury—fury that my little sister had been hurt as well as fury that she knew what being burned with a cigarette felt like. She was only here right now because she'd kept quiet, even after being shot. I wasn't sure whether the intruders would have just killed her if they'd found her under the sink, or if they'd have hauled her, injured, away to be patched up and sold.

Nevarra...

"I'm going to carry you to your bedroom," I told Sadie. "I'll try really hard not to hurt you, okay?"

She nodded, then looked back at me with fear in her gaze. "Where is Aunt Bea? Where is Nevarra?"

"Aunt Bea is upstairs. She's hurt, but she'll be okay. Nevarra... Nevarra ran when the shooting started. She's at Marissa's house," I lied.

Sadie nodded again. I knew how much pain she was in because she'd swallowed that lie without question. Nevarra would never have run. It would have been hard for her to stay under the porch, hiding and remaining silent while intruders shot up her house. I remembered the torn piece of her shirt under the porch, the lost shoe, the blood. No, Nevarra would never have run.

I wished she had.

I scooped Sadie up in my arms and carefully carried her through the front room and down the hall. Bea was standing outside the girls' bedroom door, her left arm stabilized with what looked to be paint stirrers and toilet paper. Her face contorted when she saw Sadie.

"Oh, my baby! My baby!"

Once more I forced back tears, just as upset over Bea's anguish as I was about Sadie's injuries and Nevarra's kidnapping.

"I'm okay, Aunt Bea." Sadie managed a smile. "I didn't make a sound. Even when I got shot, I didn't make a sound."

"You were so brave, baby." Bea pointed to the bedroom. "Eden's going to lay you down in your bed, and you're going to rest. I'll take care of you. Just like when you had the flu last year, honey. Aunt Bea is gonna make it all right."

Those words warmed me even though they were meant for Sadie. I remembered coming here at thirteen, angry and scared and not trusting anyone. Aunt Bea had made everything all right.

And now it was my turn to make everything all right.

I gently put Sadie in her bed, propping her leg up on a few folded towels and checking her bandages. The bottle of antibiotics went on the bedside table. Once she'd drifted off to sleep, I followed Bea into the hallway, quietly shutting the bedroom door.

Bea burst into soft sobs. "Nevarra? Oh God, Eden. Is she dead? Did they shoot her?"

This time it was me who pulled Bea close and rubbed her back reassuringly. "She's alive. They didn't shoot her, but they took her."

Bea shuddered. "That means we can find her. We can find her and bring her back home."

I waited for Bea's sobs to lessen, and then I pulled back from her. "Tell me what happened. You're the only one who got a look at these guys."

The tax collectors didn't usually enforce their own laws. They used mercenaries. It wasn't the tax collectors who'd be interested in Nevarra or the price she'd fetch on the market, although some of the demons who ran that office might be. No, Nevarra had been a little extra payment to the men who'd been paid to come here, break legs, and collect. I needed to know who they were and track them down before they sold my sister.

"Eight men." Bea frowned in concentration. "They had on vests like some kind of SWAT team. Two had rifles and the rest had pistols."

It made sense. If they'd thought I'd kept seventeen cases of bullets, then they might have been worried they'd be walking into a serious firefight. And instead they'd encountered Bea, who hadn't even been armed.

"They broke down the door, yelled at me to get down on the ground, then did a quick search of the house. Then they pulled me up on my feet and asked where the money was. I gave them the food money in the coffee can first, hoping that would be enough." Bea's lips twisted up in bitter amusement. "I should have known that eight men with weapons wouldn't be satisfied with that. They smacked me around until I told them where our stash was." Bea hesitated at this point, her eyes filling with tears once more. "Oh, Eden. They took it all. That was our money to get out of here, and they took it all."

"It's okay," I reassured her. "We'll get more money. This is just a delay. That's all."

But my heart sank. Two years it had taken us to save all that up. And now all we had to our names was what Bags had given me today.

"Then they kept insisting that you had more," Bea continued. "They twisted my arm so hard I think they may have broken it. They kept hitting me. I told them that you had hiding spots outside the house, and that must have been where you kept the other bullets or cash, because they weren't here." Bea reached out to touch my cheek. "You need to hide. They'll be looking for you, trying to find that money or those bullets."

That was pretty low on my priority list. Eventually I'd need to track down that bitch of a cop, set things right with the tax collectors, get my license reinstated. But all of that had to wait until after I'd found Nevarra.

"They were different races," Bea went on. "Dressed in camo with the flak jackets, but no helmets."

Idiots. Smart enough to put on a vest, but too arrogant to protect their heads. Maybe there wasn't much in their skulls to protect. I had a good idea who they might be. Well-funded. Organized. A mixture of races. SWAT equipment and not bothering with helmets. All that ruled out a good number of the gangs and militias.

"Tattoos?" I asked. "Hairstyles? Beards or clean-shaven?"

Bea thought for a moment. "Some had long hair, some short. Same with beards. One of them had a tattoo on his neck. It looked like…a screwdriver? No, that couldn't be right. Nobody's gonna get a screwdriver tattoo."

"Fixers," I told her. "They're a loosely affiliated mercenary group. Some of them think it's hysterical to get tool tattoos—

hammers, screwdrivers, and stuff. I've seen one of them with a very intricate tattoo of a circular saw."

Fixers had no limits when it came to what they'd do for a buck. Any job, as long as the pay was good. They were dicks, and because they weren't an organized group like a gang or a militia, they didn't have a certain place they congregated or met to do business. All job offers were sent out via group text. They might not have a leader, but somebody by the name of Bolt coordinated the jobs and dealt as their accountant—keeping track of who did what and what clients owed what. They may not have a Fixers' clubhouse, but people were creatures of habit, and members did have favored places to assemble.

It would take me fucking forever to track these eight down by visiting every bar, burger joint, or strip club in the city. I needed to move fast before Nevarra was sold and vanished into the seedy underworld of pedophilia.

I needed help. There was one name that had been whispered around the streets for as long as I'd been alive as someone who could find people and things, who could get stuff done, who could solve problems for the right price. He might be able to help me—or he might laugh in my face and throw me out on the sidewalk.

Either way, I had to try.

"I'm going to go see someone who might help me track down Nevarra," I told Bea. "Are you feeling okay enough to take care of Sadie while I'm gone?"

She nodded. "I can take care of her. I'm not hurt that bad."

I glanced down at her arm, but didn't have the luxury of calling her on that fib. I needed to find Nevarra before it was too late, then I'd worry about Bea and Sadie's injuries.

Bea went back into the girls' bedroom, leaving the door open. I went into the cubbyhole-sized space that had been my old bedroom and started digging through the closet, searching way in the back for clothes I hadn't had a reason to wear over the last two years.

Bishop was the guy's name. That's all I knew beyond the fact that he owned some scary-ass bar out northeast of Sunland-Tujunga, right at the base of the San Gabriel Mountains. I didn't know if Bishop was his first name, his last name, or some weird title, although I doubted the guy who'd been described to me was all that religious. Bishop was supposedly as scary as his bar. He allegedly got shit done, found things that couldn't be found, killed everyone who looked at him funny. Bags had told me there had been a story going around when he was young that Bishop had walked through a hail of bullets in some urban warfare, grabbed the gang leader by the neck, and popped his head off like a champagne cork. The dude had been riddled with holes, but walked away like he didn't have a scratch on him.

Clearly that was a tale that had been blown way out of proportion, but desperate times called for desperate measures. Even if this Bishop was only half the badass of his legend, he was still my best bet to finding Nevarra quickly.

I held up a leather bustier and pursed my lips in thought. Bags wasn't any spring chicken. If Bishop had been around when he was a kid, then the guy was probably using a walker by now. Unless Bishop was some sort of title? Maybe the old guy's kid had taken over? Either way, men appreciated a sexy woman—unless Bishop was gay.

Shit. I hoped he wasn't gay.

I didn't have any money beyond what we needed for food, so I'd need to approach this guy with a different sort of currency. And hope he wasn't gay.

Guessing that any man with a scary bar would probably find leather sexy, I shimmied into black leather pants and poured myself into the bustier, lacing it up so that my boobs were on full display. Then I dug through my top dresser drawer, hoping that wand of mascara hadn't completely dried out.

It hadn't. And I'd managed to find some lipstick buried in the back as well, with just enough to scrape on some color. I eyed myself in the mirror, thankful that my complexion was a clear gold, and that the mascara was enough to accentuate the curve of my eyes. As for the rest of my curves, the leather did the trick.

I walked out of the bedroom and saw Bea waiting for me in the girls' bedroom doorway, a disapproving pucker to her mouth. I couldn't help but grin, my mind going back to those dates I'd had back in high school where Bea had insisted I change clothes and wipe off half the makeup I'd had on before she allowed me to leave.

"Oh, Eden. No."

"I'm twenty-two, Bea." I handed her my Glock 17 as a backup to the one she already had, wondering how the hell I was going to manage even the little 43 with this getup on.

"You're better than this." She gestured at my outfit. "You have value beyond your body. Don't do this."

She'd been the first one to ever tell me that, back when I'd been thirteen and had discovered how easy it was to manipulate boys with a swing of my hips.

"I'll do this if I have to." It wasn't like I'd enjoy screwing some ancient dude, but to find Nevarra I'd do it. And I'd win a fucking Academy Award for the performance, too.

She sighed. "I don't want you to have to."

Me either, but desperate times…

"I don't think the Fixers will be back here," I told her as I strapped my shoulder harness over my leather bustier. "They got the money. They've got Nevarra. They'll be searching for me elsewhere."

They'd be searching for me elsewhere, intending to

torture me until I gave up the location of either those seventeen cases of bullets or the money I'd gotten for selling them.

Then they'd either kill me, or make me wish they had.

"Either way, keep both guns close. Shoot first, ask later. I'll be back sometime tonight," I told Bea.

Not for the first time I'd wished we hadn't sold our cell phones, but we hadn't been able to afford the service plan. We did have a landline, but that phone had been ripped from the wall and was currently in a heap beside the sofa. Still, I'd get a message to her if I was going to be out past dawn, even if I had to slip a kid a few bucks to relay it.

Which reminded me…

"Here." I handed her the money I'd gotten from Bags, saving a ten for myself. "For groceries or medicines, or whatever. Also, there are two more loaded magazines on my dresser if you need them."

I hoped she wouldn't need them.

"Find her." Bea glanced once more at my leather getup, and her lips tightened into a firm line. "Whatever you have to do, find her."

That's exactly what I intended to do.

I put the 43 in my shoulder holster. Then I shook my dark hair loose from its messy bun and left.

CHAPTER 6

$\mathcal{I}$ stood in front of the building, working up the courage to go in. This was the place that gang members spoke of with a nervous glance over their shoulders. I wasn't sure what to expect. Hard core mobsters? A biker gang? Ex-cons with a long history of violent crimes?

Suerte. That was the name in flickering neon over the front door. I'd been led to believe that Bishop had owned this place forever and guessed he must be of Latinx heritage to have used a Spanish word for the name of his bar. Looking at the chipped concrete block building with the faint remains of peeling paint under the eaves, I guessed it was named Suerte since anyone going in would be damned lucky to get out alive. The place didn't have a bouncer, but I assumed it didn't need one. The customers and staff inside were probably capable of taking out any trash that walked in.

Twelve blocks surrounding the place were in blackout darkness, but this bar was fully Illuminated. I listened for the sound of huge generators, but heard nothing. The silence was eerie. It was as if the building were standing bastion against the darkness, a little oasis at the edge of hell.

"Get your ass in there," I muttered. I'd done enough stalling. Time was not on my side here, and I needed to swallow the deep unease that had lodged itself in my throat, and go inside.

The music didn't screech to a halt when I walked in, but I felt as if every single patron's attention was on me. The first thing I noticed was the lack of brown faces in the crowd. The darkest person in the bar looked as though they would blister at noon without a healthy coating of SPF 30. LA had always been an incredibly multicultural city, and that included the neighborhoods here in the Valley. When the demons first burst into the scene, the one-percenters got in their private jets and got the fuck out of town. By the time the angels showed up to fight back and trash whatever was left standing, those with diversified assets cut their losses and fled. It had skewed the demographics considerably and made the number of white people huddled in this room seem odd.

No, not huddled. Crouched. Territory marked, and every one of them prepared to defend it with their life. Noted.

A few heads turned as I walked past the tables to the bar, sitting at an empty seat between two men who were glaring holes straight through me.

"Taco Bell's five blocks south, Chica," the bald guy on my left snickered.

I ignored him, keeping my eyes on the bottles behind the bar—and his reflection in the mirror behind the bottles.

The dude to my right with the long wiry gray beard snorted. "You're in the wrong place, sweetie. Around here we eat dark meat for dinner."

I forced myself not to tense up. This had been a bad idea, a very bad idea, but I didn't have any other ideas. I could spend weeks looking for Nevarra and trying to dodge the tax collectors and never find her. If this Bishop guy could help, then I'd put up with racist insults and threats. I'd put up with anything to find my sister and bring her home.

The bartender walked by, ignoring me.

"I'm…I'm looking for Bishop?" Shit. Why was my voice like that? I sounded like a teen who'd been hauled in for dealing, not a grown woman asking a perfectly legitimate question.

The bartender continued to act as if I wasn't even there.

"Bishop?" The bald guy laughed. "Since when does he screw wetbacks?"

"Bishop's picky," Scrawny Beard said. "He might fuck you, but that's it. If you want anything more than a quick screw in the storeroom, then you best move along."

Two women moved up behind me. In a more crowded bar, I would have thought they were trying to squeeze beside me to order, but I knew better.

"Is Bishop here?" I called out to the bartender again, my voice sounding loud in the abnormally quiet room.

"He can have his pick," Scrawny Beard sneered. "He's not going to be slumming it with a skank like you."

"You've got ten seconds to get out the door." Baldy eased off his bar stool.

The two women behind me shifting into backup positions.

I kept silent and focused on keeping my breathing even and my muscles relaxed as I watched Baldy through the mirror. That's how I saw him make a grab for me.

His fist closed around my hair and pulled me backward. I reacted, turning sideways and slamming my elbow into his nose. At the same time, I sent a backward kick into Wiry Beard's right knee. Spinning around on the barstool, I punched my assailant again with my fist, ducking a swing from one of the women.

Baldy wrapped my hair tight in his hand, and pulled me

against him, locking his other arm around my midsection. One of his feet hooked around mine and he yanked me off balance, throwing me down onto the ground.

I was free, but it was still four against one. The two women kicked at me, and I found myself rolling and curling in to evade their feet instead of trying to get up. I felt a hand curl in my hair once more, forcing me to my knees.

The redhead went to kick my face, and I grabbed her foot, sweeping her other leg out from under her. The brunette danced back so she didn't step on her friend. The hand in my hair tightened and fingers came around my neck.

Fuck this shit. I grabbed the hand at my neck and sent a pulse of electricity into the flesh. The man yelped, then let go of me, dropping like a sack of concrete.

Ta-da. This was my other magic trick, the one even my family didn't know about. Guess it was no longer a secret, since Baldy was twitching on the ground and cursing in a breathless voice.

The entire bar had watched me take him down, but I didn't have time to think about whatever fallout I might suffer from that. Jumping aside and putting the wall at my back, I faced the two women and Wiry Beard with my fists ready. So much for finding Bishop and begging him to help me find Nevarra. I'd be lucky just to get out of here in one piece.

The brunette grinned at me. The redhead eyed my fists and took a step to the side. Wiry Beard stayed on his barstool, cursing and rubbing his knee. I heard a few chairs scrape back, and knew from a quick glance in the mirror that I was in serious trouble.

A woman with her platinum hair in a shoulder-length flip slammed her hands on the bar. The sound was like a gunshot. Before I could blink, every patron was back in their chairs or on their stools. The brunette had backed up about ten feet, and even the redhead was suddenly giving me distance.

Correction, not me. They were all giving the diminutive Marilyn Monroe distance.

"Damn it all to fucking hell, I think she broke my knee," Wiry Beard complained.

"Oh can it, Cody. It'll heal by morning."

The woman wiped her hands on a rag and tossed it at the bartender, hitting him in the face. Her nametag said "Head Bitch" which made me think I might actually like this woman.

"She doesn't belong here," the redhead argued. "She's not one of us. And she fucking Tazed King. No one attacks King and lives."

Head Bitch fixed the other woman with a hard stare. After two seconds, the redhead dropped her gaze. "Way I see it, King attacked her. Now go sit your ass down, or some stranger with a pocket zapper'll be the least of your worries."

The redhead went to help King to his feet and got swatted aside for her efforts. The bald man finally managed to get up, spat in my direction and stumbled his way over to one of the tables.

"Bishop'll be back soon. He doesn't normally hang out here on Thursdays." HB kept her eyes on the bald man. "Can I get you a drink while you wait? On the house 'cause of your trouble just now."

I really wasn't in the mood for drinking, but I knew better than to refuse. She felt she owed me, and it would be very rude for me to let that debt go unpaid. At least, that was the excuse I was using. I never turned down a free drink. Or free food. Or free anything.

"I'd love a beer. Thanks."

I sat back on the stool. Wiry Beard promptly stood and limped elsewhere.

HB crooked a finger, and the bartender yanked a bottle out of the fridge, twisting the cap off and setting it down in front of me.

Heineken. Huh. I had no idea why I was getting the fancy beer, but I wasn't going to argue. Taking a sip, I kept an eye on everyone through the mirror and waited. No one else bothered me. By the time my beer was half gone, a blond surfer god came through the door. Every head in the entire room swiveled to watch him, mine included. King stood, still covered in blood from when I'd broken his nose and made like he was going to approach the guy.

For a second I expected a repeat of what had happened to me, only with a whole lot less hair pulling. The air in the room thickened. King leaned forward, as if he were bracing against a strong wind or getting ready to explode into action. The blond guy tilted his head, his expression a mixture of disgust and incredulity, as if a really mangy hamster had just growled at him.

Did hamsters growl? Either way, bulk-wise the odds might not be in his favor, but my money was on the blond.

"Sit. The fuck. Down." The words came out like bullets from a gun. Okay, maybe the odds were in Surfer Dude's favor after all.

King sat down as if his legs had been cut out from under him. Completely ignoring him and everyone else in the joint, the blond guy walked behind the bar, and came to a stop in front of me.

"You're looking for me?"

I almost choked on my beer. *This* was Bishop? I'd expected an older man—a way older man. And given the name of the bar, I'd expected him to look Latin-American. He was definitely Caucasian, seemed to be in his late twenties, and looked like he was ready to bench press a few large appliances before he grabbed his surfboard.

Tall. Muscular. Sun-streaked hair that flopped into his eyes and curled up at the nape of his neck. Brilliantly blue eyes and the sexiest mouth I'd ever seen. I tended to go for the dark-haired, olive skinned bad boys, but this guy was seriously fucking hot—emphasis on the fucking. Venice Beach muscle heads weren't usually my thing, but this guy took my breath away.

"What do you want?" the man demanded.

Someone behind me snickered.

"Can we talk in private?" I asked, looking around at all the patrons who were pretending not to be listening in.

"No. Spill it, then get out of here."

I winced. So much for making a sexy impression on the guy, although I doubted I looked all that sexy anymore with my hair in a knotted mess and my black leather accessorized with a coating of dust from the floor.

"I need to hire you." Might as well get straight to the point. I didn't have time for small talk anyway. "I need to find someone. Fast."

His eyes did a slow tour of my leather-clad body. "Guy knock you up?"

"No! That's…no!" I sputtered.

"How fast?" He picked up my half empty bottle of Heineken and threw it in the trash.

I cleared my throat, resisting the urge to run for it. "Tonight. Now. Right now."

"I charge by the hour, and I get paid for my time whether we find what we're looking for or not, whether whatever I'm tracking winds up dead or alive."

I swallowed hard and nodded. "How…how much is your rate?"

He quoted a number that sank every last one of my hopes. "I don't have any money. Or bullets." At least none that I could spare. Not that the box I had would be enough in trade even if I offered it up.

That gorgeous upper lip curled into a sneer. "Then go find someone else. I don't do charity work."

"Can I pay you on time? With interest?" I fought a wave of shame. "I'm good for it, I promise."

He turned. I shot out of my seat to lean across the bar and grab his arm. "Please. I'm desperate. I need you to find my sister. She's only fourteen years old. They took her from our house. I heard you…you could find people. I'll pay. I swear. I'll pay double your rate if you'll give me thirty days to get you the money. Double."

As soon as I'd reached for him, I realized my ass was in the air, and I was in a position where Bishop, as well as anyone looking in the mirror, could see a substantial amount of cleavage. The surfer god eyed my breasts, the bar lighting reflecting gold flecks in his blue eyes. A low-level electric pulse shot from his warm skin into my hand and through my body.

I sucked in a breath, which lifted my breasts and brought them dangerously close to tumbling out of my bustier.

Okay, maybe this outfit hadn't been such a great idea after all.

"Paying on her back is the only currency you're gonna get from this one," King snarled. "Actually, she's probably better paying on her hands and knees."

I ignored the comment and focused on Bishop. Yeah, he *was* eyeing my boobs, but I'd seen him tense when I'd mentioned Nevarra's age. That gave me hope.

"Please. She's just turned fourteen. You know what they'll do to her. I'm desperate. I'll do anything. *Anything.*" And I would too.

His jaw clenched. "Where was she taken from?"

I told him my address, afraid to move, breathe, or give him any reason to say no.

"I'll be there in half an hour." His eyes swept me. "We might be on foot and moving fast, so I suggest you change into something more…appropriate."

I let out whoosh of air and slid back down to my barstool. "Thank you. Thank you so much—"

My words were addressed to his back because he was walking away. Thirty minutes. Shit I'd have to hustle to get back home by then and be ready to go, and these boots weren't exactly made for walking, let alone running.

CHAPTER 7

I got home to find that Aunt Bea had made her way into the kitchen and was boiling water over the little camp stove I'd picked up a few months back. The woman's face was swollen, but she'd cleaned herself up and had a makeshift sling holding her splinted arm. Her clothes were filthy and blood splattered, but I'm sure that was at the bottom of her list of priorities right now.

"How is Sadie?" I asked her.

"Sleeping. I re-dressed that wound on her shoulder, but her leg…"

"I know." I sat down and pulled off my boots, inspecting blistered feet unused to wearing heels. "I'll find something to sell for more antibiotics and first aid supplies. And maybe pain pills, although they're hard to find."

Bea sat down across from me, swaying a bit in her seat.

"You okay?" I asked her.

"Lost a lot of blood. My heart pills mean I don't clot so quick. Bled like a stuck pig all over the hallway." She sent me a wan smile. "I'll be fine. My biggest worries right now are keeping Sadie's leg from getting infected and finding Nevarra."

Mine too.

"Someone will be here in a few minutes to help look for Nevarra. He's got a reputation for finding people." That wasn't all he had a reputation for, but Aunt Bea didn't need to know that.

She sent me a sharp glance. "I'm not happy that you went out to meet him dressed like you're walking Western Avenue."

I didn't blush at Bea's mention of one of LA's many prostitution spots because she wasn't far from the truth. Bea had never been a prude, but she'd raised us to not be so quick to think to use our bodies as commerce. But desperate times…

Not that Bishop had seemed more than mildly interested in my body.

"Marissa from down the street has a cousin who works at the hospital. Tomorrow I'll go down and see if she can ask around for a nurse or a doctor who would make a house call. Maybe they'll take trade or payments."

Hospital staff were swamped. The chances that a nurse or doctor would make a house call, even if a co-worker asked them, was slim, but it was worth a try. There was only so much Bea and I could do with a bottle of antibiotics and basic first aid supplies. Hell, I didn't even know if the medicine I'd gotten from Bags was the right stuff to counteract an infection from a gunshot wound.

There was a soft knock on the door. I waved for Bea to stay seated and went to answer it. I hadn't had time to repair the thing, so I'd leaned it against the opening, giving us little more than illusion of privacy and security.

Bishop was at the door with an absolutely huge dog that looked like some kind of Malamute, or German Shepherd-wolf hybrid. I'd assumed he'd be bringing a bloodhound, not

Cujo on steroids, but I was in no position to be picky, so I invited them in and told them I just needed a few seconds to go change.

"I'd offer you something to drink, but…" I waved a hand at the trashed house.

He grunted a reply, and I went down the hallway to my room, not wanting to keep him waiting. Grabbing some clothes off the floor, I went into the girls' room to check on Sadie as I dressed.

She was still sleeping, her brown hair spilling over the pillow and blankets. I put a hand to her head, thankful that she didn't feel feverish. Bea had put a few more towels under her leg, elevating it. It looked clean, the bandages fresh.

I shimmied out of my tight leather garb, put on a pair of cargo pants, a tank top with my shoulder holster over it, and running shoes. Then I rechecked my pistol and slid it in the holster before slipping on a leather jacket. Then I dug around in the girls' laundry basket, trying to find something that Nevarra would have worn recently that didn't get washed last night.

Downstairs I found Bea sitting on a battered sofa, talking to Bishop. The dog looked simultaneously alert and bored. And pissed off, as if he had better things to do this evening than go track down a missing child. His head swiveled to watch me, and I shivered. The thing bared a row of sharp white teeth and stared at me with dispassionate yellow eyes. I'd seen police canines take down a guy before, but compared to Bishop's dog they'd looked like Chihuahuas.

"You going to be okay?" I asked Bea. "We might be out all night."

I hoped tonight was all it would take. If not, I'd check back in come dawn and give her an update before heading out again.

"I've got the pistols. We'll be fine. You just go get Nevarra, and let me worry about taking care of Sadie."

"I'm worried about you too." I smiled and gave her a soft kiss on the one part of her face that didn't look bruised.

"I'll be fine." She turned to Bishop. "Thank you again for helping us."

I watched her head down the hallway, then handed Bishop Nevarra's shirt. "She was wearing this yesterday. I figured you'd need something for your dog to use in tracking."

Bishop took the shirt, then with an odd smile held it out to the dog. "Got it?"

The dog bared his teeth, and I swear I saw him roll his eyes.

"Tell me about her," Bishop urged. "What's she look like?"

"She turned fourteen two weeks ago. She's five feet tall and I'd guess a bit under a hundred pounds. She's slim, but wiry and strong. Her eyes are about the same color as mine. Her hair is darker with tight curls. I'd describe her skin tone as sort of medium mahogany brown. Her father was Dominican, I think she once told me, and her mom white. She's got a little scar about half an inch long above her left eyebrow."

I saw Nevarra in my mind, clear as if she were right in front of me. She'd been with Bea and me since she was six. Her parents had died in a car accident when she was four and she'd been removed from her aunt's house two years later for neglect. She'd arrived here with an emotional well run dry and a heart full of fear and defensive anger, but Bea's love was a balm that eventually soothed all wounds.

"How's she going to take this whole thing?" Bishop gestured at the overturned furniture. "The attack on your house, the men taking her. What's her likely response?"

I couldn't help but smile. "She's pissed as hell right now."

Bishop smiled back. Heat flashed through me like an unexpected strike of lightning. It annoyed me. What the fuck was wrong with me? Now was *not* the time for sexy-time fantasies.

"Good. What do you think she'll do?" he asked.

I took a deep breath, trying to keep my damned hormones under lock and key. "She'll fight at first, then she'll start plotting. Nevarra's stronger than she looks, and she's smart. If she couldn't escape in the first hour, she'll settle down and start observing her surroundings and her captors, looking for the best way to get out. She won't take stupid chances unless she thinks there's no other option."

Bishop's expression softened. "I'm glad. That means there's a chance you'll find her alive at the end of all this."

All my fears came rushing back, and I forced them aside. Now wasn't the time to indulge in them either.

"I can show you where she was hiding when they found her, if that'll help," I said.

He nodded and stood. "It might help."

"Do you have any sisters? Or brothers?" I asked as I led him through the kitchen. The dog paused where Sadie had been hiding, eyeing the bullet holes in the cabinets and giving them a quick sniff.

"I haven't seen my family in a very long time. We're estranged." He said the last with an expression that told me this wasn't a topic he was going to elaborate on further.

"Sometimes you have to ditch the family you were born with and make your own," I told him, thinking of Sadie and Nevarra. "Sometimes there's no family to even ditch."

That had been me. Two women had found an infant in a church parking lot at two in the morning, naked and screaming my head off. I'd entered the custody of the county of Los Angeles, and remained there, my parentage a complete mystery. There were blanks where my documentation should have listed my mother and father. I'd spent most of my childhood thinking that was an ideal situation, that having no family meant there were less people in your life who were in a position to hurt you when you were most vulnerable.

I used to fear a family's love was a temporary, conditional thing that would build me up with hope only to utterly destroy me when that love shifted to hate or worse, apathy. Now I lived with the fear that someone might take my family away from me. I loved. And I limited my love to a very small group who I would give my life to protect.

But there was no way I'd reveal this to some guy I'd just met—to a very hot guy who was absolutely not my type.

Find Nevarra. Pay this guy what I ended up owing him. Figure out a way to make enough money to get Nevarra, Sadie, and Bea the hell out of here and to somewhere safe. That's all I needed to be thinking about right now.

We went out the back door and down the steps.

"This is where she was hiding," I said.

Bishop nodded, stuffing Nevarra's shirt in the waistband of his pants where it dangled beside his hip. Without any prompting, the dog squeezed itself into the space under the stairs, sniffing all around. Bishop knelt down, examining the hiding area carefully, brushing a finger over a spot of dried blood and lifting it to his nose.

I frowned because blood smells like blood. Maybe he had some magic in him that he didn't want to admit to? Hell, I didn't admit to my own magic. Most people didn't want to be thought a crazy freak, and until two years ago no one even believed magic was real. It could be he was like me with only a few odd skills that didn't do much good.

I hadn't thought about Bishop having magic. There *were* mages in the city, but not in this section of the Valley. Their services cost way more than I could have paid even as of yesterday. No, he couldn't be a mage or he'd be in living in some swanky penthouse or gated house in the hills, not running a dive bar full of racist customers.

"Come on," Bishop growled.

I figured he was talking to the dog, but just in case I followed him as well. We went through the metal gate, along the side of the house, and out to the street. I thought it was odd that Bishop was leading and not the dog, but what the hell did I know about scent tracking beyond a few cop shows I'd watched on TV years ago?

The dog sniffed around. Bishop scowled at the asphalt.

I stood in absolute silence, not wanting to disturb their mojo, and trying very hard not to get in the way. The man looked up, off into the distance toward the mountains, then back at the dog. Their eyes met, and Bishop nodded.

"They loaded her into a vehicle. I'm thinking it might be quicker to track from the truck since they probably took her more than a few miles."

A vision filled my brain—a vision of Nevarra struggling as men roughed her up and stuck her in a van, all of them laughing and thinking of what kind of money they'd make selling her. My pragmatic mind tried to reassure me that they wouldn't hurt her too bad, that they wouldn't rape her. Her value would drop to a fraction of what they'd get for a young uninjured virgin, and money would be more important than sex, even if a few of them liked their partners on the young side.

I'd find her no matter how long it took, and I'd fucking kill anyone who laid a hand on her, but I wanted to get to her tonight, before she had to go through life trying to wash those kinds of memories out of her mind.

*B*ishop's truck reminded me a lot of his bar. It was a bench-seat Chevy from the '70s that looked like it had been restored at one point and allowed to deteriorate ever since. The back right fender had a dent in it the size of a bowling ball, and a long gouge down the side was rust red amid the primer gray and faded sky blue. The dog hopped into the bed with an impressive vertical leap, and I opened the passenger side door, surprised that it didn't even squeak.

The truck roared to life and Bishop eased it down the road, both windows open as well as the rear one that separated the cab from the bed. I glanced back to see the dog with his front feet on top of the wheel fender, nose to the sky. Bishop stared straight ahead, that scowl still on his face.

I didn't say a thing, but I couldn't help but fidget, wishing *he'd* say something, or that the dog would bark. Anything. I just wanted reassurance that we were still following some sort of scent trail.

Without any discernable direction from the dog, Bishop took a few turns, and merged onto the highway heading south.

"You're young," Bishop commented out of the blue.

"Twenty-two." I'll admit my tone was a bit defensive. In my mind, that wasn't young. He didn't look much older.

He chuckled. "You in college?"

I'd taken a few courses after high school, but my heart hadn't been in it. School wasn't my thing. I hadn't known what was my thing back then. I still didn't. The demons coming had ignited something in me—the need to protect my family, to keep us all safe and get us the hell out of here before we ended up like that tractor trailer on the side of the freeway. Before that I'd just been wandering around unsure what I was supposed to do with my life. Once my family was safe, I'd probably go back to the same. Nothing else sparked a fire in me. Nothing. Right now my family needed me. When they didn't, I wasn't sure what I'd do.

"Yeah. I was pre-med at USC," I told him.

He snorted.

"How about you? What were you all doing before everything went to shit?" I asked.

"Working for a bunch of assholes."

"Huh. Owning a racist bar is clearly a big improvement over that." I didn't know why I wanted to poke at this guy, especially when I needed him right now. I eyed him out of my peripheral vision, hoping my big mouth wasn't about to get me dumped on the curb, but Bishop didn't look angry. He seemed amused by my comment.

"We're only a racist bar on Thursdays." He glanced over at me, then back to the road. "Sorry King came after you. His pack…they're dicks, but they've become even bigger dicks since he took over."

"Why don't you tell them no and kick them out?"

Wasn't that the point of owning your own place? You didn't have to put up with anyone's shit?

"If they weren't hanging out at my place, they'd just be

somewhere else." Bishop wrinkled his nose in disgust. "That pack's got a few bad apples. They're not all like that."

Like King, the two women, and Wiry Beard, he meant.

"If people tolerate the bad apples, that makes them one too." I was lumping him into that category as well, hoping he wouldn't realize that and shove me out of the car. I really needed to shut up. Nevarra had been kidnapped, and if I had to put up with some guy excusing racist assholes in his bar, then I needed to do it.

Bishop shrugged. "It's not my job to clean up their mess. They're not my problem."

"They are when someone comes into your bar, gets insulted, then gets fucking attacked," I shot back. "The guy jumped me, and those two bimbos joined in. I get the feeling half the bar was seconds from piling on me when your manager-woman stepped in."

His hands tightened on the steering wheel. "King crossed a line. I'll make sure he doesn't do it again."

"Maybe you should put a sign up out front that Thursdays are only for racist slime, just to warn people." Maybe I should just shut my fucking mouth before it got me in trouble.

Bishop sucked in a breath, relaxing a fraction as he let it out. "I'll take care of it."

I rolled my eyes, thinking his idea of taking care of it wouldn't change a thing. He'd said it wasn't his problem, and I got the idea he meant it. Bishop clearly didn't like to be bothered—by dustups in his bar, by women with no money pleading for help.

But he was right. If I ever needed to go back to Suerte, I'd avoid Thursdays. King and all the racists in the world weren't my problem either. That wasn't my battle to fight—not when I had so many other battles facing me right now.

"Look, there's always going to be bad apples. They come and they go. There's no sense wasting time on them." He glanced over at me. "King's pack has been coming to Suerte on Thursdays for a long time. You're right. I need to do something about him, but assholes like him are always gonna be around. Take out one, and two more will show up."

And letting racist assholes insult and attack potential patrons in your bar was okay because something-something and "you'll never get rid of them all so why bother"? What a load of bullshit. Plus the botany metaphors were annoying me. Deciding this argument wasn't going to go anywhere, I sat back and kept my mouth shut.

"You hurt?" Bishop grumbled after ten minutes or so.

"Huh?"

"Hurt. Did King hurt you?"

Oh. For some reason I'd thought he had been talking about my emotions, as if he'd hurt my feelings. "No. I'm fine."

I was, and that was a fucking miracle. Being hauled around by my hair hadn't seemed to have caused any lasting injury to my scalp, and although a few of those kicks landed, I didn't even feel bruised. It had been a while since I'd been in a physical fight, but I clearly hadn't lost any of my skills.

We both fell silent, and an hour later Bishop turned off the freeway into Hawthorne. My stomach churned. This was Disciples territory, and it seemed pretty far for the Fixers to have hauled Nevarra. Had the dog lost the scent somewhere? Was Bishop not as good as everyone said?

Pulling the truck over to the side of the road, Bishop put it in park, grabbed the keys, and got out. I followed his lead, trailing along behind him and the dog as they turned down an alley and came to a stop in front of an old abandoned Costco.

Here? Why didn't he say anything? The silence was killing me.

"Bea said the one had a screwdriver tattooed on his bicep," I whispered. Bishop looked back at me in surprise, as if he'd forgotten I was with them. "Are you sure we're in the right place?"

"Yeah."

This guy needed to say more than "yeah."

"Is she in there?" I prodded.

Was anyone in there? The place was dark. No vehicles were nearby. The whole area was like a ghost town.

"I don't know." Bishop glanced down and met the dog's eyes. "I'm sending Bob to check."

What a shitty name for a dog. I looked after the animal in some sympathy as it trotted over to the building, vanishing smoothly into the shadows. "He looks more like a Spike, or an Ajax."

Bishop snorted. "He'd be flattered to hear that. Spike. Shit, we'd never hear the end of it if I told him."

I waved a hand in the general area where the huge dog had disappeared. "He's really tough-looking. Bob just doesn't sound right."

"Well, that's his name." Bishop grinned. It made him look even more like a stereotypical California surfer dude. "Maybe I'll start calling him Tiny, just to piss him off."

There was clearly something weird going on here. I didn't have a lot of personal experience with dogs, but it seemed more and more like Bob wasn't a normal dog. And maybe Bishop wasn't a normal human.

Not my business. If they helped me find Nevarra, they could be fucking flying alien monkeys for all I cared.

We both turned to stare at the building for a while, waiting for Bob to return with his report.

"It's spelled," Bishop abruptly told me.

"Huh?"

"Magic. A spell to avoid detection of something or some-one. That's why we lost the trail."

"That's good, right?" I began to get excited. "Nevarra's

scent trail ends here, and doesn't go anywhere else, so she's got to be inside."

"Maybe. The same magic that is shielding the building could have been used to get her out of the building and somewhere else without leaving a trail. Vehicles can be spelled. I've also seen amulets that are designed to shield a person."

"So it's magic that hides someone's scent?"

"Scent as well as other forms of detection." Bishop gestured at the building. "From the outside we can't tell if there's anyone inside because the building is spelled. It's effective against Bob's nose, technology such as scanning for heat signatures, a location spell."

"I thought spells just kept people from getting inside. Like a security system." I knew so little about magic. Hell, two years ago I didn't believe magic was real, even though I'd had my strange talents for as long as I could remember.

"Protection wards *are* the most commonly found spell around here," Bishop said. "You see this kind of shielding magic used in burglaries. If someone's going to steal a million-dollar painting, they don't want the owner finding it with a location spell, or an electronic tracking device."

"Or Bob," I mused.

Bishop chuckled. "Or Bob."

In two years of scavenging I'd never come across a magic wand, or amulet, but I wasn't sure I'd recognize one if I saw it.

"But Nevarra *could* be inside?" I asked. "Bob can't find her scent leaving. The building has some sort of non-detection spell on it. You're thinking either she's inside, or they managed to drive her out in a warded van?"

He nodded. "That's what I'm assuming."

"Do you know who owns this building?" I asked. I

doubted the Fixers, although they'd clearly brought Nevarra here.

"Disciples," Bishop spat the name out. "They move a lot of stolen product, and they're known for putting non-detection spells on their warehouses. They snatched up this building a few years back and use it for temporary storage of goods."

Then why the hell had the Fixers brought Nevarra here? Were they trading her to the Disciples? Did they intend to hide her among pallets of PlayStations and Rice Krispy Treats? Or were they meeting someone here who liked to buy preteen girls?

"Do you think she's already been sold?" I could barely get the words out.

A muscle in Bishop's jaw twitched. "I doubt it. A quick sale means lost money. She'll bring them a lot more if they auction her off or if they can contact a few big-money buyers and start a bidding war."

"She was taken by the Fixers. Why would they involve the Disciples?" I asked. "Why split the money when they could make more selling her off themselves?"

Bishop grunted. "Could be the Fixers don't have the connections or organization to pull it off, where the Disciples might. Could be they don't want to take the risk of the police catching wind of them trafficking a little girl."

I looked at him in surprise. "Why would the police give a shit?"

He shrugged. "Some still do."

When the demons had come, the police had done their best to control the situation, to limit the damage and keep people safe. I was no fan of the cops, but I saw some good ones doing good things during the riots and violence of those first few months. He was right, and for the first time in my life, I actually contemplated going to the police to report Nevarra's kidnapping. There was a fifty-fifty chance they might turn me over to the tax collectors, but if they had detectives knowledgeable about how human trafficking worked in the city, it might be worth putting my neck on the line.

"What do you know about the Disciples?" I asked him, wondering where the hell Bob was and what was taking him so long.

He shrugged again. "Not much. They stay out of my way, and I don't bother them."

I didn't reply since at that moment I saw movement over by some dumpsters. Bob slid from the shadows and trotted up to us, exchanging a long wordless communication with his master.

"Four people inside, but no kids," Bishop told me. "Your girl's scent goes in, then vanishes around the loading docks, so Tiny here thinks they took her out in a warded vehicle."

Bob snarled at the new nickname.

"He said there's lots of shit inside," Bishop continued. "Electronics and weapons. No, I'm not grabbing you a laptop."

I blinked in surprise, for a second thinking that Bishop was still talking to me. *Was* he talking to me? I couldn't imagine what a dog would do with a laptop, even a weird dog like Bob.

He couldn't be one of those shifters I'd heard about… could he? Weredog? I shot Bob a quick glance, then another at Bishop, wondering if he was one of them too.

It didn't matter. I'd find Nevarra, then avoid these people like the plague. Well, after I paid them, that is.

"I'm going in," I announced, removing my pistol from the holster and pulling the slide to chamber a bullet. Four people. I could take four. Maybe.

"She's not in there," Bishop reminded me.

"No, but they might know where she is." Which meant I'd

need to not kill them. Damn it. It would be hard enough to take down four people without getting killed myself. Now I needed to add keeping at least one of them alive to the scenario.

Bishop sighed, then looked down at Bob. "Shut up."

I didn't know what that was about and I wasn't going to ask.

"Just show us how you got in," Bishop told the dog.

We followed Bob around past the dumpsters to where a loading dock door was cracked open a foot from the ground.

"Security?" I asked Bishop. There was an alarm box by the bay doors, but it wasn't set.

"The only magic is the non-detection wards," he said. "If they have security spells, they're not activated right now."

Good. That meant if we were quiet, we'd have the element of surprise on our side.

Bob shimmied under the loading dock door without a sound, so fluid it seemed as if he were boneless. I knelt down to do the same, but hesitated when Bishop put a hand on my shoulder.

That same electricity zinged through me as it had in his bar. Damn it, the guy might be a weredog like Bob, but even that suspicion didn't keep me from wanting him.

"I won't fit," he whispered. "I'll need to open the garage door, and it'll make noise. Use the distraction. I'll wait thirty seconds before I push it up."

I nodded, not trusting myself to speak, then slid under the door with far less grace and silence than Bob had.

Although the building appeared to be several stories, it was one big open space with filthy windows stacked above each other three stories high. Inside, huge metal racks were lined up in neat aisles, each one of them loaded with pallets full of boxes. Was there even a market for all this shit anymore? Maybe the Disciples had found a way to ship all this over the border to sell to those who hadn't been abandoned by their country.

Bob was nowhere to be seen, and I wasn't sure exactly where in this huge place the four people were, so I ducked down a row, trying to keep behind the boxes as I scoped the place out. Thirty seconds wasn't very long. I hid behind a pallet full of boxes labeled coffee filters and waited, deciding my best plan of action would be to wait for Bishop to cause the distraction and let the bad guys come to me.

The garage door didn't just squawk when Bishop opened it, it shrieked. The sound was like a knife in my ears, and I wondered if he'd opened the door or ripped it clear off the track.

The noise was loud enough to cover up any shouts of alarm from the bad guys, so I ended up without the slightest idea which direction they might be coming from. Wedging myself between the crate of coffee filters and the one of paper towels next to it, I waited.

These guys were no fools. A few faint footsteps were all that clued me in as to their whereabouts. A man in dark clothes, his pistol sweeping the area before him, came into my line of sight. I held still, wanting to wait until he was past me before I did anything, but a noise in the aisle behind me had him swinging around.

And staring right at me. I scrambled backward, tripping over a piece of wood jutting out from the pallet and falling into the next aisle. Two bullets clanged against the metal shelving right where my head would have been a split second before. Firing back, I rolled behind the cases of paper towels, jumped to my feet, and ran.

Cardboard, bits of paper towels and coffee filters flew through the air right behind me as I raced down the aisle. Ducking down behind a crate, I waited until the shooting stopped, swung into view and popped off two rounds.

I was pretty sure I'd hit him, but from the return fire and his shout, it must not have penetrated anything vital. When the shooting stopped, I scooted between the crates to peer down the other aisle. There was blood on the floor, but the bad guy was nowhere to be seen, so I eased out from between the pallets, checked the aisle again and dashed across. There was no way anyone had missed hearing the gunshots. They'd all be converging here soon, and I needed to not be caught where I couldn't easily escape.

Another bullet pinged off the metal shelving.

I ducked down, trying to pivot around so I could make sure I wasn't about to run head-first into the barrel of a pistol.

The coast was clear, and I made a dash for it, weaving and ducking. I heard a few shots, but nothing came close. Where the fuck were Bob and Bishop? I was getting the feeling I was in here alone facing these four dudes. Flattening myself against a crate of canned chili, I spun around the corner with my gun at the ready and saw a body on the floor. The man's arm was partially detached from his body, and as I dashed by, I saw his throat had been ripped out.

Well at least *Bob* was helping out. At least, I assumed it was Bob since I couldn't imagine doing that sort of thing with human teeth.

One down, three to go. The warehouse was eerily silent once more so I walked along the jutting wood of the pallets, listening and briefly glancing around each corner before I ran across the aisle. Three rows back, I saw a few spots of blood and smiled. At least I knew where one of them was headed, although I wasn't about to assume this guy wasn't a threat. He might be injured and bleeding, but one stupid move on my part, and he could still blow my head off.

I followed the trail, carefully checking to make sure none

of the others were flanking me or coming around from behind. A shout and rapid gunfire came from a few rows up. I ducked low and ran, rounding the corner to see Bob grappling with my injured guy. They were on the ground, and Bob was savaging the man's arm, trying to get to his neck. The man reached out, grabbing his gun from the floor and bringing it upward. I shot, and this time my aim was true. The man's head rocked backward, the gun and his arm falling to the floor.

I spared a second to wonder if the blood on Bob wasn't solely from the bad guy before another man rounded the corner.

Two left.

I ducked back, and Bob vanished between the crates. The guy must have thought I was the more serious threat because he started shooting in my direction. I ran, weaving through the aisles as he chased me, bullets pinging off the shelves and tearing through boxes. I managed to get far enough ahead that he was no longer shooting at me, then squeezed between more pallets of industrial-sized canned chili—who the fuck needed this much canned chili?—and tried to quiet my ragged breathing. My hands shook from the adrenaline and my ears rang from the sound of gunshots in this echo chamber of a warehouse. That's probably why I didn't hear the second guy behind me until his gun was pressed against my temple.

"Gun down. Ease out slowly, and keep your hands where I can see them." His voice was breathy as he tapped the muzzle against the back of my head, punctuating his command.

He was scared. And he had reason to be. I placed my Glock carefully on the floor, then raised my hands and scooted slowly backward, hoping the other guy didn't get here in the next five seconds.

Once I was out from between the pallets of chili, he backed the gun off my head. "Stand up slowly, and—"

I spun before the guy could get the rest out of his mouth and leapt forward in a crouch. He yelped and shot wildly before I grabbed his leg and sent electricity sizzling through his body.

This was the second time I'd used this superpower today, and I wasn't sure it would even work a second time. Or how powerful the electric shock would be. I was like a human Taser, but without any control over whether I was delivering the equivalent of a static shock or something a whole lot more than a stun gun. I could numb someone's arm. I could drop them to the ground where they'd twitch for a few seconds then lay there for at least a couple of minutes. I could knock them out.

I could kill them.

It was like a game of Russian roulette which was going to come out of me, which is one of the reasons I chose not to use it unless I had to. It would really suck if I'd intended to interrogate someone, after just giving them a warning zap, and they ended up dead and smoking on the ground.

Like this dude.

Good thing there was one more guy roaming around the warehouse alive. At least I hoped so. I was going to be really pissed if Bob had killed him, leaving me no one to interrogate.

And where the fuck was Bishop?

Idiot should have just shot me, I thought, giving the body a kick. No doubt he'd intended to interrogate me as well, to figure out which gang I was with and what they were planning before putting a bullet through my head. Joke was on him. I was just as much of a killer without my gun as I was with it.

A scraping sound had me jerking my head up and diving

for my gun. I stopped mid-reach because it was Bishop, coming down the aisle and dragging the other guy behind him by the back of his shirt.

"Fuck! Tell me you didn't kill him?" I shoved my pistol in my shoulder holster before jogging over to meet him.

"He's alive." Bishop dropped him like a wet sack of flour on the floor, then motioned toward the guy as if he were that woman on a television game showcasing a particularly lavish prize. Vanna something or another I think her name was.

I snapped my gun into the holster to make sure it would be difficult for the guy to grab and use on me. Of course, that meant I'd be relying on Bishop to help if the dude was faking the extent of his injuries and attacked me. I didn't want to zap him and end up with no bad guy left to question.

Plus, I didn't want Bishop to know what I could do. *Some secrets best remain secrets.*

I hauled the guy up to his knees, where thankfully he managed to stay. One of my shots had grazed his torso, tearing his shirt and leaving a deep, bloody gash. That seemed to be his only wound.

His eyes flickered with recognition, and he spat at my feet. "You're dead, you fucking bitch. If the tax collectors don't kill you, then the one of us will. Or maybe the Disciples will kill you, since you shot up their warehouse."

Oh please. The Disciples weren't going to hunt us down for wrecking a few cases of paper products, and the Fixers weren't organized enough to bother avenging a few dead members. But the rest of his threat rang true. I needed to make sure I stayed clear of the tax collectors until I could either get their money or their bullets from that cop. If I continued to elude their mercenaries long enough, they might send a demon to get me. Then none of my nifty magic tricks would be able to save me.

I eyed the screwdriver tattoo on his neck, and tried to

keep from ripping this guy's head off. This was one of the guys who'd broken into my house, beat up my foster mother, shot Sadie and taken Nevarra. I'd enjoy killing him.

"Where's the girl?" I demanded.

He grinned up at me. "Gone."

I started to reach out to grab him, but felt the tingle of sparks along my fingers and decided against it. I couldn't trust myself right now, and I needed to know where they'd taken Nevarra.

So instead I unsnapped my pistol and drew it. "Where? Who has her?"

"Fuck you." He spat at my feet once more.

I shot him in the knee.

He toppled over, clutching his leg and swearing. I waited a few seconds for him to get ahold of himself. Then I asked my questions once more.

"You'll never find her." He sneered.

I contemplated shooting his other knee, but didn't want to risk him bleeding out...yet. So instead I kicked his injured leg.

"Did you guys sell her to the Disciples? Who in the Disciples handles their human trafficking deals? Where did they take her?"

"Fuck you," he gasped, his eyes meeting mine.

This guy wasn't going to tell me anything. No matter what I did. He knew he'd die either way, and preferred to go out with the upper hand. I took a step back, clenching my fist in frustration as I tried to think of what I could do to torture additional information out of this guy.

"Let me." Bishop's deep voice washed over me.

I turned to see him watching me with an impassive expression on his face, Bob at his side. Bob's expression was far from impassive. The dog was totally judging me.

As if he could do any better.

The Fixer also seemed to have forgotten about Bishop's presence. He glanced at the other man, and terror creeping into his eyes. Damn it, I was the one with the gun, and here he was practically wetting his pants at an unarmed surfer dude. Although to be honest, Bishop was pretty scary for a jacked-up guy with blond hair, blue eyes, and a beach boy tan.

Bishop walked over to the man and took his shirt in a fist. "Look at me."

The Fixer's eyes were everywhere but on Bishop, but at the man's command, his gaze slowly dragged upward.

"Where is the girl?" The words were soft, and seductively smooth.

My legs felt weak. *I* wanted to answer the man, and I had no idea where Nevarra was.

"I…I don't know. I don't know where they took her." The man's eyes never left Bishop's. A thin line of drool rolled down his chin. "She's worth a lot—worth more than some used-up runaway from the streets. She's young. She's the perfect age. And she's clean, cared for. She'll bring a lot of money but we don't have the contacts to get her to the buyers, so we made a deal with the Disciples."

"What sort of deal?" Bishop's one hand tightened in the man's shirt.

"Finder's fee, then five percent of the sale." The man licked his lips. "They'll probably auction her off to get the best price, so we won't get paid for another few days, or maybe a week depending on how hot the bidding is."

I tried to steady my breathing trying not to think of what Nevarra was going through, but I couldn't help but ask. "Is she unharmed? She's still…no one touched her?"

Bishop jerked the man. "Answer her."

"No one's gonna fuck with merchandise that valuable," he said. "She had a cut and some bruises, but that's it."

I felt like I was about to throw up. "Where did they take her? Which member of the Disciples handles this sort of 'merchandise'?"

Bishop didn't have to jerk the guy this time.

"I don't know where they took her. None of us do. Disciples ain't gonna tell us that," he said. "I don't know who handles that sort of sale for them."

"You're telling me you turned over someone worth a lot of money to some rando in another group? And you're not worried they're going to screw you over?"

He grinned. "We got enough up front that if they screw us over, it's no big deal. Plus, we'll get 'em more if they pay up the rest. If not, then they won't get the opportunity next time."

I started to pace. All we had was this worthless sack of shit, and he didn't know where Nevarra was, or who took her. Someone with the Disciples. None of that was going to do squat for helping me find my sister.

"Who was here for the trade?" Bishop asked the man. "Tell me what happened?"

"Kurt knows someone, and he called it in once we left the house with the girl. They said to meet here. There were six of them. A tall guy with black hair and a scar down his face was running the show. He checked the girl over, then he and Kurt came to an agreement."

I frowned. "How tall?"

"Taller than me, so six three? Six four? He was a white guy. Fender. That's what the other guy called him. Fender."

I sucked in a breath.

Bishop shot me a quick glance. "You know this guy?"

"Know *of* him." I frowned, trying to think of where Fender might have taken Nevarra to keep her safe until they could sell her.

"After they made the deal, Kurt got cash and bullets, and

Fender got the girl. He told us we could pick out a few things from the warehouse as a bonus—cell phones or computers if we wanted. Kurt left me and Hunter to pick shit out. Two Disciples stayed back to make sure we didn't take too much and to lock up after we were gone. We grabbed what we wanted, but there was this case of brandy in the back, so we figured we'd all have a drink. Then we heard you breaking through the garage door…"

Kurt. I'd need to remember that name, since he was probably the Fixer tasked with collecting me. And Fender… Damn it, I needed to talk to Bags. He'd know where the Disciples liked to hang out, and he'd be my best chance of knowing where Fender could be found.

"You done with this guy?" Bishop asked.

I nodded, still mulling over how I was going to get in to see Bags when I heard a crack.

Blinking in surprise, I saw Bishop let go of the man, dusting his hands off as he turned away. The Fixer slid to the ground, dead, his neck broken. No, his neck wasn't just broken, his head was turned around Exorcist-style. I shuddered, thinking what sort of strength it must have taken to do that. And Bishop had done it casually, effortlessly.

Yes, I had a weird attraction toward the guy, but fear was starting to edge that attraction out. I did not want to get involved with this guy. Nope. Not even a booty call.

Except I owed him, and I'd already implied that sort of payment was on the table. Shit. I had no doubt I'd enjoy the hell out of having sex with Bishop. Hopefully he wouldn't kill me when we were done. My mind instantly detoured to visions of Bishop naked, my hands running over hard tanned muscles, my tongue tasting his skin.

"You know how to find this Fender guy?" Bishop asked, pulling me out of my reverie.

"No, but there's someone I know who might be able to

tell me where he can be found." Unfortunately, I'd need to wait until morning. I didn't know if Bags slept at the pawnshop or had a house somewhere, but either way disturbing him this late wouldn't be a good idea.

I ran a hand through my hair. "I'll go see him first thing in the morning."

That would give me time to formulate a plan, and to make sure Bea and Sadie were okay.

The dog looked up at Bishop, meeting his gaze. They exchanged a wordless communication, then Bishop turned to me.

"I'll talk to a few people. See if I can find him at my end. Put out some feelers on your sister. Other than that, there's not much more I can do right now." He gestured to the dog. "If you find something we can track, come see me. Otherwise, we won't be any further use to you."

That statement seemed to annoy him. It depressed me. He'd been the one guy I thought could find Nevarra for me and find her fast. Without Bishop, I was on my own.

Either way, I'd availed myself of this guy's services. Hopefully his hourly rate didn't include travel time.

"How much do I owe you?" I squirmed. Not that I had any money. I'd probably be making payments to this guy for the next decade. Or as King had said, on my back.

The dog made a weird coughing noise as if he could read my mind.

Bishop shrugged. "Nothing until you find her. You bring the girl home, then come see me, and we'll set up some sort of payment plan."

Time was money, and he'd spent a couple of hours out here with me tonight. I had no idea how much he earned at the bar, and that dog looked like he ate his weight in food every day. Surely the guy would want something, even if it was a quick blowjob in a back alley.

"But your time… Maybe I can give you a…deposit?"

His gaze drifted to my lips, and I wondered if a blowjob was exactly what he was thinking himself. Then he shook his head. "I don't take that kinda payment." Then he went on before I could reply: "If you're ever in my bed, it's because you want to be there, not because you're paying back a favor or think you owe me something."

I was relieved and disappointed. Relieved because I didn't want to be a whore—to this man in particular. Disappointed because I wanted him. *And* because this meant I'd probably be paying him off for the next few months, or years. So much for getting my family out of here anytime soon.

But it would be worth every penny if I got Nevarra back safe. Bishop might not have found her, but I had a strong lead, a direction to pursue. The Disciples. Fender.

He stepped forward, reached out as if he were going to touch my face, then dropped his hand back to his side. "When your sister is back home, then we'll discuss compensation."

Why was he being this nice when he'd been a bit of an asshole in the bar? My suspicion flared, and I immediately searched my mind for an ulterior motive. Why was he not worried about payment? For all he knew, I could find Nevarra and skip out before I even gave him a dime.

Although the guy had a reputation for finding things and people. I was pretty sure he could track me down if I ran out on my debt. It's not like I could afford some sort of non-detection spell myself.

Bishop turned to leave, then paused. "Actually, since we're here…"

* * *

BOB WASN'T THRILLED about riding in the bed of the truck surrounded by cans of chili and paper goods, but Bishop had yanked a laptop out of a stack of brand-new computer equipment for him, so he'd stopped snarling at us. I'd taken the cash off the dead guys, along with their guns. I'd also grabbed a few other things. With my license pulled, I couldn't risk pawning anything, and knew Bags's shop was probably under surveillance right now. We'd need to barter for what we needed, and while bullets were the currency of the street, toilet paper was the currency of suburbia.

And canned chili, hopefully.

Bishop had snagged a random assortment of stuff—a few pressure washers he'd found in the back, a case of gourmet beef jerky, a huge box that contained a deluxe massage chair, and some high thread-count sheets. I'll admit that I was eyeing the sheets as well, but since I didn't own a king-sized bed, I opted to pass.

Bishop pulled the truck up to the curb and glared at the front door propped against the opening. "You need to fix your door."

"No shit, Sherlock," I snapped, exhausted and emotionally drained worrying about my family. "It's kinda low on my priority list right now."

But he was right. I did need to fix it to keep out the neighborhood animals, the insects, and the riffraff that might think the house was vacant and ripe for looting. Maybe while I was at Bags's I could see if he had some hinges I could grab. And lumber.

Bishop grunted, then completely surprised me by getting out of the truck and helping me unload all the shit I'd lifted from the warehouse. He even carried it into the house for me and set the boxes next to the couch. I watched him leave through the crack between the front door and the door jamb, noticing that Bob had leapt into the front seat where I'd previously been. I stood at the door until he'd driven out of sight, feeling oddly empty without him by my side.

Oh no. No, no, no. I hadn't felt this tingly needy feeling in a long time, and I wasn't about to feel it now, especially not for a scary, muscled surfer dude who was probably a weredog or something.

Nope. No way.

CHAPTER 9

I debated the wisdom of staying at the house with Bea and Sadie. Whoever was hunting for me knew I lived there and might be back. Oddly that's what made me decide to stay. I'd rather be there to defend my family than spend a sleepless night worried about injured Bea trying to defend herself and Sadie against intruders.

Bea was in the girls' bedroom, struggling to stay awake, the pistol by her side. I checked on her and Sadie.

"Get some sleep," I said.

The house was eerily silent. No one ever realizes how much ambient noise there is until it's gone. Without the electricity, there was no hum of the refrigerator, no whir of a fan, no buzz of a streetlight. I was even more on edge with the door broken and propped against the frame. There was nothing I could do about that right now, but I could at least try to clean up a bit and try to rid it of the visual reminders of what had happened today.

It was dark, but the moon filtering through the curtains gave the room a monochromatic light. I'd always had incredible night vision, and it wasn't like I could sleep, so I swept the broken items into a corner, righted the furniture, and tried to duct tape the cushions back together, covering my crappy repairs with blankets. The broken tables I set to the side, hoping that I might be able to glue the pieces back together come morning. When I was done, the place didn't look quite so trashed.

Just before dawn I heard the hum of the refrigerator kicking on, and saw the light outside flicker. Rushing to the kitchen I checked to see if we had water.

Bingo. First I filled the ice trays and put them into the freezer, then I started refilling all the plastic jugs and containers we used to hold water, just in case we were out for any length of time. Digging out the remains of the ground coffee, I filled the maker, set it to brew, and headed upstairs to check on Sadie and Bea.

Bea was kneeling beside Sadie's bed, sponging her off with a damp rag. Sadie twisted in the sweat-soaked sheets, her eyes glassy. Pink stained the bandages wrapping her leg, and I worried her restless stirring was making the wound worse.

Fear stole my breath. Wasn't it too soon for her to be running a fever? Had infection set in already? She needed a doctor, but we had no money for a house call, and the hospital was so overrun that she'd have to sit in a crowded waiting room for eight or more hours before even being seen.

"I'm going to run down to Marissa's early this morning and see if her cousin found a doctor or nurse who would make a call on credit." Bea's voice was soft and low, but under the soothing tones I heard her worry.

They were my family, and I hadn't protected them. Sadie...what if she died? And Nevarra might be facing things worse than death. What good was I if I couldn't help the people I loved? I reached out to touch Sadie's forehead, feeling the heat radiating off of her. Then I felt tears sting my eyes, spilling over as a sob I couldn't hold back broke free.

I never would have broken down like this in front of anyone but Bea. She's the only one in my life who had ever seen me cry. With a clucking noise, the woman gathered me into her arms and rocked me just like she'd done when I'd been a scared and rebellious teen.

"She'll be fine, Eden. We'll get her medical care, and she'll be just fine. And you'll find Nevarra and bring her home."

"What if I don't?" I choked out all my fears. "What if I can't find her? What if Sadie gets worse and loses her leg or dies? What if they come back and kill you both while I'm out looking for Nevarra?"

Bea squeezed me tight, stroking my hair. "Stop this right now. You are not alone, Eden Alvaro. And unless you've forgotten, you're a twenty-two-year-old young woman, while I'm a fifty-two-year-old woman. You three are *my* responsibility. Yes, I need your help, but you're not expected to do all this on your own."

I sniffed and wiped my eyes as I pulled from her arms. "But it's my fault this happened. It's all my fault."

"Honey, it's nobody's fault but those assholes who came barging in here, shooting the place up and demanding payment for things you never took. You were set up. Blame them. Blame those mercenaries. Do *not* blame yourself."

I sniffed again. "But Sadie's really bad off, and you're injured. I need to find Nevarra, but there's you and Sadie. And how am I supposed to earn money to get us out of here when my license is pulled and I've got a price on my head?"

I felt so weak pouring all of this out onto her shoulders, but I'd learned at the age of thirteen that Bea had wide, strong shoulders—wide enough to carry all of our burdens. She'd never think less of me for having my doubts. She'd never look at me with anything but pride and love, even when I felt absolutely unworthy of either.

Bea reached out and took my hands. "You ask for help, that's how—just like me. I'm going to stay here and take care of Sadie, and I'm gonna ask neighbors and friends for help. You ask your friends to help you find Nevarra. And when all this is over, I'll keep working at my job, sewing and making soaps, while you deal with this person who set you up and get your reputation back along with your license."

It all sounded so doable when Bea said it. There was the plan, laid out as smooth as a newly paved road. In my panic I'd been able to see no more than a few steps ahead, but sitting here with Bea I could suddenly see for miles.

There was only one problem with her solution—I didn't have any friends to rely on for help.

From the front of the house came a series of loud banging noises. We sprang into action, Bea grabbing the pistol she had beside Sadie's bed, and me grabbing mine from my shoulder harness.

"You stay here," I told her. "Keep Sadie safe."

She ignored me and nearly gave me a heart attack as she looked out the window. "There's no truck or car on the curb. They either parked down the block or walked here."

If it had been the Fixers, they would have just driven right up to the curb, or maybe straight through the front of the house. I chambered a round, and slid sideways along the hallway wall toward the living room.

Bang, bang, bang, bang.

Shit, was that someone *knocking*? A neighbor who was checking on us, or checking to make sure we were dead before he looted our house? Although I'd assume a neighbor would call out and come right on in since the door was only leaning against the opening, or at least come in after a soft, polite knock.

Bang, bang, bang, bang.

It didn't sound like a knock at all. It sounded like someone was hammering.

Then I heard a whirring sound that I immediately recognized as a drill. Bea and I exchanged equally confused looks, then I pivoted around the corner of the hall to see a boy who looked like he should be still in high school attaching a brand-new door to the frame.

I stood in the middle of the hallway and watched him for a second, shocked that this kid was fixing our house. Who the hell was he? And why was he repairing our door?

I glanced back at Bea, saw her put down her gun. I didn't know this kid, and was a bit edgy with everything that had happened yesterday, so opted for a different approach.

"Drop the drill," I yelled, pointing my pistol at the kid's chest.

He jumped back a step, lifting both hands and the drill in the air when he saw my gun. Then he let out a string of curses in Spanish.

"Eden! For heaven's sake, he's Carlotta's boy, Javier, from down the street."

Carlotta's boy. My mind ran down the few neighborhood families I knew by name. Was this the kid that came by to check on the girls when Bea was at work? Or the one whose older brother had tried to steal my bike last year? Or the one whose sister I'd beat up back in high school for making eyes at Drew?

Either way, I didn't recognize him, and I didn't trust him.

Bea pushed past me, easing my gun to the side with her hand. Then, I was the one cursing as she blocked my shot.

"Fucking hell," the boy swore, this time in English. "They tell me I have to come here and fix these things for you, but they don't tell me some *puta* is going to try to blow my head off for it."

Puta? This kid who looked barely older than Nevarra had actually called me a puta? If Bea hadn't been standing right in my way, I would have shot the kid. Or at least shot at him.

"Please excuse my foster daughter," Bea apologized. "I'm sure you can see we had a rough time of it yesterday. She's a little on edge about it."

I was more than a little on edge.

The kid leaned sideways so he could see me around Bea's considerable bulk. "Bad guys don't come fix your door, Chica. Maybe you should think about that before you go pointing a gun at somebody."

Bea shifted, blocking my view once more. "I truly appreciate your helping us, Javier."

He leaned the other way to scowl at me. "Mom said I needed to. And she told me I'm not supposed to ask you to pay me, either. I wouldn't be doing this if she hadn't ordered me to. I don't care if you have a door or not."

"Your mom is very kind," Bea told the boy. "Please thank her for me. Why don't you take a break and have a cup of coffee?"

The boy followed Bea into the kitchen. Now I remembered him, that little kid that used to follow Adriana and me around, tattling on us if he caught us smoking. I watched him, wondering how this kid had seemingly gone from five years old to fourteen or fifteen overnight. There had been an elder brother as well—one I'd drooled over when I'd first come here. I hadn't seen him in nearly a decade. I hadn't seen Adriana in years either. I guessed they'd both moved out after high school, where I'd stayed.

I slid my gun into the holster, still keeping it free and handy, and went over to see exactly what Javier had been doing when I'd come down the hallway and threatened him.

Wow. He *had* been fixing the door. He'd already replaced part of the frame, and was beginning to put on new hinges.

The new door that was propped next to the broken old one looked like it should be at the entrance of a Rodeo Drive jewelry store. It was thick steel with blurred bullet-proof glass panes that were covered with decorative steel panes. Aesthetically pleasing, and I was pretty sure it would take a small bomb to get through the thing. An intruder could always swing around to the back of the house, or go through a window, but battering at this door would give us enough warning to be ready to fight back, or to escape.

Was I a bad person that I immediately wondered who he'd stolen this door from? And what motivated his parents to send him over here first thing in the morning to install an expensive steel door on our modest little house?

Yeah, that probably did make me a bad person.

I glanced toward the kitchen and narrowed my eyes, trying to calculate the risks of leaving this kid here with my family. Adriana had been okay, and I never heard anything bad about Carlotta or Luis, but I didn't know this kid, and I was spiraling into a panic mode where I didn't want to trust anyone.

This was ridiculous. Bea trusted him to come by and check on the girls while she was at work. She clearly knew the family better than I did. Besides, I couldn't stay here and stand over him with a loaded gun while he finished with the door. The clock was ticking on Nevarra's safety.

Forcing myself to trust that the teenage neighbor kid fixing our door wasn't something I needed to worry about right now, I tried to put my fears away and headed into the kitchen. There I poured myself the last of the coffee, and exchanged glares with the kid while Bea chatted on about neighborhood gossip.

"You almost done with that door, Javier?" I continued glaring at the kid over the edge of my coffee mug.

His mouth firmed into a tight line. He put the coffee cup

on the counter and stomped out of the kitchen. A few seconds later I heard the drill once more.

"Eden, he's helping us out," Bea scolded. "You don't seriously think he's installing a heavy-duty door on the front of our house as a pretext for robbery?"

Probably not, but as Bea had said, I was edgy after what had happened last night. Bea and I headed back into the living room where she muttered something about checking on Sadie and left me behind to drink my coffee and watch Javier as he finished the door. He swung it back and forth a few times.

"You gonna stay here and stare at me while I put new glass in your windows?" he asked once he was satisfied that the door latched properly. "Because if you are, then I'm going to say 'fuck you' and just go home."

I needed to go see Bags. I needed to find Nevarra. I was absolutely torn between leaving two of my family behind and staying to protect them. Then I remembered my conversation with Bea. She wasn't so injured that she couldn't protect herself and Sadie. A broken arm didn't mean she couldn't shoot that gun. And besides that, Bea had ways of dealing with conflict in a non-violent fashion that I obviously lacked.

"I have to go out." I stepped closer to the boy. "If I come home and find either one of them has so much as a split end, I'll hunt you down and kill you. Got it?"

"What the fuck is wrong with you, lady?" The kid held up his hands as I took another step toward him. "Okay, okay. I get it. Like I'm gonna hurt some old woman and two girls."

Just in case I went back to the girls' bedroom and gave Bea one of the extra guns I'd stolen from the warehouse last night—a sweet SIG Sauer P226—with a fully loaded magazine, because clearly it would be best if she had three pistols to defend herself and Sadie with.

Then with another threatening glare at the neighbor kid, I headed out.

Getting in to see Bags was going to be a bit tricky. Normally I just strolled right on up to the door and inside, but I was sure his place was currently under surveillance. The tax collectors were clearly hot to bring me in. After not finding me last night and trashing my house, the Fixers would probably assume that I'd gone to ground somewhere. A person could only hide for so long, and with my salvage license no doubt suspended, I'd need to pawn stuff for cash at a place where I could do it off the record. That required the salvager to have an established relationship with the pawnshop. Bear State had been my go-to, and even though they'd tossed the place and smacked Bags around, they knew I wouldn't have many, if any, other options.

They were right. I didn't. Not just for fencing salvage either. I could trust Bags. I knew he'd be straight with me, not turn me in, give me information, protect me from anyone who wished to do me harm.

He was a friend. I guess he'd always been a friend, but in my weird paranoid mind, he'd only just moved into that category last night.

After parking a few blocks away and making a round-about approach, I crouched behind a crumbled concrete retaining wall and watched two men loiter in the general vicinity of the pawnshop. One had taken up a post on the east corner of the short block, making the absolute minimum effort to conceal his intent. Besides puffing away on a cigarette, his body was tense, his expression sharp and alert as his gaze darted up and down each street. The dude on the west corner was at least *trying* to look like a homeless man propped up against a lamp post, but he had to have been the cleanest, best-dressed homeless man I'd ever seen. And if that didn't give him away, the clearly visible hip holster did.

Obviously the Fixers hadn't sent their best and brightest to do this job. The bounty on my head might be sizable, but it must not have been big enough to have everyone lining up to take on boring-as-shit surveillance duty. Still, with their positioning, it would be hard to get past these two morons unnoticed—at least if I went through the front or emergency side doors. What they, and probably just about everyone, didn't know was that there was a cellar door into the pawnshop. It looked as if it had been rusted shut and chained up for decades with rotted leaves and old trash littering the stairway down, but Bags was too smart not to have a back way out in case he needed to make a quick escape from the shop. The chains were attached to nothing but the door itself, and the rusty-looking hinges were only painted to look that way. The door would swing open with absolute silence. The lack of a doorknob deterred anyone attempting to get in, but I knew there was a pressure plate, cleverly hidden behind some ivy, that would pop the door open.

I just needed to get around to the back of the building and down the stairwell without either of these two goons seeing me.

My opportunity came in the unlikely guise of a junky trying to score. A battered yellow Toyota Camry slowed down at the corner where the smoking guy stood, the passenger lowering the window as the car rolled to a stop. The Fixer tried to wave the guy on, but he clearly was desperate for a buy. After a brief argument, the Fixer decided to put out his cigarette, pull out a baggie from his pocket and do a little deal on the side.

That left the fake homeless man.

The moment he turned to look down a side street, I made my move, moving low and quick to the back of the building. Not waiting to find out if I was seen, I headed down the steps, careful not to slip on the mildewed leaves. At the door,

I grimaced and stuck my hand into the spider-filled ivy to push the pressure plate. The door silently popped open. I shuddered and frantically brushed the spiders from my hand as I darted through.

"Bags? It's me," I called softly waving to the camera in the corner. There was a silent alarm on the door, and I really didn't want to get shot while coming up the steps to the store. I waited, not only to make sure that Bags knew it was me, but just in case there were any customers upstairs. After a few minutes, the upstairs door opened, spilling thin golden light down the stairs.

"Come on up, Eden," Bags whispered down the steps. "Keep close to the floor and go to the break room. I'll be there in a few."

I did as he said. The break room was a six-by-eight space with chipped linoleum flooring, some mismatched cabinetry, a bar sink, a dented fridge, a stained coffee maker, and an electric hot plate on a Formica counter. A small but sturdy wooden table sat in the middle of the room, its surface covered with cigarette burns and brown rings. Two hard chairs sat next to the table. In the corner was a cot with a rumpled set of sheets and a lumpy pillow. I searched the fridge, grabbed a soda, and sat down at the table to wait.

I didn't have to wait long before Bags came in, propping the door open and positioning his chair so he could see out to the shop before sitting down. He looked better than he had last night, but the makeshift splints on the fingers of his right hand would be a hindrance if he needed to shoot someone. Good thing Bags was almost as decent a shot with his left hand as he was with his right.

"How's your family?" he asked practically before his butt hit the chair. "Shit, Eden. I didn't even know you had a family. Mom and Dad? Husband and kids?"

I didn't know if Bags had a family or not either. We never asked, never discussed those things.

"My foster mom, Bea, and two foster sisters," I told him. "Bea got beat up. Sadie, the youngest, was shot by accident while she was hiding. They took my other sister, Nevarra, with them. She's only fourteen."

Bags knew exactly what that meant. He swore, a pulse jumping in his throat as he clenched his teeth. "Damned Fixers. Have you found her yet? Did you go to the police? You need to see Bishop. Whatever it costs."

"I already saw Bishop. He tracked Nevarra to a warehouse in Hawthorne. The Fixers sold her to the Disciples. The trail is magically shielded, so Bishop can't help me further, but I got some information. The guy from the Disciples who brokered the deal and took Nevarra with him was a tall, thin, white guy with black hair and a scar on his face."

"Fender." Bags grunted. "Nasty son-of-a-bitch."

"That's who I was thinking it was too. Tell me about him, about the Disciples. Tell me everything you know."

"The Disciples." Bags thought for a moment. "They keep their own storerooms, barter and fence a lot of their stuff directly and off the books to avoid taxes. I don't see them all that often, but I know they're a big group, structured with lieutenants and sub-bosses. They don't claim as much physical territory as the Gray Dogs, but they work their business all over the state. They're not the sort of gang that pushes dope or sells laptops off the back of a truck like the Dogs do. They deal with distributors and companies. They sell and barter in bulk, establish connections between sellers and buyers, ensure safe deliveries and commerce transactions."

"So, they're middlemen running protection rackets?"

Bags held up his hand and wiggled it back and forth. "Kinda. Not the sort of protection racket where a local pool hall pays them monthly or gets tossed. They'll go to somewhere like Conway Food Products and offer to make sure their food shipments actually make it to the grocery stores or restaurants."

And all of this had sprung up in the last two years. I shook my head, amazed at the agility and enterprising nature of some people.

"They take risks and go for the big jobs, leaving the little stuff to other people." Bags glanced out into his shop, then leaned in close. "They have the means to actually handle the big jobs. Automatic weapons. Military grade crap. Those armored tanklike transport vehicles. Bombs. Magic."

My palms were sweating just thinking about all that. And here I was with a couple of pistols. I was so outgunned.

It didn't matter. Outgunned or not, I had no choice but to go up against these guys.

"And Fender?" I asked.

"Scary as he is, he's not even one of their Lieutenants. He's a team lead at best, and their top gopher/knee breaker. He and a guy named Piers handle most of the Disciple business in the Valley. I don't think he'll have your sister with him. He would have picked her up and delivered her to someone else."

Great. This was going to be one long follow-the-breadcrumb trail to find my sister. Hopefully, she hadn't changed hands too often, because each time she went to another person and another location, the longer it would take me to find her.

"Who do you think Fender might have transferred her to?" I asked, hoping to cut out some of the middlemen on this and head right to where Nevarra was likely to be.

"I honestly don't know. The only side of the Disciples I really know about is their protection racket and who they use to fence their stolen goods. If the Fixers brought the Disciples in, that means they probably have a division in their organization that deals with human trafficking." Bags shrugged. "It makes sense. They play big, and there's big money to be had in selling people."

"Someone has to know who those people are," I mused. "You can't run a human trafficking operation if no one knows you've got people to buy."

"I think most of it is done online." Bags dug in his pocket and pulled out his cell phone and a pen, then grabbed a crumpled, greasy napkin and started writing. "Here. This is who you might want to call. I also wrote down where the Disciples like to congregate in the Valley."

An auto parts place and a fast food joint. At least it was a starting point. But it wasn't the Disciples' hangout locations that had me staring at the napkin in disbelief, it was the name and phone number Bags had written down.

"Detective Sarah Juke?"

"I knew her father; he was an honest cop." He pointed to the napkin. "I've known Sarah since she was a baby. I got invited to her birthday parties, sent her a card when she graduated from the academy. I trusted her dad, and I'd trust her too."

I couldn't believe Bags was recommending I walk straight into the lion's den. "I can't go to the cops. I'm in the system from some shit back when I was a teen. And I'm flagged right now because of this mess with the taxes. She'll turn me over to the Fixers, or give me straight to the tax collectors."

"Maybe. Maybe not." Bags lifted his hands. "From what I know of Sarah, I don't think she'd turn you in. All I'm saying is you've got a kid sister who's about to be sold to the highest bidder. Sarah worked for the LA human trafficking division before the demons came. She's still here and on the force, and although she might not be in that division anymore, she's got to have contacts and information you could use. She's someone you want to talk to."

I eyed the napkin again, weighing my chances. "What makes you think what she knew from two years ago is still applicable today?"

"Because I'm pretty sure it's still most of the same players, they're just bolder and busier now than they were two years ago." Bags leaned forward and tapped the corner of the napkin. "We had Gray Dogs, Fixers, Disciples, and the militias before the demons came, they just were smaller and more careful. Someone back then knew how to sell bodies, who the buyers are and how to get the most for a kid, then they're still doing it today."

He had a point. I was still going to track down some of the Disciples and see if I could find out who had Nevarra, but if this Detective could also get me some names, it would help.

I stuck the napkin in my pocket, thanked Bags for his assistance, then snuck out the back door.

CHAPTER 10

I needed a phone—a phone that couldn't be traced to me, but one on which I could receive a return phone call. That meant I needed to steal one because I didn't want to waste the little money we had left on a burner.

As much as I wanted to take down one of the Fixers watching Bags's place and rob him blind, I didn't. First, any phone I lifted off one of the Fixers was bound to be traced and I didn't want those guys knowing where I was. Secondly, killing one of the guys watching the pawnshop would probably work that group up into even more of a frenzy. Right now, finding me would be a payday for them, but nothing more. Killing one of their surveillance guys would make finding me personal. They'd know it was me who'd killed one of the men watching the pawnshop where I was known to go. I wasn't going to risk it, not even for the satisfying sense of vengeance killing one or both of them would give me, and certainly not for a phone.

I needed to lift it off a civilian. As much as I hated stealing from a regular old Joe or Jane, it would be safer than stealing from a bad guy.

So, I drove into Burbank, eyeing the people who were heading to work, stopping off to get gas or a paper or a cup of coffee. My pickpocket skills were subpar at best and I was feeling a little guilty, so I bypassed the obviously blue-collar folk and looked for someone driving a late model car who looked like he or she might be heading into an office job.

My luck seemed to be turning around because while I was getting gas, I saw a man who looked like he was heading to the golf course pumping gas into his BMW at the pump next to mine. We nodded at each other, then he dashed in to grab a cup of coffee, leaving his phone in the cupholder.

I was gone before he'd even paid for his caffeine fix, and rode a few blocks before I pulled over and examined the phone.

Hoping this was going to work, I dug around in one of my pockets. Lock picks. A bungee cord. A multi-tool. Ah, there it was.

I pulled out something that looked like a memory stick with an adapter for just about any phone, computer, or electronic device. This thing had cost me more than my surveillance camera jammer, but it was about to be worth every penny. Picking the correct adapter, I attached my thingie to the phone, and pushed the little button on the end.

It worked its own kind of electronic magic, and in five minutes had bypassed the phone's passcode and deactivated it. I had no idea how my own magic worked, and even less idea how this thing worked, but work it did.

Sticking my thingie back in my pocket, I dialed the number Bags had given me on the crumpled napkin.

"Detective Juke."

I almost dropped the phone when a woman's voice answered the phone instead of a machine. It was just past seven in the morning and I hadn't expected the detective to actually be in the office.

"Fucking prank calls." The woman hung up before I could pull myself together enough to answer her, meaning that I had to dial the number a second time.

"Detective Juke?" I blurted out before she could say anything. "I need your help. My foster daughter was taken yesterday. They're going to sell her. I was told you could help."

I figured the police would be more sympathetic if I pretended to be Bea, who was an upstanding citizen and a CPA, as opposed to a twenty-two-year-old with a sketchy past who was wanted for tax evasion.

"Did you file a missing person's report?" The detective's voice was harsh and accusing, as if it were my fault that Nevarra had been kidnapped.

"No. Not yet. My other sis—daughter was shot in the home invasion, and I have to stay here and take care of her. I was told you could help me. Please. She's only fourteen."

"Give me your address, and I'll come over to take a statement and file the report." Her voice didn't sound any more sympathetic than before. I was beginning to regret this whole thing. The police never helped, especially people like me. This woman was annoyed. She probably hadn't even had a cup of coffee yet.

But I was desperate, and as much as I distrusted the police, I did trust Bags and he said this detective might be able to help me find Nevarra.

"Can you just take the information over the phone?" I tried to sound panicked. It wasn't difficult because I actually was barely holding on.

There was a moment of silence on the line, and I thought that maybe the detective had just hung up on me in frustration.

"Tell me what happened, ma'am."

Definitely frustrated. But I'd gone this far down the path,

so I figured I might as well keep going.

"A bunch of men broke into our house yesterday looking for my oldest foster daughter. She's twenty-two and hasn't lived here for years, but I guess she must have used our address for her salvage license. They took all of our money, beat me up, shot my youngest, and took my other foster daughter with them. I recognized the one man's tattoo. He was a Fixer."

"I see."

I felt sweat trickle down between my breasts. She didn't believe me. This had been a colossal waste of time. I was better off tracking down Fender than trying to get this cop to help me.

"I need to see you," the detective said. "And before you hang up on me, know that your daughter is probably listed on a sale site right now, and if we don't move fast, we'll never find her."

I hesitated, knowing the woman was right, but also knowing that I would be of no help to Nevarra if I were in jail or in the hands of the tax collectors. And as much as I needed assistance, I trusted *my* ability to find Nevarra more than some cop.

"If she's pretty and fourteen, then you don't have much time. A girl like that will fetch a lot. There aren't a lot of people in the city that do that sort of human trafficking. The Fixers don't deal in prostitution or trafficking, so they most likely sold her off to another gang."

"The Disciples," I blurted out. "I...I heard them say they were going to sell her to the Disciples. Cash up front for a deposit, then a percentage commission once she was sold."

I heard the detective suck in a breath.

"Then we need to move fast. I need to meet you, Eden Alvaro."

This time it was me who sucked in a breath. She knew my

name. I was calling on a stolen phone. I'd never mentioned Bea or Nevarra's name, but she knew *my* name. My finger hovered over the disconnect button, but I hesitated, because if this detective was smart enough to know the Fixers did enforcement for the tax collectors, and to run a search on all delinquencies that were serious enough to warrant excessive force, all while we were talking, then she was a woman I wanted helping to search for Nevarra.

"I can't." I looked around, wondering if I should ditch the cell phone, and if they could trace the call and find my location. Fuck, they could already be on their way. In seconds I could be surrounded by patrol cars, hauled in, handed over, all while Nevarra vanished into the underworld of sexual slavery.

"I don't give a rat's ass about what you're not reporting from your salvage runs. All I care about is finding your sister. Those tax collectors can rot in hell for all I care."

I wanted to believe her, but I had firsthand experience in how convincing cops could be. They always seemed to be on your side, sympathetic, understanding, then next thing you knew you were headed for juvie.

But I didn't have much choice. I'd deal with my own problems with the Fixers, the tax collectors, the bitch who set me up later. Right now, Nevarra was my priority. I'd meet this cop, and if she pulled anything, I'd take her down. Then I'd deal with the repercussions of killing a cop later, along with all the other shit I had piling up on my list.

"Okay. Pasadena. The coffee shop on Marengo and Union. Six o'clock this evening. There are a few things I need to do first," I said as she began to protest at the delay.

I heard the detective sigh. "Okay. I'll be there. Alone, so don't shoot me. And Eden? Don't do anything stupid, okay?"

I hung up on her, because I was about to do something stupid—something really stupid.

CHAPTER 11

 I headed to the first of the two places Bags had written down—the one he'd heard Fender hung around—not so much because I thought I'd find Nevarra, or even Fender, there, but because there was a slim chance I could beat information out of someone, and I needed to do something. I couldn't just wait around, and I couldn't put Nevarra's safety on this one cop's shoulders.

There were risks in what I was doing, and not just the risk that I'd get killed, or turned in for a bounty. I was well aware that if someone in the Disciples found out I was coming for them, hunting them down, then they'd lock Nevarra away so tight I'd never find her. They needed to not worry about me, not even know my name. We hadn't left anyone alive at the warehouse last night, and I was sure when the Disciples had discovered the bodies, they'd chalked it up to a robbery by a rival gang. We *did* take a bunch of their shit. They'd never connect that crime with me—which was exactly what I wanted.

Vultures had a reputation. We were thought to be cowards who avoided any sort of violent conflict. We swooped in, grabbed the goods, then got the fuck out. We hovered around the edges of fights, only joining in if we had to defend ourselves. If the Disciples thought about me at all, they'd be imagining me hunkered down in some hidey-hole, trying to get across the border with the loot and the money. They'd never imagine that I'd risk my hide looking for a younger foster sister; I'd not risk my hide picking them off one at a time until I managed to find out where she was being held.

I had to be stealthy. And I couldn't leave any survivors to snitch on me.

The "no survivors" thing didn't bother me. It was just one more thing that made me a freak, one more thing I had to hide from everyone. Oh well.

The address Bags had given me was a car parts place. The Disciples had taken over what had once been an AutoZone store, surrounding it with a tall chain link fence that had loops of wire around the top, as if it were a prison yard. Instead of keeping the bad guys inside, the Disciples were clearly hoping to keep their stock from walking out the door. The warehouse from last night had been secure, but this place had once been a retail store complete with glass windows and doors, and a layout that invited customers to come in to shop.

From the fence and the guards milling about outside, the only customers the Disciples wanted coming into this place were their own gang members or other organized crime groups looking to swap for car batteries and parts, not Joe Citizen picking up a pack of windshield wipers and some of those pine tree air fresheners to hang from the rearview.

There were stacks of fancy rims, some on and some off the tires. A pile of catalytic converters sat off to the side. Several high-end cars were lined up behind the fence in various states of being parted out.

Two guards were all that I could see at the moment, and they were doing a shitty job of watching the store. The bigger guy leaned against the wall, a pistol held loosely by his side. The other guy was making out with a woman beside a Ferrari that was up on blocks.

It was the perfect opportunity for me to slip by while the pair of them were distracted, but just as I went to sneak around the side, I looked back and saw that what I'd thought was a passionate embrace was one-sided.

The woman was struggling. And she was losing out against a guy nearly twice her size.

Damn it all. I didn't have time for this, but I wasn't about to just walk away. I also wasn't about to go rushing in and get shot by the bored guard with the gun.

There was about twenty yards between me and the building. Along the way were two more cars, a metal trashcan that was probably used for a warming fire on cooler nights, and a set of expensive spinner rims on fat tires next to what looked to be a brand spanking new outboard motor.

I held my hand up and pushed, just like I'd done when deflecting the balls Sadie and Nevarra threw at me. The tires were a good distance away and a whole lot heavier than children's balls, so all I managed to do was rock that stack a little.

The motion was enough to catch the attention of the dude standing guard. "Something's over there behind the wheels."

Rape-guy didn't even pause. "Probably a rat or something."

I pushed again, harder. The stack rocked and one of the tires fell off and rolled a few feet away, knocking a set of rims over with a clang.

Rape-guy's head jerked at the noise, but he all he did was swear and turn his attention back to the woman.

The guard walked toward the tires, bringing his pistol up.

Shit. I'd wanted them both to investigate, although if I could separate them it might be easier for me to take them down one at a time. Holding my palm flat, I pushed once more and sent the fallen tire rolling past the car and around the edge of the building.

Now the guard swore and trotted after it. "Those fucking tires are worth a fortune."

"If those Dub rims are dented, Fender'll have your head," Rape-guy called after him as he struggled with the woman.

I slipped around the edge of the car and darted to the next for cover, putting me in better view of the side of the building where the tire had come to rest. This next thing was going to be tricky. I'd either bring the guard down without a sound, or he'd scream loud enough that Knife-guy would come running with his dick out. Either option would work, so I waited for the guard to pocket his pistol and pick up the tire in both hands by the rim before sending a jolt of electricity across the courtyard, into the metal, and into the guard.

The guard fell to the ground, convulsing, the tire still in his hands. I ran to him keeping the electrical pulse up for seven seconds. The dude wasn't smoking, so I assumed whatever I was doing it wouldn't kill him. Not that I cared whether in the end I killed him or not. I just didn't want him getting up anytime soon, or dying before I could question him.

I snuck around the side back to the other guard who was still struggling with the woman. Walking as quietly as I could, I came up behind him. Unfortunately, the woman gave me away, her eyes widening with surprise as she saw me over Rape-guy's shoulder.

He shoved the woman to the side and spun around, pulling a knife from his waistband. The woman fell to the ground, her legs tangled as she went down. With a snarl, she kicked out at Rape-guy, catching him in his left ankle. It didn't do much more than make him swear and kick back at her before trying to hop out of her reach, but it was enough. I grabbed at his hand with the knife, feeling a sharp sting as the blade sliced my arm. Then I stepped into the guy, slammed my head into his nose and employed my stun gun superpowers.

Men are idiots. They always expect women to fight like they do. I was shorter and slighter built than this guy, so I didn't have his arm reach or his arm strength. He outweighed me by close to seventy pounds. I could punch until my fingers fell off and I wouldn't win against him. The only way I'd prevail is if I went for his vulnerable areas fast and hard, if I closed in, kept him off balance, and let his weight and bulk work against him.

Sadly, my stun gun powers failed me this time, which left me having to fight a much bigger opponent who had a knife. I attempted another head butt, which he was smart enough to evade. He pulled his arms in closer, slashing the knife toward me. I wasn't strong enough to overpower him, and my hand, slick with blood, slid off his wrist. The blade raked across the front of my jacket instead of my neck. I felt a sting, then a wetness on my chest.

Fuck, I needed my gun, even though shooting would bring whoever was in the building running. I couldn't afford to be exposed, but I couldn't afford to be dead either. Not that I could reach my gun with both hands frantically trying to keep the guard's knife from slicing me to ribbons.

This whole thing was not going down as planned. My arm shook as he brought the knife upward and turned it. Fucker was going to stab me, and I wasn't strong enough to do anything about it.

A whack sent the man against me with enough force that I nearly fell. The knife dropped from his hand, and he slid to the ground, blood gushing from his head. The woman stood behind him, her shirt twisted and torn at the shoulder. She was holding a tire iron in both hands and as I watched, she proceeded to cave the guard's face in with three more blows.

So much for questioning this one. Hopefully, I hadn't fatally electrocuted the other guy.

The woman tossed the tire iron aside, cursing the man in something that sounded like Russian. She spat on him a few times. I waited until she was done, then quickly went through the guy's pockets, taking the knife and some of his money, before tossing the rest of the cash at the woman who was trying to straighten her shirt with shaky hands.

She froze and glared at me. "I'm not a whore."

I shrugged. "Then be a thief. That's what I'm doing."

She flashed me a crooked smile and grabbed the cash from the ground. We both ran, her toward the street and me around the side of the building.

The guard was still on the ground. I checked for a pulse, then did some cursing of my own when I realized he was dead. Fuck. I was hoping to find out if Fender was here, or at least find out where Fender was before I killed this guy.

There would be more gang members inside, but I doubted it would go over well if I waltzed in the front door covered in blood and asked to speak with Fender.

Guess I don't have any other choice.

If I was going in, I was going in prepared, so I grabbed the dead guy's gun, then took his cash as well, because there was no sense in leaving good money behind.

First, I assessed my wounds. The cut on my chest was shallow and had already stopped bleeding. The one on my arm hurt like fuck. I wiped the blood on my pants, and decided it wasn't deep enough that I needed stitches or immediate medical attention.

Hugging the building, I worked my way to the back

corner. A quick glance told me there were no other guards outside, and the only two entrances were the main one in the front, and this steel door in the rear of the building. Whoever this Fender was, he was either an arrogant ass, or cheap. Only two guards? Okay, maybe that would have been enough if they hadn't both been on the same side of the damned building, one of them getting his rocks off while the other chased a spinner across the lot.

The back door opened, and I knelt down behind an oil drum. A dark-haired man stepped outside, holding a cigarette. He was built like a piece of beef jerky with a clean-shaven face and a high-bridged nose that had a hook at the end. He took a few puffs, then pocketed the lighter, kicking a rock over to prop the door open.

This wasn't Fender. I eyed the doorway, wondering how many more were inside, if Fender was actually in there or not. If I could manage to grab this guy, I might be able to find out if he knew anything about Nevarra or Fender—and then kill him before anyone knew I was out here. It wasn't a perfect plan, but I was going to have to improvise and go with the flow.

The man smoked while I contemplated, weighing my alternatives. Soon he'd notice that the guards were oddly silent and nowhere to be seen. Soon he'd head back inside and I'd lose my chance to grab him out here alone. Making a decision, I pulled my pistol from the holster, thankful that I'd already chambered a round. Pistol in one hand, stolen knife in the other, I took a breath, hesitating as the man dropped his cigarette, ground it out with the heel of his boot, then unzipped his pants.

For a second I wondered what the fuck he was doing, then I heard the sound of water and realized he was peeing onto the frame of an Acura sedan. I lived with three women.

I'd forgotten how cavalier men were about yanking it out when they needed to go.

It was the perfect opportunity. I walked up behind the guy, shoved my pistol against the back of his head as I wrapped my other arm around his waist and slid the knife up against his cock.

He abruptly stopped peeing and slowly raised his hands out to the side of his waist. "Your life really worth some cash and a pair of spinners?"

"I don't want your money or a set of rims. Where's Fender?"

He laughed. "What, he knock you up or something?"

Why did everyone assume I was pregnant? "Where's Fender?" I repeated.

"He's not here. Try down around the airport."

I believed him. A man with a knife against his dick tends to tell the truth.

"I'm looking for my sister. Fender had her last I heard."

He shrugged. "That Russian bitch? Butch and Blade are probably giving her a ride out front. You wanna join her?"

I tucked the knife in closer and felt him tense. "Not her. The little girl Fender picked up from the Fixers last night. He took her. I need to find her, or find Fender."

The man's breath came out in a hiss. "I don't know nothing about little girls. I don't fuck with that perverted shit. None of my boys do. Fender neither. He doesn't screw kids."

"Where is he?" My finger tightened on the trigger. One wrong move and this guy was going to be minus a chunk of brain as well as his dick. "Fender picked her up. Does he keep the girls with him until they're sold?"

"Fender's just a pick up and delivery guy," he scoffed. "He wouldn't have her. I don't know who he'd take a kid to. That's not part of the business I deal with. I just manage the chop shops and parts sales. That's all I do. I don't know nothing about kids."

He was lying. I don't know how I knew this, but I did. Pushing him closer to the Acura, I nicked him with the knife. He let out a high-pitched scream, then shut up as I pressed the blade so tight the slightest move would emasculate him.

"Who has my sister? Give me a name." Someone probably heard that scream, which meant I had seconds until one or more guys came to investigate, even if they thought it was the Russian girl screaming.

"Desiree, you crazy fucking bitch," he breathed out in a pained whisper. "He would have taken a kid to Desiree. She runs that side of our business."

"And where's Fender?" I demanded.

"Fuck if I know."

"You said he's down by the airport. Where?" I couldn't go searching all over LA for this guy, and I doubted *by* the airport meant *in* the airport. Fender could be anywhere from Torrance to Hawthorne, and that was way too much ground for me to cover.

"I don't fucking know."

I didn't have any time left for this. And unfortunately, I didn't have a lot of options that would allow me to kill this guy silently, so I pulled the trigger at the same time as I yanked the knife up and away. Blood and brain matter all sprayed all over the Acura frame.

I ran, my sliced arm stinging and still bleeding as I held tight to my pistol, my other hand and the stolen knife wet with the man's blood. I ran, and didn't look back, my ears ringing so loudly from the gunshot that I couldn't tell if someone was after me or not. Darting down side streets, weaving in and out of alleys and crossing main thorough-fares, I didn't stop running until I was a good mile away. People looked, but then quickly turned away, not wanting to know what was going on. Just another day in New Hell, seeing a blood-splattered figure fleeing with a gun in one hand and a knife in the other.

I washed off in a public fountain that still had a few inches of oil-slicked water in it, then yanked a bandana out of my cargo pants to tie around the cut on my arm. I was pretty sure I looked a mess with a slice across the front of my jacket, and splattered blood all over my clothes. But that didn't matter because I had a name.

Desiree. I hadn't expected a woman to be allowed into the Disciples as more than a groupie. Clearly the gang was more enlightened than I'd thought, although not so enlightened that they thought twice about selling kids into slavery.

I still didn't know where Nevarra was, or how to find this Desiree, or even Fender for that matter, but I was getting closer. And if I had to interrogate and kill every Disciple one at a time, I'd find them. Then I'd find Nevarra.

CHAPTER 12

*O*nce I cleaned most of the blood from my hands and arm, I backtracked, got my bike, and headed to the second address that Bags had given me. The chance that Fender would be there was slim to none, but whatever Disciple hung out there might know where I could find him or this Desiree. Then I planned on stopping by Suerte to see if Bishop could shed any light on the information I'd gathered.

I pulled into the lot of an In-N-Out Burger in south Burbank, checking the address before driving around to the back and parking my bike where I could make a fast getaway if I needed to. There was a sweet black Harley Roadster a few spaces down. I admired it. Then I admired the helmet sitting on the seat. If it was still there when I came out, I was so going to steal it.

The helmet, that is. As much as I was drooling over the Harley, I liked my old bike too much to give it up.

The Disciples weren't the typical gang with geographic territories, they were a broad organization that handled certain types of business all through southern California. If a gang had a lot of clout, the Disciples would pay a toll for doing business in their area. Otherwise they flipped the local gang the bird and did whatever they wanted without interference. The auto parts store didn't surprise me. The fast food joint did. But even members of organized crime needed to eat, and we locals did love our In-N-Out Burgers.

I left the Harley alone, for now, and walked in, not sure what to expect. In-N-Out wasn't a franchise organization. I got that a member of the Disciples might come here regularly for lunch, but Bags had made it sound like they had some sort of office set up here. It was weird, but *everything* was weird in LA, especially the last two years.

Scanning the customers, I dug a ten out of my pocket and got in line behind a very sweaty teenage boy, and a man who looked as if he might have spent the morning on the inside of a cement mixer. It was a bit late for the lunch crowd, but there was a family with two loud toddlers parked at a table close to the exit, a woman with a gigantic fountain drink smack in the middle of the room, slouched in her chair and reading a book. A bald man with a tight, sharp dark beard lining his jaw sat in the front right corner. His back was to the wall, his table stacked with papers. He looked ridiculously oversized crammed into the little plastic seat, like someone had squashed a heavyweight boxer into a children's playset. Tattoos covered his bronzed arms, and a pair of mirrored Aviators shielded his eyes. He had to be one of the Disciples. Everything about the guy screamed gang.

I got a soda and made my way toward the man, not quite sure how to handle this situation. It was one thing to hunt down bad guys in a warehouse, or outside a building full of stolen auto parts, it was another to start a gunfight in a burger joint with innocent civilians eating ten feet away. There was a family with toddlers here, for heaven's sake.

The man suddenly looked up and pulled off his sunglasses, his eyes locking on mine.

Crap. What should I do? The guy looked to be in his late twenties, and was pretty hot in a jacked-up, tattooed, bad-guy kind of way. Should I flirt? Act like I was hitting on a good-looking guy in a burger joint? I would have totally tried that approach, on a day where I wasn't wearing blood-covered clothing and a ripped jacket.

Surprisingly the guy waved me over with a grin that I got the feeling was supposed to look friendly. It didn't look friendly. It looked like he was about to chomp me in half and gnaw on my bones. Still, I'm an idiot so I went over to his table, hoping if we got into it he'd be a good enough shot not to kill the little kids.

"I'm Piers and you must be…Andre Delgado." The guy looked down at the paper in front of him and shook his head. "Fuckers downtown screwed up again. I'm guessing it's Andrea and not Andre?"

What the hell was he talking about? I stared at him for a few seconds before my brain kicked into gear. "Yeah. Is that a problem?"

"It is, but I'm not going to turn you away when you drove all the way from Crenshaw. Sit. Sit. I'll bet traffic sucked giant donkey balls."

I dropped into a chair across from him. "It's LA. Traffic always sucks giant donkey balls."

He chuckled, then steepled his fingers and regarded me. "I hate to tell you this, honey, but Disciples don't bring on women unless they're working a corner or someone's bitch. I respect that you look like you can handle yourself in a fight, but we're not the gang for you. Unless…" He pursed his lips, dark eyes focusing on my face then traveling down to my boobs.

Piers. Bags had mentioned that name as being someone

who occasionally worked for Fender. That was a connection I wanted to use, if only I could figure out how to bring it up without getting shot.

Looking at the paperwork in front of the man I saw a list of names, addresses, and phone numbers as well as a second list of job titles. It seemed that Piers had turned this In-N-Out Burger into his recruitment center, and today was the day for interviews. Hopefully Andre Delgado didn't show up, because I was going to run with this and see what I could get. Hopefully I wouldn't have to pull my pistol.

"Do I look like I turn tricks?" I leaned back in the tiny plastic chair and tried to appear badass.

His mouth twitched. "I'll bet you clean up real nice. Besides, some guys are into hot, tough women."

I got the impression he was including himself in that group. "I prefer to make my money in other ways and keep the banging strictly recreational."

He grinned. "I can respect that. Unfortunately that's the only job I can offer you right now. Now if you're looking for some recreation, *that* I can offer."

He was pretty hot, although these arrogant guys tended to be shit in bed. The edge of danger that would come with fucking a gang member was a real turn-on. It made me want to take a chance, even though the experience might end up being less than satisfying.

Maybe later. Right now I needed to find Nevarra, not screw a tattooed guy in the back room of a burger joint.

I returned his cocky grin with one of my own. "You *sure* you don't have a job for me? Because I heard you guys make exceptions now and then when it comes to working with women. Desiree, for example."

Piers sucked in a breath. "You might look tough, but you'll never be in Desiree's league. Unless you've got horns and wings, that is."

Desiree was a demon? Damn, that would really complicate things. I felt pretty confident about my odds against a human, especially if I could take them by surprise. But a Demon?

"I'm sorry you came all this way for nothing, but Disciples just don't work with women." He leaned back in the plastic chair and spread his arms wide. "Not my policy. If it were up to me, you'd be in. It's not up to me, though."

He knew Desiree. He might not know her personally, but he might know where I could locate her. Fender had given Nevarra to this Desiree. Demon or not, she was the best lead in finding my sister.

I pouted and leaned forward, pressing my boobs together and wishing the neckline on my T-shirt was a few inches lower. "See, I've heard otherwise. I've heard when it comes to your team, it *is* up to you. I might not have horns and wings, but I've got skills. If you made an exception for Desiree, then I don't see why you can't make an exception for me."

His gaze lingered on my chest for a few seconds before he lifted his eyes to meet mine. "I can't force the other guys to respect you and I don't want to spend all my time listening to them bitch and moan, or driving you to the hospital because they knifed you. It's not gonna happen, honey."

"Then get me a job with Desiree's team." I pointed to the papers. "I'm pretty sure she and her team won't have any problem working with a woman."

"Do you realize what that division does? They deal in trafficking. They're pedo-pushers." His face twisted with disgust. "I fucking hate that shit. Look, maybe I can get you some contract work helping out with the whores, but trust me, you don't want to mess with the trafficking side of the business."

I shrugged, trying to put aside the fact that this guy had just gone up a few notches in my opinion. "We all have to do shit we don't like nowadays. I don't like pedos either, but business is business. These little kids…they deserve to be kept calm and comfortable. That's not a job for a man. That's a job for a woman. I'm a woman, and I need a job."

He sat back in the chair, his expression turning thoughtful. "I've heard there have been problems. Kids cry, and refuse to eat, or make themselves sick. Sometimes they hurt themselves."

I forced a smile to my face. "Like you said, I can clean up nice. I'm young, and I'm female. I can make things easier for them. I've got two sisters. I know how to set little kids at ease."

Piers crossed his arms and frowned. I sat absolutely quiet, because this was one of those instances where the first person who spoke lost.

"You really don't want to do this, Andrea." He leaned forward. "You said you've got sisters…how are you gonna feel when you get attached to these kids and in a week or two they're gone? And you know what's going to be happening to them? How are you gonna sleep knowing that?"

Damn it, I kind of liked this Piers guy. I hoped I didn't have to kill him. And I really hoped he didn't have to kill me.

"I don't want to do this, but I need a job. And if I can make a difference in these kids' lives before… I just need a job. I'll do it if I have to, and deal with the sleepless nights."

He sighed, actually looking disappointed. "Gotta run this by a few people. This isn't an open position for us, and someone needs to clear the budget. Plus, Desiree likes to hire her own people. She'd probably need to meet with you first."

Fear and excitement warred within me. Desiree would know where Nevarra was. And I got the idea that she was probably more likely to turn me into a pile of broken bones and torn flesh than anyone else in the Disciples.

"That's cool. I'm happy to meet with her anytime,

anywhere. Oh, but I've got a new phone," I recited the number of my stolen cell phone, watching as he wrote it down.

"Good." He crossed out the other number he'd had for Andre Delgado. "I'll call or text you as soon as I know something."

I stood and picked up my drink. "Do you think I'll at least get an interview by tomorrow? I really need work within the next few days."

Piers stood as well. "I'll do what I can, but no guarantees."

"Where does Desiree work out of? Maybe I can just swing by today, since I'm up here." It was a long shot, but I didn't want to have to wait for a phone call, and there were probably thousands of women named Desiree in LA. Even if I could manage to get a list of names and addresses, I wouldn't find the right one in time to save Nevarra.

And if she was a demon…I doubted demons were in the phone listings.

Piers shrugged. "Downtown somewhere? Fuck if I know." He eyed me once more. "Sure you don't want to take an hour off for a little recreation?"

I hesitated. It had been so long since I'd had a man's hands on me…

The timing sucked. I needed to find Nevarra. After I had her home and safe, then I'd think about a one-and-done.

"Tell you what," I purred. "You get me an interview with Desiree. That will definitely put me in the mood for some recreation." I put the straw between my pursed lips, took a long drink of my soda as my eyes met his, then I lowered the cup, smiled, turned around, and walked to the door.

I tossed the remains of the drink in the trash can, swiped the helmet as I walked by, got on my bike, and headed north.

Horns and wings. That was going to be a problem. If Desiree was a demon, then I really didn't have any way of defending myself against her or taking her down. I doubted my stun gun skills would do more than piss her off, and although I could fill her full of bullets, I'd heard demons could shrug them off like they were Nerf darts.

I needed one of those guns with the white muzzles—the ones that could negate a demon's powers as well as other magic. Unfortunately, they were expensive and not as easy to find as regular guns. The cops had them. Some gang members had them. In all the years I'd known Bags, none had come through his pawn shop. How the hell was I going to face this woman without one? She'd kill me with a flick of her taloned hands.

Bishop. The guy had a weredog buddy. He could compel people to spill their secrets. He could twist someone's head around like a fucking top. I wasn't sure how he'd stack up against a demon, but if I was going to need to go up against Desiree, he was the one I wanted by my side.

The parking lot at Suerte was empty. I wasn't even sure they were open, but the door wasn't locked, so I went on in, plopped down at the bar, and waited. After a few seconds, HB peeked around the corner of what looked to be the store room.

"Give me a second. I'm checking kegs for the order."

She vanished without waiting for a reply, leaving me to look around as I waited. The bar was furnished with an eye toward easy cleanup. Stainless steel, vinyl, tan walls with high-gloss paint. The bar was oak planks with a layer of poly that was probably two inches thick. The floor was the only thing that hadn't held up to the regular use. The wood was scuffed and scratched as if someone routinely dragged the metal tables around. Or perhaps it was clawed animals that had been dragged around. I could imagine Bob would do some serious damage to a wood floor.

HB popped out of the store room, wiping her hands on a cloth. "I assume you're here to see Bishop and not grab a beer?"

I nodded. "I got some additional information on who might have my sister."

She poured me a glass of iced tea while I told her the abbreviated and sanitized version of what went down at the warehouse last night as well as my activities today.

"A demon?" She shuddered. "Are you sure?"

"No," I confessed. "The Disciple I spoke to hinted that she was a demon, though. Given that this particular gang doesn't work with women, it makes sense."

"You really don't want to mess with demons," she warned me.

"No, I don't, but I might not have a choice. She's got my sister. She's the only lead I've got. If Fender handed Nevarra off to this Desiree, then she's my only link."

HB leaned her hands on the bar. "Have you ever been up close to a demon before?"

Not voluntarily. They tended to cluster downtown, which meant I avoided downtown. I'd seen the occasional one at a distance here and there, and made it a point to drive in the other direction as fast as possible, praying the whole way that it hadn't seen me.

"There was one that came down our street a few years back. We locked the doors, turned off all the lights, and stayed inside. He tossed a few cars, then went on his way."

She grimaced. "He picked up the cars and threw them?"

"No, I mean he broke into them and stole shit. He was a little guy. Slimy. Had a tail. Kept jacking off on people's lawns. We still have a foot-wide brown spot by the driveway where nothing grows." I didn't want to think what that demon-ejaculate would do to a human partner.

"Sounds like a Low. They don't have a lot of power. They're easier to kill than the other demons."

"The guy had acid sperm," I countered. "How is that not a lot of power?"

"A Low can't hold you in place with his gaze. A Low can't create a convincing human form, not that even the high-level demons bother to hide their real nature anymore."

"A Low can't activate the gates to Hel, or teleport himself and a victim. He can't split atomic particles with a thought, or rearrange the molecular structure of the air around him into a weapon of pure energy. He can't survive without a physical form to anchor his spirit-being."

I spun around to see Bishop walking across the room toward us. The guy didn't make a fucking sound. I hadn't even heard the door open.

He shook his head, the faint smile at the edge of his mouth belaying the stern expression of his blue eyes. "I'm assuming you've gotten yourself into trouble with a demon?"

"Not yet," I told him. "So far I'm only in trouble with the Fixers and the tax collectors, although if the Disciples figure out that I killed three of their guys today, then I'll be in trouble with them too. Oh, and if that Disciple I met with at the In-N-Out knows I stole his motorcycle helmet, he's probably going to be pissed. Or maybe not. He wants to fuck me, so he might overlook the helmet thing."

Bishop snorted. "Not likely. You're hot, but you're not that hot. So what's up with the demon?"

A thrill ran through me that Bishop thought I was hot, quickly followed by disappointment that he didn't think I was hot enough to even overlook minor theft.

"The guy that wants to bang her said her sister was given to a demon named Desiree," HB chimed in.

"No," I corrected. "The guy whose dick I cut off told me Nevarra was turned over to Desiree, who seems to be in charge of the gang's human trafficking operation. The guy who wants to bang me is the one who hinted that this Desiree is a demon."

Bishop snorted. I think it might have been a laugh, but I

wasn't sure. "Is this a normal day for you? Slicing off dicks and offering to screw men for information and favors? I'll admit it's a great follow-up to last night, where you killed a few guys and robbed a warehouse."

"Hey, you robbed a warehouse too!" I protested. "And I remember you and Bob doing your share of killing."

He shook his head. "Woman, you are nothing but trouble. I'm pretty sure your first name is trouble."

"Actually it's Eden," I told him.

He laughed. "That has to be the worst name ever for you. Eden. Seriously? You are about as far from the Garden of Eden as anything on this planet. No, your name is Trouble."

I was kind of insulted by that, but whatever. I wasn't here to win friends and influence people, just to get whatever information and help I needed to find my sister.

"Back to the subject, I think I convinced the guy who wants to bang me to get me a job interview with Desiree. She's my only real lead to Nevarra," I explained.

"What about that Fender guy?" Bishop asked. "You're better off going after him than someone who might be a demon."

"That's plan B," I told him. "If he turned Nevarra over to someone else, he might not know where she's being kept. I'd rather go with the last person who was known to have her."

He walked up to stand beside me. "Suicide by demon is your plan A?"

I felt a bit sick in my stomach at that. "Hopefully I live long enough to get my sister and return her safely home."

"Sounds like suicide to me," HB chimed in cheerfully.

"Do either of you know anything about this Desiree?" I asked. "You both seem to know a lot more about demons than I do. Maybe she's one of these Lows and all I have to worry about is acid bodily fluids."

"I don't know any demons personally," HB announced.

"I haven't heard of a demon named Desiree, but that's not surprising," Bishop said. "Names have power. They can be used to bind and control. Demons often have a long string of names. If you know them all and know their order, then you have a significant advantage. That means demons are constantly making up new names for themselves. They might be Horace this decade, and Justin the next."

Crap. I was hoping he would know something about her —something that might help me prepare at least a minimal defense. I wanted to know what I was going up against, but it seemed I'd be walking into this demon's lair blind. If Piers came through for me and I got an interview, that is.

Maybe Bishop was right. Maybe I'd be better off going with Plan B and staying away from this demon. But time was ticking. I needed to find Nevarra. And the quickest way to do that was to stick my head into the lion's mouth.

"Thanks." I slid off the bar stool. "I appreciate the info. And the tea."

I headed for the door, a bit surprised that Bishop followed me out.

"How's the other little girl? The one who was hurt?"

He knew about Sadie? Had Bea told him last night while I'd been getting ready?

"I'm worried about infection setting in." I told him. "We've got some antibiotics, and first aid supplies, but neither Bea nor I are trained in medical care. I really don't want to have to take her to the hospital, but we might have to."

Bishop grunted and kept walking beside me, pausing as I reached my bike.

"Let me know if you get a scent again, and I'll bring Bob out," he offered.

"I will."

Even though I knew it would cost me each time I used his services, I was grateful for the offer. I slid my stolen helmet over my head, then straddled the bike.

Bishop eyed me for a second. "Good luck. And try not to get killed, Trouble."

I kicked my bike to life and pulled away from the bar thinking that I was going to need all the luck I could get.

* * *

I HAD to knock on the new front door since I didn't have a set of keys. Something twisted painfully in my chest to see Bea answer it instead of one of the girls. I was so used to one of them peeking at me through the window first, and demanding I tell them the phrase each of them had come up with to let them know everything was okay.

My favorite color is bacon.

There's a penguin in the backyard.

I'd give anything to rewind back two days. Anything.

"How is Sadie?" I asked, noting the worry in Bea's eyes.

"Feverish. Her leg is hot and swollen." Bea's voice shook. "Marissa dropped off some food this morning, and I asked again if she could get her cousin to send a doctor or a nurse over. If she can't get anyone to come by tomorrow, I'm going to take Sadie to the hospital."

The hospital. Where Bea and Sadie would sit and wait all day just to be seen, where nurses, doctors, and staff were so shorthanded that medical care sometimes came too late. Out in the waiting room, Sadie would be exposed to all sorts of germs, feverish and in pain without even a bed to lie in. But she *needed* medical help. If we couldn't get someone to make a house call, then the hospital was better than watching her die of infection here in our home.

I went to the girls' room and sat on the bed beside my littlest sister, feeling the heat from her before I even put a hand on her forehead.

"I've given her some aspirin, and more antibiotics," Bea whispered. "I was about to start putting cool cloths on her when you came in."

Sadie's eyes drifted open. "Eden."

"I'm here, sweetie." I smoothed the damp hair back from her forehead.

"Where's Nevarra?" she asked, turning her head fitfully.

I glanced over at Bea, who shook her head. She hadn't told Sadie what had happened, and it was better off if we kept it that way.

"She's staying at a neighbor's house for a while," I lied.

"Where are the elephants and flowers? They came to visit me. Elephants squeezing under the bedroom door then blowing up huge like party balloons."

Fever dreams.

"The elephants went home," I said. And hopefully they wouldn't be back.

"I saw an angel," Sadie abruptly said, her fevered gaze suddenly locked onto mine. "He was so beautiful, so bright that it hurt to look at him. He was gold and pink and dove-gray like a sunrise on the beach. So beautiful."

I clamped my lips tight and blinked hard. I knew she'd been hallucinating, but still couldn't hold back a hard shiver. When the demons had come, we'd put our faith in the angels to save us. My faith was already shaky at best, but two decades of being dragged to mass had left me with certain expectations about the messengers of God.

Those expectations had been quickly shattered. The angels battled the demons, destroying even more of our city and state. They'd killed demons, sent a huge number of them back to hell, then they'd left.

They'd flown off and forsaken us, leaving us to deal with the demons that remained and the ones who quickly returned from hell. Even our own country had abandoned us. They might be beautiful as Sadie said, but I'd given up any hope of being saved by angelic beings from on high.

"The angel stood next to the elephants and spoke to me." Sadie closed her eyes. "It wasn't words. His voice was like bells, like wind chimes. He told me I'd live, that my leg would heal."

I slowly let out a breath and forced a smile, because if Sadie believed, that was all that mattered. "He's right. You *are* going to get better. You'll be up walking around again in no time."

"I told him he could take my leg if he'd just bring Nevarra back to us. I'd trade him my leg if Nevarra was safe, if she was back home." Sadie looked at me again. "I know she's gone, Eden. I know they took her. They took my sister. They *took* her."

She knew. I hadn't wanted her to worry, but we were past that now. "Nevarra will be fine, Sadie. You concentrate on getting well, and let me take care of bringing Nevarra home."

"The angel told me I was a brave girl. He said he didn't want my leg, and that you'd find Nevarra. I made him promise, Eden. I made him promise to help you find Nevarra. Because angels always keep their promises."

Like fuck they did.

I reached down and took her hand. I wasn't sure what was stranger—that Sadie in her fevered hallucination had tried to bargain her leg away for her sister's life, or that she'd badgered an angel into helping me.

Me. The least likely person to ever be receiving heavenly aid.

"Don't you worry about any of this." Bea smoothed a

damp cloth over Sadie's forehead. "Eden and I will take care of everything. Don't you worry one bit."

Sadie closed her eyes once more. "I miss the elephants. They were nice elephants. Maybe we'll get married."

"You want to marry an elephant?" It wasn't the weirdest thing I'd heard in the last few days, but it was up there.

"Or an angel. If I marry an angel, we'll all go live in heaven." She turned her head to the side and whimpered. "I wouldn't hurt if I were in heaven."

She wasn't going to die. And she sure as fuck wasn't marrying an angel. I was *absolutely* not ready for any of us to go live in heaven.

I sat beside Sadie for a while as she slept fitfully, watching as Bea lay cool cloths on her face and chest. A tense knot formed in my chest, growing until I could barely breathe. What was I going to do? Bea was covered with bruises, her arm still in the makeshift sling. What if it was broken? What if the bones weren't lined up and it healed wrong? She needed X-rays, possibly surgery. She didn't need to be sitting here in pain trying to take care of Sadie.

And Sadie… Even if she somehow managed to fight off this infection, would she ever walk again? Would she ever be completely free of pain? How much nerve and muscle damage had she suffered when that bullet ripped through her leg? They both needed me to care for them. And Nevarra needed me to find her.

What if the Fixers came back looking for me? Bea was in no shape to fight them off. What if they killed Bea and Sadie, then lay in wait and murdered me when I came home tonight? They were probably watching the house right now. They'd probably called in reinforcements when they saw me come in. They'd pick me off as I left, or storm the house. I'd die. Bea would die defending me. Sadie would die alone in a bedroom with no one to care for her. No one would come for Nevarra. She'd be sold, raped, beaten, starved, tortured, and killed, and all the while she'd cry, wondering where I was and why I didn't come to save her.

Everyone I loved would die. The only people in the world who mattered to me would die horribly and there was nothing I could do to stop it.

A hand rested on my shoulder, and I realized my breath was coming in sharp panicked gasps. My chest felt as if someone had pummeled it with a sledge hammer.

"Easy. Breathe in two three four, breathe out two three four."

I did as Bea said, my body reacting instinctively to the warm cadence of her voice. The four count became six, then eight and the tightness in my chest began to loosen. The hand on my shoulder eased me against a soft warm body, the other arm encircling me. Bea's lips touched my forehead and it felt almost like a blessing.

"I am not going to die. Sadie is not going to die. You are going to find Nevarra and bring her home."

"The Fixers…"

"Will regret they ever came within a mile of this house." Her hands smoothed my hair. "Dave Rickard chased off one of them this afternoon with a hail of bird shot. Christopher Hammond set up some battery-operated alarms across our back fence. The whole block is taking shifts doing patrol duty. Genevieve Planteaux is drawing wards on the street at the intersections and along the curb."

I snorted. Genevieve Planteaux's only magical powers were probably in her head, but what did I know? Either way, the Fixers would be wary of crossing a bunch of chalk symbols that might be nothing, or might make their skin erupt with agonizing boils.

Bea's hand smoothed my hair once more. "We haven't had much in the way of problems here. Some cars broken into and stolen, some vandalism. That's it. Even after the fights were over and the angels left, the worst we had was that sad excuse of a demon wandering down the street, jacking off, stealing stuff from cars, and yelling profanities. Oh, and that cute little kitten with the laser eyes."

That kitten had been terrifying. No one dared breathe until the thing crawled under the fence into the landfill transfer station and headed north.

"The gangs leave us alone," Bea continued. "None of us have anything worth stealing—and nothing worth getting shot over. What happened to us yesterday scared people. If a bunch of armed hooligans can roll up to *our* house, bust in the door, shoot Sadie and steal Nevarra, then it can happen to anyone."

"Anyone who gets set up by a cop and has the tax collectors after her," I added.

Bea made a shush noise. "All they know is we got attacked. And that means it's time for the whole block to get together and start protecting each other. I'm not saying the Fixers won't be back, but if they come, they'll be facing some seriously pissed off residents."

The Fixers weren't like the Disciples. They took a job for the money and wanted to make sure they came out alive and uninjured at the end of it. With a neighborhood full of vigilantes and the streets lined with runes of unknown power, they'd probably just decide to grab me elsewhere. It was one less worry on my mind.

"Sadie..." I turned to look at my sister.

"I am perfectly capable of caring for your little sister. We'll get a doctor or nurse here within the next day, or I'll take her to the hospital. And you better believe we're not going to be sitting in that waiting room all day long waiting to be seen. You know me better than that."

I couldn't help but smile. Bea was kind, understanding, loving, but if she needed to defend one of us, a pack of starving lions wouldn't stand a chance against her.

"Trust me to take care of us while you find Nevarra," she said.

"But your job. What about your job?" I was running out of things to worry about, and that was a rarity.

"If I lose my job, I'll find another. I've done it before, you know. We've all figured out that we can cut back. I've got sewing skills I can trade for food. And you'll get things straightened out with the tax collectors and start earning again." Bea's hand continued to stroke my hair.

"We lost all of our savings." And I owed Bishop a small fortune for his help.

"We'll save again," Bea reminded me, her voice soothing. "And we'll leave when we can. Until then, we'll make the best of what we have here, just like all these other people are doing. Not everyone can just pick up and leave, Eden. Some have to stay and fight to make their homes a better place. If that's what we end up doing, I won't be sad about it."

We'd dreamed about making a life across the border, where we didn't have to wonder if there would be water or electricity each day, where the schools would be open and Bea could go to work knowing the kids were in classrooms learning, not cooped up in the house afraid to go out. I wanted that for us. I wanted that for them. I didn't want to have to stay here and fight tooth and nail for every scrap we had, only to have it all blown away because some crooked cop lied about my take.

Speaking of cops…

"I need to go." I stood and leaned over to kiss Bea on the cheek.

"Get something to eat before you leave," she told me. "And I got the phone working again. Call me if you're not coming home tonight."

That was one of the benefits of good old-fashioned land-line phones that didn't need electricity to work. They were sturdy. Evidently it took more than ripping the cord from the wall and throwing them across the room to break them.

I left Sadie to Bea's care, changed my clothes and cleaned up. Then I headed down the hallway to do as my foster mother said and grab a bite to eat, noticing my surroundings for the first time.

The house looked…great. I may have had my doubts about Javier, but the kid could hang a door. And replace windows. Everything was unpainted. A few of the windows were smaller than the original ones, so Javier had built in the frames with layers of two-by-fours. No trim had been put on, but everything was sturdy, safe, and weatherproof. He'd even repaired the broken coffee table with a combination of wood glue, putty, and screws.

It would do. And I was grateful—grateful enough that I was glad to see that Bea must have given the boy one of the industrial-sized cans of chili and a packet of toilet paper to take home to his family.

When I walked into the kitchen I was even more shocked. Not only had Javier replaced the shot-up cabinets with a collection of mismatched doors and drawers, the other neighbors had obviously been by as well. The food… I was pretty sure that the chicken, noodle, and cheese casserole had come from the Rickards down the block since Shelly was famous for her casseroles.

Besides that, there was a plate of empanadas, a hot pie that smelled of steak and onions, three loaves of banana nut bread wrapped in cellophane, and a tin of snickerdoodles.

All this time I'd been ignoring our neighbors, feeling as if we could rely only on ourselves, but when tragedy happened, they'd come through. Javier had been sent over to make repairs. A neighborhood watch had been formed. Everyone up and down the street had come over with food.

They cared. Or maybe they just figured there was safety in numbers, and if they helped us, we'd help them when they needed it. Probably the latter.

Yep, that was my suspicious, paranoid nature kicking in once more.

I opened the fridge and saw a gallon of whole milk. Beside it was a bar of chocolate with a little bow on it and a hand-written note in a childish hand that said "get well soon, Sadie." For the second time, I felt tears welling up in my eyes.

I didn't really know these people, and I hadn't wanted to. I'd called this house home since I was thirteen, and I'd recognize most of the neighbors if they walked past me on the street, but that was it. Whether it was curiosity, self-interest, or kindness that had brought them to deliver gifts of food to our house, I was grateful.

The electricity was on so I warmed up a bowl of the chicken noodle casserole and a couple of empanadas in the microwave, eyeing the clock and estimating my travel time to Pasadena.

A vibration in my pocket made me jump and about gave me a heart attack.

The phone. It was amazing how I'd gotten used to not having one. I pulled it out of my pocket and checked it hoping it was Piers telling me he'd set up a meeting with Desiree.

The text wasn't from Piers but someone named Amanda who wanted to know if I'd be home late since she wanted to make reservations at Guido's for dinner.

Guido's. Damn. I hadn't eaten out in years, and a mid-level place like Guido's sounded like a royal banquet to me. I texted Amanda back, telling her I'd be home on time, feeling a twinge of envy for the phone's owner.

It might have been a long time since I'd eaten out, but that chicken casserole and the empanadas were better than I'd had in a long time. I rinsed and wiped my bowl, checked once more on Sadie and Bea, then headed out.

CHAPTER 14

*D*etective Juke didn't look anything at all like a Sarah. She didn't look much like a Juke either. She was tall and lean with olive skin. Dark freckles scattered across a round face and broad nose. Her hair drew the eye and held it, a bright red teased out into an afro. She wore black leather pants, a white silk shirt with a low V of a neckline, and a black leather vest. A matching shoulder holster held a pistol whose make and model I couldn't quite determine. Her belt held a coiled bull whip on one side and a set of handcuffs on the other. I blinked wondering if she was perhaps the secret love child of Zorro and Little Orphan Annie.

"Alvaro." She stood and shook my hand, which wasn't something I was used to. Then as I sat, she waved the waitress over and ordered us both coffee and some blueberry scones.

I wasn't used to that either.

Before I could orient myself to the strange turn of events, this woman who looked nothing like a cop suddenly became one.

"Let's get started on your missing person's report." She pulled a sheet of paper out of nowhere, like a magician and clicked a pen. "Name, address, and phone number."

She knew my name, but I gave it to her anyway. My address? I wasn't about to make the same mistake twice. I'd used my real address on my licensing paperwork, and that's how the Fixers had gotten to my family. I hesitated, trying to think of a fake one to give her, and before I realized it I'd given her the address to Suerte.

Ha. I envisioned the cops showing up at the bar to arrest me and being chopped to mince by Bishop, his staff, and the patrons. They'd probably feed the body parts to Bob.

The detective took down the information, including a description of Nevarra. I was careful to skirt over what exactly had caused the Fixers to perform a home invasion and kidnapping, even though she already knew about my issues with the tax collectors.

When I was done, Juke had me sign the form, then slid it somewhere under the table.

"It's been a crazy few days. Three members of the Disciples got whacked at the old auto parts store over on Sutter Avenue." Her dark eyes narrowed. "A brunette woman was seen running from the area right after a gunshot killed one of their lieutenants—Crow, was his name. Someone blew his brains out and left him with his dick hanging by a tendon."

"That sounds terrible." I tried to compose my expression into one of shock and horror, like a normal person at hearing of such a thing. I'm pretty sure I failed.

"Word on the street among the Disciples is the killer was a Russian woman who's the girlfriend of a lower level member and whom two guards had decided to rape. The guards are dead, so that does seem to point to this Russian woman. Although how she managed to electrocute one of them, and why she stuck around to blow Crow's brains out and emasculate him while he was taking a piss seems a little perplexing." Juke shrugged. "Personally, I don't find it perplexing. A woman raped by members of her boyfriend's gang might be angry enough to take out the lieutenant who had sanctioned the rape."

I cringed a little, hoping the Russian woman didn't end up dead in an alley because of what I'd done. If she was smart, she'd have taken that money, ditched the low-level Disciple boyfriend, and headed out of the city.

"How the heck do you all know any of this?" I asked. "I can't imagine the Disciples calling the police to report a homicide, or in this case three homicides."

At that time our coffee and pastries arrived. Juke smiled thanks up at the waitress and took a sip, waiting for the other woman to leave before she continued.

"Employees at a store across the street called it in. Between you and me, no one gives a rat's ass about three dead Disciples. Or about two other Disciples and two Fixers that got iced during a supposed robbery at a warehouse last night. But it's important to stay aware of these things, just in case they connect to something we do give a rat's ass about."

I liked this woman. She was a cop, and I was predisposed to hate cops, but Juke seemed a really unusual cop. I guess in order to remain a member of the police force in New Hell, you kinda had to be weird.

"I don't know anything about these shocking crimes," I lied, "but I have come into a bit of information. I've learned that a Disciple named Fender most likely handed my sister over to someone named Desiree, who supposedly handles their prostitution and human trafficking businesses."

Juke snorted, then picked up a blueberry scone. "I could have told you that without you needing to slaughter three gang members. Not that I'm complaining, mind you."

"I don't know what you're talking about. I was nowhere near that auto parts store today," I continued to lie.

She ignored me. "If you'd have told me two years ago that I'd be turning a blind eye to vigilantism, hell, even encouraging it, I would have laughed until I passed out. This is one crazy fucking world we live in now. Do we follow the constitution even though we're no longer part of the U.S.? Do we even bother to Mirandize suspects anymore? How do we prioritize cases when no one gives a shit and our budget has dropped to pretty close to zero because there's no government, no property taxes, no nothing."

"We've got government," I pointed out. "I voted last year."

I hadn't voted last year. Why bother? I was pretty sure most of New Hell felt the same. And I wasn't about to discuss tax revenue. Nope, that was definitely a topic I wanted to avoid at all costs.

"Desiree." Juke finished chewing the last of her scone and wiped her hands on a little white napkin square. "First thing you've got to understand is none of us is really sure who Desiree is. We've never seen her. We've never had a good lead on her. All we know is that whoever the hell Desiree is, she's been heading up this operation for almost a decade."

A decade. If Desiree really was a demon, then she'd been here long before most of us even knew demons existed.

"Look." Juke slid a messenger bag out from under her chair and put it on the table. It was black leather. Of course. "Let me show you how these auctions are done, and then you'll realize that trying to stop these fuckers is like cutting the heads off a hydra. I'm not saying we shouldn't keep at it, but that it's something we'll probably be fighting forever."

She pulled out a folder and slid it over to me. The first few pictures were screen shots of what looked like the home page of an exclusive dating site. "This is from a bust eight years ago we did in conjunction with an FBI task force. It took the federal UC almost two years to infiltrate the group and get onto the site as a buyer."

I had no idea how long undercover operations lasted or how they worked, but *two years*? These trafficking groups were very careful who they did business with. They likely had a group of known buyers and were reluctant to allow new ones in even if they were throwing a whole lot of money around.

I didn't have two years to build their trust, or the money to support a cover. I'd need to instead rely on brute force and the fact that I was crazy and motivated enough to lose my life bringing Nevarra back.

I looked at the pictures of the website. "So your UC made contact and worked his way in all through the internet? Or did he have to meet people in person at some time or another?"

"He had to socialize with the right people so they could vouch for him, but this entire operation was done over the internet. He met one of the sellers in person. That's how we knew the Disciples were involved. One of our Vice guys made him. It was a lucky break, because the gang keeps their human trafficking as a stand-alone business so a drug raid wouldn't normally have exposed it."

"But that was eight years ago," I mused.

She nodded. "They kept that side of their business separate due to logistics back then, but I'm not sure if they bother anymore. We've got no feds to rely on now, and we've got the budget of a neighborhood popsicle stand."

That meant crime was nice and comfortable out in the open, and the cops needed to pick their battles. I thought about the hit on the jogger, and all the cases of bullets in the trunk of that car. With everything that had happened in the last two years, cops with an inclination to be dirty felt free to do whatever they wanted.

I turned to another photo and saw a sheet of mug shots. None of them looked familiar, although eight years later they could have been dead, still in jail, or operating out of the city.

"Someone tipped the Disciples off," Juke explained. "We had to move early and didn't get their top tier. We snagged enough people and evidence to make them suspend their human trafficking operations for a while. They focused mainly on the other sides of their business until two years ago."

When the demons came and all the criminal elements flexed their muscle and felt confident bringing their doings out into the sunlight.

"These guys," she tapped the sheet with the mug shots, "were guarding a group of kids. We caught them and rescued the kids. We also found a photo studio with equipment to do stills and video that they could post onto the 'net. They had a pay-per-view site and would use the less 'pristine' kids for that. Runaways and teen prostitutes. Buyers could still place a bid on them if they liked what they saw, but the real money was selling the ones that looked like they came from nice wholesome families and had never been touched. Those were just posed in their photos and carefully guarded until they were sold. We got eight kids out of there with this bust."

She reached over and turned the page to three photos of missing child alerts. Just three? Did no one care about the other five?

"Four arrests at the scene. We hammered them hard and managed to get them to turn on two more, plus we got the names of three buyers. Two of the buyers slipped through the cracks. There just wasn't enough evidence, and they had expensive lawyers. The six Disciples were convicted. We offered deals left and right, but no one would give up the top dogs. They were terrified. The only thing we got out of them was that the operation was run by someone named Desiree."

"No one even gave a description of her?" I asked.

Juke shook her head. "None of the guys we arrested had ever seen her in person. All they knew was that she went by Desiree. They didn't even know her last name. I don't know if she's black or white. I don't really even know if she's a she. That's it. Two-year-long operation. Six guys in jail. Eight kids returned to their parents, although I'm pretty sure a few of them were back out on the street within a week."

I turned the page and saw a photo array of the kids. Six girls and two boys, all looking to be under the age of fifteen. Different races. And different backgrounds, from the wary, hard expression on a few of their faces. I hesitated, my eyes were drawn to a light-skinned black girl. She was one of the older ones—about fourteen I was guessing. There was something familiar about her. Something about the wide set of her eyes and the firm, almost masculine, lines of her square chin. I looked closer. Her dark curls were tucked behind an ear decorated with three earrings—a turquoise turtle, a coral fish, and a silver snake that edged up toward the cartilage.

I recognized the jewelry, and suddenly recognized the face. Eight years had thinned out her cheeks and sharpened the lines of her jaw and chin, but the eyes were the same.

I was looking at a childhood photo of Telaney Miller.

I *knew* her. Fuck, I'd just seen her yesterday at the Gray Dog and Southside dustup. She was a fellow Vulture, a scavenger I respected and admired and she'd been a victim of human trafficking. I hadn't even known. Although that would hardly be the sort of thing you'd confess to business acquaintances.

Telaney Miller. I reached out to touch the photo, wondering what her life would have been like if eight years ago the feds and local police hadn't raided a human trafficking operation. Knowing Telaney, she would have beaten her buyer to death with a sex toy and been free within a week of her purchase, but maybe that was me just being optimistic. Telaney was tough as nails now, but this girl in the photo looked lost. Scared. My stomach churned, envisioning her used-up body buried in a shallow grave or tossed into a lake. Or if she'd been lucky, maybe she would have been resold for prostitution after she'd gotten too old for her pedophile buyer.

I had to find Nevarra. Gritting my teeth, I closed the folder and slid it back toward the detective.

"Think they'd be stupid enough to use the same place?" A girl could always hope.

"I doubt it. They know we're understaffed and that there's no FBI task force backing us up, but they learned from what went down eight years ago." Juke pulled another set of photos out of the messenger bag and handed them to me. "I know a few people with mad tech skills and managed to squeak in to see their website, although I got booted in less than five minutes—not long enough to trace the IP through all the server bounces."

My hands shook as I opened the folder, expecting to see Nevarra's face staring up at me. Thankfully the first screenshot was a homepage with a countdown to an auction.

"They set the auction end date when they have one kid, then continue to add other kids to it as they acquire more, up until the last day," Juke said.

I took a breath, let it out, and flipped the page. Four children stared back at me—a boy and three girls. A cherub faced, blond haired boy who looked like he should be attending kindergarten, a girl with blue-black hair and creamy skin who looked to be just on the edge of womanhood, a teen with a thick head of golden-brown hair and bright blue eyes, and a girl who looked to be about Sadie's age and of mixed Asian heritage.

No Nevarra. I was equally relieved and terrified. I hadn't

wanted to see her picture in this folder, but if she wasn't part of this auction, then where was she? Had they killed her? Sold her off without any sort of bidding? Kept her for themselves?

Swallowing hard, I pushed the folder back to the detective. "She's not there. Nevarra. My sister. She's not one of those four kids."

"I got that screenshot this afternoon," Juke replied softly. "She wasn't up for sale as of then. I was lucky to get that far in before I got booted off the server. It asks for a security key at random intervals. I'm afraid if we try too much, they'll change the whole thing." She put the folders back in the messenger bag. "If you click on the pictures, there's a profile of each child. I only caught a glimpse of that level, but I know there's a spot to place a bid."

"How close are you to getting them?" Fuck, I felt like I was going to puke right here in the coffee shop.

"Not close. We've reached a dead end as far as finding out where they are or who Desiree is. The few Disciples we've pulled in on other charges won't talk. We can't find where they're holding the kids, or where they're running this auction from. We've got people on it. *I'm* on it when I'm not getting yanked into homicide."

That wasn't the answer I wanted to hear. "I thought you could help me. I thought you were closing in on these guys. It took you two years with the FBI to bust them the first time. How many kids got sold off before you raided them? How many kids are going to get sold this time before you find them? *If* you ever find them, that is."

She held up her hands. "We're doing the best we can with what we've got. You work your angle. I work mine. If we can share information, then eventually we'll get these guys—and Desiree too."

I pushed back the chair and stood. "What part of 'they've

got my sister' did you not understand? I'm not doing some long-term case with you. I'm trying to find her and get her out of there before they sell her."

The detective stood as well. "And how exactly are you going to do that? Run around killing Disciples until you get lucky? Or until they kill you?"

"If I have to, then yes." I stormed out of the coffee shop, not looking back.

I wasn't a detective. My investigative skills were nil, but I was really damned good at smacking hornets' nests and running away really fast. I had a few leads, and if they didn't pan out, I'd start swinging and hope I made enough of a stink that someone ran off to Desiree and led me there.

As frustrated as I was with Detective Juke, meeting her hadn't been a waste of time. I knew more about how the auctions worked. I knew that they didn't have Nevarra up for sale on the site as of this afternoon. And I knew one of their previous victims.

I didn't have Telaney Miller's number, and all I knew about where she lived was that she'd moved somewhere in Silver Lake. I wished I'd gotten her address or some way of contacting her when I'd seen her at the accounting day raid, but at the time I'd had no reason to think I'd ever need to call the woman. We weren't really friends. Acquaintances, that's what we were. Trusted business associates.

Damn, I wish I had her phone number.

Figuring there might be one person in the Valley who knew how to contact Telaney, I snuck back to Bags's place. There were two new guys standing around out front watching the pawnshop with more attentiveness than the previous two, so instead of trying to sneak in, I called him. He didn't pick up, and the store was clearly closed, but I left a message anyway and drove back toward Sun Valley.

It was a half hour before my phone buzzed in my pocket.

I pulled it out, hoping it wasn't Amanda pissed off because the phone's original owner had stood her up at Guido's.

The text was from an unknown number telling me to be at Artemis Books on Oxnard and Willow Crest in an hour.

Was this Bags being careful and texting me from one of the burner phones he had in the store? Was this a message for the former owner of the phone? Was it Piers trying to get lucky? Although I doubted Piers would have me meet him at a used bookstore, so I crossed that idea right off. It might be from Bags. Either way, I was tired of driving around, waiting for something to happen. I'd go to the bookstore, and if it was for the guy who was supposed to be having dinner with Amanda at Guido's, I'd just go home.

I got to the bookstore fifteen minutes early. Artemis Books was in a strip mall. The concrete façade had been painted robin's egg blue. There were bars over the windows and a metal door that looked like it should have been on a bank. It took some serious effort to pull the thing open, but I managed. A weird static shock rolled through me as I entered—not quite like what I could do with my stun gun abilities, but similar. It made me pause, wondering if the business had some sort of magical security. My head didn't explode, and I felt no further electric shocks, so I kept walking.

Inside, the bookstore was dim, the only light from a few strategically placed lamps. A glass counter stood off to the side about halfway through the store. There was an enormous old-school cash register on it, which seemed sensible given how often the electricity went out in the Valley. The entire rest of the store consisted of row upon row of wooden bookshelves, stacked two deep in places with books. The place smelled of lemony wood polish, and leather with the faint odor of mothballs.

"Hey! Hi there!" A man waved at me from around the side

of a bookshelf at the back of the store. "Just unpacking some new arrivals. Let me know if I can help you find something specific."

I thanked him, then ducked down the nearest aisle to browse and wait for whoever might show up, whether it be Bags, Piers, or some stranger looking for the guy who used to own this phone.

Pulling one of the books at eye level off the shelf I glanced at the cover. Albert Joissen. *The Early German Alchemists*. I opened it to a random page and saw a wall of text in a miniscule font about Hennig Brand and his various attempts to create gold from urine.

Ew.

I put the book back and selected another, looking for something to occupy my time as I waited, preferably something that wouldn't completely gross me out. How the hell did someone come up with the idea that they could turn piss into gold? True, they were both yellowish, and if you whacked someone hard in the kidneys, their pee might have enough blood in it to make it kinda gold colored, but gold-gold? What the fuck had this Hennig guy been smoking?

The new book I'd pulled out was a translation of various lost Akkadian tablets, one which expanded on the Epic of Gilgamesh, and another that held a fractured story of the exploits of a resurrected Enkidu. I'd always had a love for fairy tales and folklore, so I read on and was startled when I looked up at the clock over the doorway to find that it was half an hour past my meeting time.

No one had come in after me, and I hadn't received any phone calls. I frowned at my phone, trying to decide whether I should text the number back and risk being outed as a phone thief.

"That's an excellent book."

I looked up at the employee who was standing a few feet

away. He was short—right around my height—and so thin that he looked as if a strong breeze would send him rolling down the street. His brown hair was shaved in an undercut around the sides and back, and long enough on top that it looked like he had a horse's mane instead of hair. He flipped the mane to the left and grinned at me.

"There's some water damage on the cover, and the glue's starting to break, so I can let you have it for fifteen dollars."

If I'd had fifteen dollars, I would have given it to the man. I wanted to read this book. I wanted to take it home and read it to Sadie and Nevarra, to tell them the tales that people had listened to four thousand years ago, but all I had in my pocket was eight bucks. I'd been giving any other cash I could scrounge up to Bea, and had only allowed myself to keep ten. After the soda this afternoon, that ten was now eight.

I put the book back. "I've only got eight bucks to my name right now, and I can't buy a book with it, no matter how much I want to."

Hopefully he wouldn't kick me out. I'd spent most of my childhood being kicked out of stores when the employees realized I had no money. Maybe if I stuck around another half an hour, whoever I was supposed to meet would show up.

"You're not here to buy books then?" The man flipped his hair to the right, still smiling. "Then you must be here looking for answers?"

I hesitated, thinking this guy was about to deliver a religious sermon along with a pamphlet about Jesus.

"No. I was supposed to meet someone here, and they didn't show."

"Ah. A date."

It really wasn't any of this guy's business, but I felt bad for hanging out in his store and not purchasing anything. Not a soul had come in since I'd been here. Maybe he was lonely and chatting with me was a welcome break from stocking shelves.

"Not a date. I'm trying to locate a business acquaintance of mine. I left a message with a friend who might know how to reach her, and got a text saying to come here but no one showed up. Sorry to have wasted your time."

"Do you want to use the store computer to see if you can look your business acquaintance up? Right now we've got electric, and the internet is up."

That was super nice of him. Of course, he'd probably look over my shoulder to make sure I wasn't downloading malware, but it wasn't like I would be searching anything confidential.

Although…

"Thank you. I'd appreciate that."

He led me behind the counter and opened up a laptop that had been hidden by the huge cash register. Salvagers had to be licensed, and there was a database of our names and license numbers along with contact info available to the public. They didn't put our addresses out there for everyone to see, but if a Vulture had e-mail or a phone number they wanted published, it would be in the listing.

I didn't have either since I didn't consistently have a cell phone or internet, and I hadn't wanted to list the landline number at Bea's. The people who looked up and contacted salvagers did it because they wanted us to keep our eyes open for certain items—items they were willing to pay top dollar to recover or purchase. The spots I worked in the Valley didn't tend to yield rare, unusual, or magical items, so it never seemed worth the bother for me to put in a contact number.

Luckily Telaney hadn't felt the same. Right next to her name was a phone number. The employee pushed a pad of pink sticky notes and a pen over to me and I jotted down her number.

"Thanks."

"No problem at all. Is there anything else you need? Someone else you need to look up?"

I hesitated partly because I didn't want to take advantage of this guy's helpfulness, and partly because I had difficulty trusting anyone, let alone some random shopkeeper at a used bookstore.

Screw it. Although if I was going to look for something that might get this guy fired, I felt I should at least give him a head's-up.

"My fourteen-year-old sister was taken by the Fixers yesterday and turned over to the Disciples to be sold in a human trafficking operation. She wasn't listed on their sale site as of this afternoon, but she might be now. All I know is that someone named Desiree runs all of this for the Disciples, and that she might not be human. If I could find the website, I'd like to see if my sister is listed, and if I can trace it somehow to a location."

The clerk flipped his mane of hair to the other side and made a click noise with his mouth. "Desire isn't human? Is she an elf? Demon? Shifter? Chimera?"

I blinked, hoping there weren't chimeras running around LA. With the way things had gone over the last two years, I wouldn't be surprised.

"Someone hinted that she's a demon. But what I really care about is finding my sister and bringing her home. I don't know if I can find the website or even get in if I do. The police can't manage to get all the way through the site security. It's probably on the dark web, and you might get in trouble if we try to pull it up with your work computer."

The man laughed. It was a wheezy, smoky sound as if he

were a three-pack-a-day kinda guy. "Nah. Don't worry about that. Here. Let me see what I can do."

He pulled the laptop over toward him, and I got to stare at the back of the lid as he typed. Light flashed from the screen as he worked, reflecting orange off his light brown eyes. He mumbled, clicked his tongue a few times, let out a few curse words, then finally turned the screen around.

I gawked, unable to even think clearly for a second because the guy had gotten in. I had no idea what sort of computer savant was working in this bookshop, but the FBI was really missing out on an incredible employee.

The webpage had three columns of pictures with a name in bold and a short description under each. The page heading said these kids were "Currently Available In Los Angeles." The four pictures that Detective Juke had shown me earlier were there along with three shadowed out boxes marked "Coming Soon": Blake, described as seven, Caucasian, and "angelic"; Lotus, described as ten, Asian, and "exotic"; Josie, described as fourteen, mixed-race, and "stunning."

Bile burned the back of my throat as I clicked on Josie. She was touted to be "fresh and virginal, a young teen and just beginning to bud into womanhood." The cheerful description went on to say that the buyer could finish Josie any way they wanted as she was "healthy and eager to please."

I shut the lid of the laptop and drew in a ragged breath. Josie had to be Nevarra. None of the other "coming soon" descriptions matched at all. She was fourteen, and although she wasn't light skinned, she could be categorized as mixed race. Stunning definitely fit. Nevarra was a beautiful girl.

Coming soon. They didn't even have a picture of her up yet. I saw a box to click for a bid amount, but it was at zero. Her profile probably hadn't been up long enough for anyone to have put in a bid. That should have been a good thing. She was still there. She hadn't been sold yet. And if what had been on the countdown page was correct, the bidding was to go on for at least a few more days. This was good. I had time—time to talk to Telaney, to hunt down this Desiree. Time to rescue Nevarra before anything bad happened to her.

Yet all I could think about was that horrible description, as if my sister were a puppy or a foal for sale and not a young girl.

"I tried to trace the website to a location, but couldn't. There's also nothing on there about anyone named Desiree."

I cleared my throat. "It's okay. Thanks."

"Is there anything else I can do for you?" The clerk's voice was soft and gentle.

I shook my head. "You've been such a huge help. And I don't even know your name."

"Alfie."

Poor guy to be saddled with that as a name. I assumed it was short for Alfred or something. Alfie. Hadn't that been a sitcom back before I was born about a furry alien?

I forced a smile to my face. "I'm Eden. And thank you again. As soon as I have some money, I'll come in and buy some books."

He raised a hand and extended a leather-bound book to me. It was the one on the Epic of Gilgamesh, and the Enkidu stories. I'd put it back on the shelf and hadn't recalled him pulling it back off.

"For you. Pay me when you can."

I took a step back. "Oh, I couldn't. You don't even know me, and you've already helped me so much. I don't want you to get in trouble with your boss, either."

He grinned and flipped his hair to the left. "I am the boss. Here. Take it. I insist."

I'd always had a hard time accepting gifts. Bea had once told me that when I refused a gift, I was insulting the giver. It was still hard for me, but I made it a rule that if someone offered a gift three times, I would graciously accept.

Unless they were fae. I'd read enough fairy tales growing up to know better than to accept any gift from the fae, no matter how many times they offered.

I peered at Alfie, trying to make sure he wasn't an elf. No pointed ears. And fae were supposed to be astoundingly beautiful with perfect symmetry of features. Alfie was kinda ugly.

"Are you sure? It might be a long time until I can pay you back."

"Then consider it a gift." He practically poked me with the book this time.

"Okay." I laughed and took it from him, holding it tight to my chest as if I were a schoolgirl carrying a textbook. "Thank you again."

"You're welcome, Eden," he called out as I walked to the door. "And tell Sadie I hope she recovers quickly."

It wasn't until I was climbing on my bike that I realized what he'd said. I'd never mentioned either of my sisters' names, and I hadn't told him about Sadie.

I pulled out the cell phone and looked once more at the text that had sent me to the bookstore. Just who the hell *was* Alfie, and who had sent me the message?

CHAPTER 15

There was a blue Mini Cooper parked in the driveway behind Bea's car when I got home. I immediately tensed, then forced myself to relax, thinking that the Fixers would hardly show up to grab me driving a blue Mini Cooper.

Parking the bike beside Bea's car, I took a few seconds to dial the number I'd pulled up for Telaney. She didn't answer. No surprise there. I probably wouldn't pick up a call from an unknown number either. I left her a message asking her to call me back, then went around front to the door, pulling my pistol out, just in case the one of the Fixers did drive a blue Mini Cooper. The door was unlocked, but I knocked and called out as I opened it.

Bea poked her head around the corner of the hallway. "We're in the girls' room," she whispered barely loud enough for me to hear.

"We?" I knew it couldn't be Nevarra, but I still dropped my backpack and raced to the bedroom hoping she'd managed to escape and make her way home. The "we" wasn't

Nevarra, but a woman, hooking a bag to an IV pole and giving Bea instructions in a calm, soothing voice.

"This is Doctor Mwangi." Bea practically radiated relief as she introduced the woman. "This is Eden Alvaro, the eldest of my foster daughters."

I reached over to shake her hand. The doctor was an ebony-skinned woman with neat rows of braids that followed the curve of her head, ending right at the nape of her neck. She wore a pair of rumpled mint-green scrubs and a white shirt with what looked like dancing cacti on it.

The woman could have been wearing a leather nun's suit for all I cared. I was just thrilled that Sadie was receiving professional medical attention.

"Doctor Mwangi is a pediatric oncologist over at Children's Hospital," Bea told me. "But she said she's done regular rotations in the ER, so Sadie is in good hands."

Likewise, I didn't care if the woman was a veterinarian, I was just happy someone was here who had access to whatever we needed to get Sadie to heal.

"I brought a portable X-ray machine and from what I see there are no bone breaks, but I'll know better once I can see the films on something bigger than my phone." Dr. Mwangi scooted the IV stand closer to the wall, then bent down and ran what looked like a plastic wand over Sadie's forehead.

"Did you X-ray Bea's arm?" I'd been concerned about her as well.

The doctor nodded. "A hairline fracture. Nothing to worry about, as long as she takes it easy." She waved a finger at Bea. "No mountain climbing until it heals, you hear?"

I chuckled to hear her mock-scolding Bea like that.

"I'm not worried about me, but Sadie. Do you think the bullet might have nicked the bone?" Bea's brows furrowed. "Will the muscles in her leg be okay? Will they heal right?"

She wanted to know if Sadie would have a limp the rest

of her life. If she'd have chronic pain. If she would be able to even walk properly. I worried about those things too.

"I really can't tell if there's any minor bone damage right now, or how extensive the muscle damage is. At this moment, my goal is to keep infection at bay, to let the wound drain and keep it clean, and to keep her fever from spiking. After she's stable, and the swelling and fever are reduced, we'll run some additional diagnostics and if needed, we'll consider surgery as well as think about what physical therapy she'll need to regain mobility."

Fear washed over me. Surgery. Physical therapy. Regaining mobility. I'd been so focused on Sadie surviving this whole thing that I hadn't begun to think about what a long road she'd have to recovery, or if she'd be permanently disabled.

"Let's see how she is in another few days. I've got her on fluids and antibiotics right now, and I treated both wounds and changed the dressings. If the swelling and fever are reduced, then I'll take more X-rays, and maybe see if I can borrow a portable ultrasound." The doctor handed Bea a business card. "Call me if her fever spikes above 101, or if you're getting any more of that yellow pus on the bandages. Change them every four hours. If she doesn't come around by the morning, or isn't eating by tomorrow noon, call me. I'm going to try to swing by tomorrow evening to check on her, but I want to know of any changes so I can bring appropriate medicines, okay?"

How much was all of this going to cost? It was one thing for Marissa to have her cousin ask a nurse to come by and check on Sadie, but this was a level of care that rich people paid for. We didn't have anything beyond a bunch of food from the neighbors, a case of industrial-sized canned chili, and a case of toilet paper. I owed Bishop. I now owed this doctor.

We'd never get out of here. We were trapped in LA just like those company-store owned miners I'd read about in high school. Yes, we could skip out on our debts like so many people did, but that wasn't me. I couldn't do that. If I owed someone, I paid it, even if it meant I had to sleep in a ditch and eat out of a dumpster to do so.

"I don't know how to thank you for this, Doctor Mwangi." Bea sat down in the little chair she'd placed beside Sadie's bed. "My children are everything to me."

"As they should be." The doctor smiled and put a hand on Bea's shoulder. "I'll be back tomorrow. Please don't hesitate to call me if she worsens."

I motioned for Bea to stay with Sadie and escorted the doctor to the door. "I'm assuming Marissa's cousin works with you," I said, not sure how to phrase this. "It means so much to us that you came to help, that we didn't have to haul Sadie to a hospital in her condition and wait all day for her to be seen. I just want you to know that I'll pay you. Whatever it takes, whatever the final bill is, I'll pay you. Anything Sadie needs, please go ahead and do it. MRIs, medicines, equipment, or anything. I'll find the money and I'll pay you, I swear it."

She stopped by the door and turned to face me, her smile brilliant and her eyes kind. "Eden, it's been taken care of. There will be no bill for this. Someone once saved my life, and they asked me to come here. I owe them far more than medicines, equipment, and medical care for a gunshot victim. And even if I didn't, I can't refuse care to a child. Every day I fight to give kids with cancer just one more good year, or month, or day. I would never refuse to help your little sister."

I clamped my lips hard to keep them from trembling and blinked back the tears in my eyes. Why the fuck was I crying all the time lately?

"Marissa's cousin has some amazing friends," I choked out. How much did we owe to our neighbors? Neighbors that I'd barely looked at twice, barely knew their names? Casseroles and neighborhood watch programs were one thing, arranging for this level medical care for free was another.

Dr. Mwangi's smile turned sly. "I've got no idea who Marissa is, or her cousin. I can't reveal who arranged for me to provide care for Sadie. Just know it will all be taken care of, including physical therapy when she's ready. All I can tell you is that you've got a guardian angel, Eden Alvaro."

I watched as she walked out the door, down the walk, and into her Mini Cooper. I stood by the window as she drove off, all the time wondering what the fuck she'd meant. A guardian angel? Clearly that was metaphorical since the angels who'd fought during the demon wars hadn't given two shits about any of us.

Someone arranged for Sadie's care. Someone had texted me and sent me to Artemis Books and to Alfie. Was it the same someone? It was kinda creepy to think there was a person rich enough to fund private medical care texting me on a stolen phone and knowing things about me that I'd kept private. I could see a guardian angel watching over Bea or Sadie, or even Nevarra, but me? Nobody cared about me besides my immediate foster family and Bags. I'd never had anyone who helped me without an ulterior motive besides Bea and my sisters, and maybe Drew when he'd lived here.

Drew? No. I hadn't seen him since he walked out over five years ago. And I doubted that even if he'd managed to strike it rich, he'd bother. No, it wasn't Drew who'd done all of this for us.

But if not him, then who?

CHAPTER 16

Telaney had called me back around midnight and told me to meet her at some ungodly hour of the morning in front of a yoga studio a few miles from her home. Traffic was shit at that time of the morning getting out of the Valley, so I was a few minutes late and sadly in need of a cup of coffee when I walked up to her in the parking lot of Sunrise Yoga. At her feet was a dead woman clad in screaming pink tights and a pink tie-dye shirt. All the blood clashed violently with the pink.

"This isn't quite what I envisioned when you told me to meet you here." I pointed to the body.

"What, you thought I was actually doing a yoga class or something?" She snorted. "I'm too late. Damn it they weren't supposed to do the hit until after the 7:00 a.m. class."

That was the problem with scavenging. If your intel was bad, the bodies would be picked clean before you even got there.

"Fuckers took her purse and tossed her car." Telaney pointed to a shiny red Audi a few spaces over. "The only things left were a handful of condoms and this." She pulled a tube of Sisley lipstick out of her pocket and pulled the cap off. "Number eight, sheer coral. Fifty bucks a pop last time I checked. Want it? Coral's not my shade."

I considered that for a moment, unable to imagine Telaney wearing makeup, let alone coral lipstick. She was probably thinking the same about me. Coral wasn't my shade either, so I politely declined.

"Suit yourself." She shrugged and stuck it back in her pocket.

"Why is someone targeting a yoga studio?" I asked as we resumed our positions staring down at the body.

The real question was why was there even a functioning yoga studio here anymore. People were so weird. Demons in the city, violence all around, and there were still enough of them clinging onto a semblance of normal life to keep a yoga studio open.

"Because it's where she went every Saturday morning. Kirstin VonMarten." Telaney's foot reached out to nudge the body, then withdrew, as if she'd decided the risk of blood-stained tennis shoes wasn't worth it. "She was married to some big studio dude with connections."

I eyed the silky blonde hair and strawberry daiquiri colored nails. "Someone sending the big studio dude a message to get back in line?"

Telaney shook her head. "Nah. She left him for some other big dude with the Palisades Militia. Her ex felt that was an intolerable blow to his manhood and put a hit out on her."

Fucking dick. Two dogs fighting over a bone, only the bone had been a woman with a life, fifty-dollar coral lipstick, and a recent manicure.

"I'm assuming the Palisades Militia is going to go after Big Studio Dude now?"

"Yep." Telaney sighed. "If I can actually get the timing right on that one, I'll score big. Wanna team up?"

It was a rare generous offer, one I hated to turn down.

"I'm smack in the middle of something else right now. Plus, there are a few issues with my license that I need to straighten out first." I liked Telaney. I didn't want to be the cause of the tax collectors scrutinizing her doings under a microscope.

"Next time then." She gestured toward the body. "Wanna grab the tights?"

I snorted. "Hell no I don't." They were downright hideous and covered in blood. Plus wrestling Lycra tights off a dead body wasn't something I really wanted to attempt.

"Actually, I came out here to ask you a few questions, not scavenge on a hit."

She took a few steps away, clearly not interested in the hot pink tights either. "You said you had something important you needed to ask me? Is there a job you need my help on? Is it about the accounting day hit Thursday where everything worth salvaging went up in a giant fireball?"

"It's kinda personal. Can we go somewhere more private?" I wasn't about to dredge up memories or out the woman's past right here in the open like this.

She eyed me with curiosity. "Sure. I only live a few blocks away. We can walk."

I left my bike, figuring it would be safe in a yoga studio filled with luxury cars, and followed Telaney. Three blocks later we were walking up to a house with freshly planted petunias blooming cheerfully beside the porch.

Outside of the occasional big job, Telaney liked to work close to home. She'd once told me that there might not be anyone waiting with the lights on for her, but she still tried to be in the door with her bra off and her feet up before nightfall.

Two years ago, Silver Lake was a hipster paradise. There'd been a coffee shop on every block. The walls and pavement had been covered with graffiti art that had nothing to do with gangs or tagging. The plentiful stores sold local crafts and weird shit like wire pyramids that were supposed to preserve food. Nearly every restaurant had served Asian fusion, and the bars proudly featured local indie bands and solo acts. Modern architecture abounded, and the namesake reservoir was ringed by a lovely trail that had been filled with fit joggers and residents walking their dogs as they sipped their double-shot dirty chai lattes.

The majority of the hipsters had defaulted on their mortgages and fled east. The banks that now owned these homes were stuck. No one was going to pay the exorbitant, inflated prices they'd loaned out for these little tiny homes, so they either wrote off the huge loss, or were still carrying the dead weight on their books, hoping no one noticed and their stock didn't plummet.

With three quarters of the homes vacant and in foreclosure, looted and abandoned, others moved in. Silver Lake was now a squatters' rights neighborhood. If you lived there, it was yours—just make sure you locked everything up tight, or you were liable to come home and find someone else squatting in your "acquired" home.

Telaney's home was a square, one-story cottage-style block house whose stucco finish had been painted a light mint-green. White wrought iron posts supported the slightly sagging porch roof, and a huge picture window took up the entire left half of the house. It had to have been all of eight hundred square feet at most, and two years ago it would have sold for just under a million dollars. If the attempts at landscaping didn't clue me in as to how much Telaney cared about her home, the interior did. This wasn't just some convenient rent-free flop house, it was her home.

Telaney had made serious inroads in repairing the damage looters had done. Holes in the walls were patched, and sheets of drywall that must have been damaged beyond repair had been replaced. The oak floors had been recently sanded and polished. A few items of furniture looked new, and others had nice slipcovers hiding any damage. A cut-glass vase full of tulips sat on the dining room table.

"Don't mind the mess." She waved at the dove gray walls that were dotted with spackle and primer. "I need to give it all another good sanding before I paint."

I sat where she indicated and admired her home, wondering how much work she'd needed to put into it to make it livable, and if there were any other decent homes in Silver Lake that were unoccupied. For a moment I had a little daydream of my own place with a comfy sectional sofa, a bedroom big enough for a king-sized bed, a bright sunny kitchen with stainless steel appliances, a fenced in backyard with a little pond. Maybe I'd have a small dog, or a cat, and I'd have Bea and the girls over twice a week for dinner. If I had a date, I could bring them home afterward. We'd drink champagne and get busy, scattering clothing all over the house as we disrobed. We'd fuck on the sectional, on the kitchen counters, against the patio door, then end up in my huge bed, tangled in sheets with legs entwined. In the morning we'd walk around naked and drink coffee, maybe screwing in the shower before I kicked him out so I could get to work.

Why was that date in my mental wanderings Bishop? The idea of him naked in bed with me had me feeling rather breathless.

It was a ridiculous fantasy. He'd thought I was hot, but not *that* hot. And he wasn't my type. And as far as the house went, there would be no sense in me spending a lot of time wrestling a foreclosure away from a bunch of squatters and fixing it up when Bea, the girls, and I were planning on getting out of here and across the border as soon as possible.

Telaney came back in with two mugs of coffee and a striped glass bowl full of chips. She put the bowl on the table, handed me one of the mugs. It said "Not Today, Satan" in bright red letters on the glossy white finish.

Sitting down in a chair across from me, Telaney grabbed one of the chips. "So what's up? Does this have something to do with your license? I heard some bitch set you up and you're in trouble."

"Tangentially." Wow, I finally got to use that word. I took a sip of the coffee, then went on. "I was at that accounting day job when the Fixers came looking for me. They took my fourteen-year-old sister and sold her to the Disciples."

Telaney sucked in a breath. "Oh Eden, I'm so sorry. What can I do to help?"

The offer surprised me—especially because I could tell she meant it. Hopefully what I said next didn't have her rescinding that offer and kicking me out of her home.

"Eight years ago, you were rescued from human traffickers. I need to know everything and anything about that group."

Her hand shook as she put her mug down on the table. That look of shock and betrayal in her eyes felt like claws in my stomach. *I thought we were friends*, the look said.

Before she could deny it all I leaned forward. "It was the Disciples then, and it's the Disciples now. That same woman, Desiree, still runs the operation. They have Nevarra. She's only fourteen. I found your picture from the raid eight years ago completely by chance. No one else knows, and no one else is going to know whether you say anything to me or not, but I'm begging you to help me. I'm begging you to help me save Nevarra."

Telaney sucked in a ragged breath, her eyes haunted and focused on something about six miles past my left shoulder. I watched and waited, hoping after she dealt with the shock of having the bandage ripped off an old wound, she wouldn't throw me out on my ass.

"I try not to think about that time." She picked up the mug, then put it down again. "I try to pretend it was all a bad dream. My mom searched for me. The neighborhood helped put up fliers. They had vigils. After six months, she gave up hope of finding me alive, but still hounded the police to keep searching for my body."

"They had you for six months?" That couldn't have been right. She would have been sold by then, but the police raid found her with the other kids, as if she had been newly kidnapped.

"I was older than most of them—the same age as your sister. Fourteen-year-olds can fetch a good price if they're pretty and they look young and innocent." Telaney's laugh was bitter. "I'm not pretty now, and I wasn't then. I didn't have the right look to appeal to the pedophiles who are eager to throw a ton of cash for someone to satisfy their sick fantasies. So, I became a video girl."

Cold skittered down my spine. Juke had mentioned that some girls were used for pay-per-view videos. Raped on camera, and broadcast for anyone with a credit card to see. I wanted to tell her to stop, to let her return all these memories into a locked box in the back of her mind, but I couldn't.

Nevarra.

"I'm so sorry, Telaney."

She waved my sympathy away. "I kept my mouth shut when the cops came. I was in shock. For years I kept thinking I was dreaming and that I'd wake back up in that hellhole. It wasn't just the trauma though. I was fourteen. My mama was all I had. If I had given the police names and locations, it would have gotten out, and I knew they wouldn't have been able to keep us safe. So instead of naming names, I let my emotions burst through the dam and flood me. All the police knew was that I'd been raped, and that they'd kept me there for six months. I saw a dozen kids come through that room and leave when they'd been sold—a dozen that they never found."

God. There was nothing I could say to that, no words to express my sorrow.

Telaney swiped a hand across her eyes. "I knew there wasn't anything I could do to help those other kids—hell, I was just a kid myself. I buried it all, believing that if the Disciples started up with that side of their business again, they'd just stick with prostitutes and not risk dealing in kids."

She looked up toward the ceiling, took a deep breath, and leaned back in her chair before she lowered her gaze to meet mine. "Desiree is one sick fuck. She meets the clients. She tells everyone what she's got to sell, what's a hot commodity—although any kid under the age of sixteen is worth bringing in according to her. She scripts the videos. She directs the photoshoots as well as the costuming and props all to make sure the 'merchandise' is presented in a manner that will get the clients stoked up and willing to bid high." Telaney's eyes glazed with that distant focus before she snapped her attention back to me. "She's not human."

If I'd had any doubts, she'd just banished them. "Desiree is a demon?"

Telaney shrugged. "Fuck if I know exactly what she is, but she's definitely not human. She moves funny. There's something weird about her eyes. It felt like she was a monster wearing a skin suit or something. It freaked me out. It freaked all the kids out. It freaked out the most badass dudes in the Disciples too."

"But that was eight years ago," I mused.

"I know. No one believed in demons back then. Everyone thinks they came here two years ago, but what if they've been walking around among us for decades? Centuries? Since the fucking cavemen?"

"Shit." I remembered what HB and Bishop had said, combining that with what I'd gleaned over the last two years. Demons were rumored to be invincible, powerful beings who could regenerate in a flash, blast cars across the road, rip the soul right out of your body and take you to hell for eternal torture. How the fuck was I supposed to defeat something like that?

I wasn't. All I needed was to find a way to get Nevarra, to sneak in and grab her then sneak out, all without coming within a mile of this Desiree.

"There's a place they'll be keeping the kids." Telaney stood and began to pace. "It's got to be somewhere they can put in cots, somewhere with a bathroom or a porta john, but limited entrances—somewhere kinda remote or in an area where no one is going to look twice if they hear a voice screaming for help. They'll have guards."

Fuck, that could be anywhere. Abandoned roadside motel. Unused warehouse. Rural foreclosed property.

"But that's not how you're going to find them." She stopped pacing. "Jimmie didn't get caught last time. If they're running this operation again, then they're using Jimmie. Desiree liked him. Called him an artist. He's the one that does the photos and the videos. He works with Thumbs, who's the IT guy."

"Thumbs?"

She made a quick movement with her hands, as if she were texting. "Thumbs. There aren't many guys with his skill who the Disciples can trust to run the auction and video website."

"So Jimmie goes out to wherever they're holding the kids and does the pictures and video." All I'd need to do is find this Jimmie and trail him twenty-fourseven. They'd want pictures of any new kids, and probably additional pictures to add to the website to spur on additional bids as the auction progressed.

"Back when they had me, they did some pictures where they held the kids, but Jimmie was also renting a studio. He wasn't going to haul all that crap out to some warehouse when he could send a van to get the kids and bring them to a place with all the right lighting and setup."

Damn it. This was LA. There had been a million small studios for rent before the demons came, and probably a million and a half now. I couldn't search every studio, and even if I did my chances of catching him at the very hour he was renting the place were slim to none.

Telaney vanished into the kitchen and came back with a pad of paper and a pen. "Here. Jimmie's got a day job." She handed me a piece of paper with a name and address on it. "James Pollina. He should know where the kids are being held. He'd come by every now and then when I was there to snap quick photos of new kids to use in planning the photo shoots."

"Sounds like a real professional." I shoved the paper into one of my pockets, envisioning me putting a bullet right between James Pollina's eyes.

Telaney caught her bottom lip between her teeth. "I was there six months, Eden. I did a lot of videos. Jimmie...he took production seriously. We'd be there all day. I saw stuff like his day-job business cards, his cell phone calls."

I got the feeling Jimmie had been a very hands-on director. It made me want to shoot him even more.

"How do you know he still works at the same place?" It had been eight years, after all.

Telaney turned away. "Because I keep track of him. I stalk him on social media, on LinkedIn. I want to make sure I never accidentally run across him. I can't ever see him again. Not after everything he saw…and did."

Jimmie was a dead man, just as soon as I found Nevarra.

"And this Thumbs guy?"

She shrugged. "Him I don't know about. Desiree and the Disciples trusted him, so I'm sure they're still using him, but I only saw him a few times when he swung by the studio to pick up pictures and videos. I don't know where he lives, where he works, or his real name."

I reached over and grabbed her hand, squeezing it before letting go. "Thank you. I'm sorry that I had to put you through all of this. I owe you big time."

She walked me to the door. "Just find your sister, and find her fast."

"I'll find her," I promised Telaney. "I'll find her, and I'll bring you Jimmie's head in a bag."

I had no idea why I'd said such a grisly thing to her. It just felt right. It just felt…right.

She laughed. "I don't want his head, but if you'd snap a quick picture of his dismembered dick and balls and text it to me, I'd be eternally grateful."

I promised to do just that, then I left, walking back to the yoga studio. It was a Saturday but some people worked on a Saturday. I'd go to West Hollywood, and if Jimmie was working, I'd lure him away from his desk. Then I'd make him tell me where they were keeping Nevarra. And if he wasn't working, I'd break into his office and search it for some sort of clue, because I couldn't just sit around and wait for him to go to work on Monday. Either way I'd figure something out. Wing it and hope I got lucky.

I was definitely feeling lucky when I saw the helmet still sitting on the seat of my bike. It was a sign. This was going to be my lucky day, I could just feel it. I'd find Nevarra, take her home, and maybe the money fairy would have stopped by the house and left ten thousand dollars in small unmarked bills for us.

Ten minutes later, I realized luck was a fickle bitch. I had a helmet, but I'd flooded my bike. Now, it wouldn't start. I stared at it, cursing silently and wondering what the fuck I was going to do. I doubted anyone in the yoga studio had tools or motorcycle repair knowledge and West Hollywood wasn't exactly walking distance from Silver Lake.

But it *was* hitching distance. I didn't have time to fix my bike right now, not when I had a man to see about my sister. It was rush hour. For once I wasn't covered in blood. I'd just catch a ride with someone, beat information out of Jimmie, find Nevarra, then come back for my bike later. It wasn't like anyone was going to steal a 1989 Yamaha Fazer. Worst case scenario my newly stolen helmet would be gone when I returned.

It was pretty much the only option I had, so I left my bike with a pat and a promise to return, and started walking west.

CHAPTER 17

There wasn't as much traffic in Silver Lake as I'd hoped for—at least not the kind of traffic that would give a hitchhiker a lift. I walked for half a mile, eventually catching a ride with a couple of guys heading north on Sunset. I got out when they turned west onto Santa Monica Boulevard and stuck my thumb out once more. It soon became clear that today was not my day to hitch, so I went with plan B and decided to steal a car.

There was a U-Haul to my right with trucks stacked behind an eight-foot chain-link fence topped with barbed wire. Down and across the street was the hospital complex—two hospitals for the price of one, all squashed into a single block. There would be vehicles in the parking lot, but I didn't feel right stealing a car from people at a hospital. I eyed the U-Haul place, but that guard with the shotgun looked like he meant business, and driving a box truck around the city wouldn't be fun.

I kept walking past the Metro station stop. For probably the first time in my life I wished it was still in service. Pharmacy. Pharmacy. Medical center building—although from the looks of it, it had been abandoned.

And there, on the south side of the street, was a familiar sight. I grinned, jaywalking across Sunset and nearly getting mowed down by a Honda to stop in front of the parking lot for the Church of Scientology. If I were to walk down L Ron Hubbard Way, I'd pass by the huge complex ending on Fountain Avenue with the ridiculously ostentatious main building façade.

I wasn't here to worship, so instead of heading for the front door, I made my way to the parking lot.

It was slim pickings. Older cars were a heck of a lot easier to steal than the new ones. I could pop the door on a 1982 Mustang, knock the ignition off, stick a couple of wires together, and be on my way, but this 2019 Dodge Challenger in front of me would have an alarm, keyless start, and probably a tracking system. There were tools to bypass all of that, but I didn't have any with me, and I definitely didn't have the time to mess with complex computer systems. No, I needed an old car, and weaving through the parking lot, I despaired I'd find one.

Two Caddys, a Lexus, three BMWs, the Challenger. Fucking Scientologists and their wealthy members.

Bingo. A Jeep. The nice thing about Jeeps was that they hadn't changed much since World War II. It had a hard top on it, but even if it was locked, I could get in by using just my multitool. Peering through the driver's side window, I looked to make sure there wasn't a steering wheel lock, or something else I couldn't bypass with what I had in my pockets.

I saw a reflection behind me in the window, but not soon enough to spin out of the way. A hand grabbed the back of my head and drove it forward. I twisted, taking the blow on the side of my head and not my nose. My skull was hard, my nose wasn't, and an impact there would have my eyes watering and my mind spinning when I needed to be able to see clearly and think fast.

Even with a hard skull, it hurt. I kicked back high and felt the give of a knee joint hyperextending. The man screamed and shifted backward and enough to the side that I was able to spin around. Grabbing his shoulders, I smashed my head into *his* nose then let go and grabbed for my pistol. A hand gripped my wrist and twisted before I could pull the gun from the holster. Now would have been a good time to have a hip holster on the left side. If I lived through this, I'd need to remember that.

Two men crowded me, pressing my back against the Jeep while the one guy recovered. I kicked out but they were too close to get enough power behind the motion to do anything but maybe bruise a shin. I did manage to knee one guy in the thigh before they spun me around and held me tight against the vehicle. A zip tie clamped my wrists together tight enough that I felt it cutting into my skin. Still, I thrashed around, trying to get enough of an opening to make a break for it. I could run with my hands behind my back. If I could manage to get away, I'd deal with the zip tie later.

"Damn, this bitch is squirmy," one of them commented breathlessly. "Can't I just shoot her?"

"Bounty pays for her alive," another growled as he leaned a shoulder into the back of my knees, held my ankles, and zip tied them. "There's no payout for her dead."

"And if she's dead, she can't tell us where the money is," a third added.

Fixers. I doubled my efforts to get free, only to fall over onto the pavement as they abruptly let me go. I might be able to run with my hands zip tied behind my back, but there wasn't jack shit I could do with my ankles tied together.

They all laughed, as if me squirming around on the asphalt of a parking lot was the funniest thing they'd ever seen. One put a foot on my shoulder, reached down, and pulled my gun from the holster. He kept his foot in place while the others searched me, flipping me over to make sure they'd checked every pocket for weapons. They felt me up more than necessary along the way, because clearly I might have a knife surgically implanted in one of my breasts, or shoved in my ass or vagina. The whole time they made lewd comments about what they might enjoy doing to me.

It wasn't about sex; it was about intimidation, about making me feel powerless. I was fairly immobilized with my ankles and wrists tied, but I was far from powerless. I thought about using my stun gun powers to melt the restraints, but I'd never done that sort of thing on plastic before and I wasn't sure how long it would take. I could see that the pistol one of them was carrying had a white muzzle. If I started generating electricity and melting the plastic zip ties, all he had to do was shoot me and whammo. No more magical stun gun powers.

I needed to go into strategy mode, to think and plan. I didn't want to make this situation any worse than it already was.

Once the Fixers were done groping me, they picked me up as if I were a dead deer and carried me to one of the nearby Cadillacs. Had they been tailing me and just happened to use the church lot to park the car, or were they Scientologists coming out of a service or meeting and me being here trying to steal a Jeep was just a lucky break?

The answer to that question hardly mattered, but I spent some time pondering it as they rolled me into the cavernous trunk of the Cadillac, and closed the lid. I heard the mumble of their conversation, the slam of the car doors. Then I felt the jolting of the car leaving the lot and heading down the road.

No sooner had the car started then I heard a growling

noise. I had no idea what was making that noise, but I could tell whatever it was, it was in the trunk with me. Hopefully it was equally restrained and muzzled, because there wouldn't be much I could do to defend myself if I were attacked right now.

I had quite a bit of time during the drive to contemplate the Fixers' possible religious beliefs as well as wonder where they were taking me. I'd assumed we would have headed downtown where they'd drop me off with the tax collectors, get their bounty, and go, but we were on the road for too long and driving at too great a speed for the relatively short trip downtown.

They'd mentioned keeping me alive not just for the bounty, but so I could tell them where the money was. That meant they were going to take me somewhere quiet and secluded, and apply sufficient inducement with fists and knives for me to tell them where I had hidden either the cases of bullets or wads of cash from the sale of said bullets. That was going to really suck because I didn't have cases of bullets or wads cash—and no amount of slicing body parts off me was going to make either of those two things miraculously appear.

I could try to melt the restraints now, and then surprise them when they opened the trunk to get me out. There had to be something in here I could use to fight them off enough to get away—a tire iron or a jack.

The other occupant of the trunk growled again, very close to my ear.

An angry Chihuahua. I'd seen those dogs in action and they were terrifying little monsters. Shoving a pissed off Chihuahua in one of their faces would be the equivalent of putting their head in a blender and pushing puree.

It growled again.

Of course, I'd probably get the crap bitten out of me first

just trying to grab it. And with my luck the Chihuahua would decide to attack me instead of the Fixers, adding to the number of things I'd need to fight to get away.

In the end I decided that I really didn't want to try to melt my restraints while I was being driven around in a large steel box of a vehicle. I had no control at all over the level of wattage or voltage or whatever I was putting out. For all I knew I'd try to melt my hands free and end up with an electrified car with three dead men and possibly a dead Chihuahua careening down Sunset Boulevard. We'd smash into something and then I'd probably die because while I didn't seem to have any problem grabbing a high voltage wire, being flattened by an oncoming dump truck full of gravel would probably do me in.

Damn it. Why couldn't I have been born with a more useful magical skill, like teleportation?

The car made a few fast turns, and I slid around the enormous trunk a bit, smacking into what felt like wire fencing. The thing inside growled again, and I realized that thankfully the angry Chihuahua was caged.

Why the fuck did three gang members have a Chihuahua in a cage in their trunk? I suddenly wondered. And why were they driving a Cadillac? And attending the Scientology church?

The Caddy started bouncing like a fucking pogo stick and I once more questioned these guys' choice of vehicle. Something with a stiffer suspension would have been better for these roads, although being stuffed in the bed of a truck, rolling around on a grooved liner would have been a whole lot more uncomfortable than the cushy, carpeted, luxuriously large trunk of the Caddy.

Even with the soft suspension, I was sore by the time I felt the car come to a stop. My wrists had swollen up around the zip tie and were raw and bleeding. My shoulders were cramping up from having my arms behind my back. My legs were in good shape though. As soon as the car stopped moving, I tried to pivot around so that I could launch a joined-leg kangaroo-style kick once the trunk was opened. Unfortunately, I'd become completely disoriented bouncing around inside the trunk, and when they opened it, I found I was facing the wrong way.

Fuck. My. Life.

I got a quick look at the growling animal in the wire cage as they pulled me out of the trunk. It wasn't a Chihuahua after all, but some sort of groundhog with claws the size of my fingers and teeth like a row of chipper shredder blades. What the fuck? Were these Fixers also moonlighting as animal control, picking up rabid groundhogs before attending a Scientology service, and snatching me up for a bounty?

"Bring it in," the taller Fixer, the one whose nose I'd bloodied, instructed the other two.

"Like hell." The swarthy one with a goatee took a step backward. "I'm not getting anywhere near that thing."

I realized they were talking about the groundhog. The Fixers must really be stretching it if they were recruiting guys like these—Cadillac-driving Scientologists who were afraid of a groundhog. The thing in the cage growled again, a long line of viscous drool extending from one of its fangs. Okay, I could excuse their groundhog fear. Plus, I'd read about what people had to go through getting rabies shots, and it sounded pretty horrible.

"We can't leave it in the trunk, you idiot. If it dies, we don't get a dime, and it's worth almost as much as the girl."

Really? My worth equaled that of a rabid groundhog? Damn, that hurt.

"Fuck you, Raymond." Goatee reached into the trunk and did the back-and-forth thing with his hand a few times until he worked up the nerve to grab the cage handle and haul it out. The whole time the groundhog stared at him with beady red eyes, foam decorating its upper lip. The growls were now punctuated with high-pitched shrieks that reminded me of YouTube videos I'd seen of wildcats.

Raymond and the other guy dragged me into a one-room cinder block building and propped me up on a chair. The door and windows were missing and looked as if they'd been gone for years. There were stains on the floor that I suspected were old blood rather than motor oil. I'd gotten a good look around as they'd hauled me inside and seen nothing. Dusty tan dirt and gravel road. Unmown wild grasses. A clump of trees off in the distance with a mountain range shadowed in a smoggy, dusty fog farther away.

An old filling station or one-room shop in the middle of nowhere. Great. If I managed to get away and run for it, I'd make a nice clear target with nothing to shield me besides a few miles of grass and dirt.

Goatee put the cage with the rabid groundhog down in the back corner of the building. None of them were carrying my stuff in a bag or in their hands. For a second I thought maybe they'd left my gun, knives, and other gear in the car, but then I saw a familiar pistol butt sticking out of Raymond's waistband.

I liked that gun. It was my absolute favorite, and I wasn't about to leave here without it.

"Where's the cash?" Raymond asked.

Before I could answer, Goatee slapped me across the face. An open-handed blow can hurt almost as much as a fist if done right, and this guy knew what he was doing. Thankfully, he let me recover a bit, so I could attempt to reply.

"A cop set me up. I don't have either the cash or the cases of bullets." With any luck they'd give up and just turn me in for the bounty that was out on my person.

"A cop set me up," the third guy mimicked with a high-pitched voice. "It was someone else. It wasn't me."

He stepped forward, elbowing Goatee out of the way so he could get eye level with me. That meant I got a good whiff of him—cigar smoke and onions. Lovely.

With a quick flick of his wrist, Cigars had a knife in his hand. "Where's the money?"

Damn it. It wasn't just any old knife, it was one of mine. Cigars put the knife right at the edge of my neckline and dragged the tip in a vertical line, drawing blood. Trying to ignore the sharp sting of the wound, I sent a little trickle of electricity into my wrists and ankles.

"I don't have the money." I spat in the guy's face to back him up hoping he wouldn't catch the not-so faint odor of burning plastic.

Cigars didn't budge and backhanded me even harder. I nearly fell off the chair, and lost enough control that the electricity surged.

"What the fuck's that smell?" Cigar asked.

I might have been able to play it off, but my pants chose that moment to catch on fire. I yelped. Cigar and Goatee yelped. Raymond cursed and yanked off his T-shirt, flailing it at my jeans in an attempt to put out the fire.

Both sets of plastic ties snapped, but my mind had detoured from escape to not-burning-alive. I screamed and tried to kick the flames off the hem of my pants. Electricity had no effect on me, but I was pretty sure I wasn't flameproof.

The fire lasted about two seconds—long enough for me to realize I needed to get my head back in the game or I was going to lose my very slight advantage. I dropped down low in the chair and kicked high into Raymond's face just as the three of them realized what had happened.

"She's loose!" Cigar shouted, reaching for his gun —*my* gun.

I'll be damned if I was going to be shot with my own gun, so I jumped to my feet, grabbed Raymond and spun him in front of me to use as a human shield.

That maneuver doesn't work so well when the shield isn't being kept compliant by a weapon. Raymond slammed his head backward into my face, then tried to flip me over his shoulder and to the ground. The guy clearly hadn't taken enough martial arts classes when he was a kid, because all he managed to do was whack my nose and make the pair of us stagger to the side.

Pain bloomed through my nose, nearly knocking me flat. It was all I could do to hang onto Raymond and try to blink the tears out of my eyes. I heard a gunshot and felt the spray of concrete chips against my shoulder. Fuck this shit. If I didn't get control of the situation right now, I was going to be back in that chair, and I was pretty sure this time Goatee and Cigar weren't going to be just slapping me for answers.

That bounty probably just said alive. It didn't say I had to arrive with my bones in one piece and all my blood on the inside of my body.

I sent a small current of electricity through Raymond and accidentally killed him. Clearly my phaser was never set on stun when I was in stressful situations because that was so not supposed to happen. I tried to hold him up and pretend he was just napping, but the guy was over two hundred pounds, so I sagged to my knees under his weight.

"She's got magic!" Goatee shrieked, reaching for the gun with the white muzzle.

I gave up trying to hold Raymond upright and grabbed the pistol out of his waistband just as Goatee fired. He hit me on my left breast. My left arm went numb and I gasped for air as the bullet punched against my chest. As soon as it hit, the bullet broke apart and spread a blue splotch across my shirt.

Paint balls. That's what the manufacturer used to carry the spell that temporarily negated magical ability. It worked against shifters, demons, angels, and it worked against me.

Goatee shot again, this bullet missing me and painting a blue splotch on the cinder block wall behind me. I returned fire, but my aim went wide with the unfamiliar weapon. Raymond was sprawled onto the floor and not much use as a shield, so I dove for Goatee, taking two more paint ball bullets to the chest and accidentally kicking the cage with the rabid groundhog on my way.

Now I had a shield. "Drop the weapon, or I'll kill him." I might not be familiar with Raymond's gun, but I was confident I could put a bullet through Goatee's head with the muzzle pressed against his skull.

"Think I fucking care? Less people to share the bounty with."

I pushed Goatee away a split second before his head exploded out the back. Cigar pivoted, lowered his aim, and squeezed another round off, this one taking out my right knee. I dropped to the ground, unloading my magazine at him and thinking that Cigar was a much better shot than I'd given him credit for.

I'd been shooting wild, a Hail Mary of bullets as I fell. I hit the wall a few times, and something metal. A few sounded as though they went into flesh. Not Cigar evidently because as I crashed on the concrete floor I saw him running toward me.

It was the last thing I saw before the butt of his gun hit my temple.

CHAPTER 18

I woke up achy on a hard concrete surface. I blinked a few times, holding very still, trying to think and plan what I should do before Cigar realized I was awake. There was a pair of legs in front of me and I focused on them as I catalogued my injuries.

My head throbbed and my nose hurt. Everything else felt…okay? How the fuck could my leg feel okay when that asshole had shot me right in the damned knee?

I'd figure that out later. Right now, I was just going to be grateful for small miracles and hope that the leg would hold me when I sprang to my feet and tried to choke the life out of Cigar before he emptied a shit ton of bullets into my stomach.

The legs bent and a face appeared in my line of vision. It wasn't Cigar's face and this man didn't smell like tobacco and onions. He smelled like sandalwood and the mist off the ocean, and he looked like a surfer god.

Bishop. I blinked at him, then looked around at the concrete block one-room building minus door and windows, at the chair, at three bodies sprawled across the ground in a sea of blood, at a rabid groundhog snarling in a wire cage.

"Figures I'd find *you* here, Trouble." He rocked back on his heels and looked around. "What the hell happened?"

I eased into a sitting position, bending my left knee and amazed that was even possible. Then I gingerly felt the side of my head. Dried blood. A minor lump. No cracked skull or brains leaking out, so I guessed I was okay. My wrists had soot from the burned chair and restraints, and the bottom two inches of my pants were charred and burned off in a jagged hem. Maybe I'd set a new fashion trend. Acid washed was so yesterday. Burned hems were totally this year.

How the hell was I okay? I should have a broken nose, black eyes, and a massive concussion. I should have a knee torn to shreds by a bullet. My head and nose weren't nearly as perplexing as my knee. The pants showed a bullet hole and were covered in blood, but my knee didn't have a scratch on it. Nothing. I'd *felt* the shot hit my knee. I'd gone down, unable to support myself. Why was my knee okay?

Had my magic suddenly become more than minor telekinesis and human stun gun? I'd been shot in the fucking knee. Gunshot wound. Broken kneecap, destroyed ligaments. Muscle, bone, and nerve damage. And here I was fit to jog a 5k.

What. The. Fuck.

Fighting for your life tends to pull your mind away from injuries, but I'd been in enough fights that I knew when I was seriously hurt and when I was not. I knew that bullet had ripped through my leg. I knew how bad it was as I'd fallen to the ground.

But… How could I have magic healing when I'd been shot multiple times with the white muzzle anti-magic gun? Was the weird healing thing not-magical or not affected by the hits? Had the anti-magic spell worn off, and I'd magically healed my knee as I lay unconscious on the floor?

Whatever. I'd think about this shit later—after I found Nevarra.

I struggled to my feet, Bishop not even giving me a hand, and looked around. Raymond was no longer smoking, but lay dead by the back wall. Goatee was sprawled across the floor in a giant pool of blood, a big-ass bullet hole coming out the back of his head. He was still leaking brains. How long *had* I been out? It couldn't have been that long if the blood was still fresh. But...I looked down at the paint splotches on my shirt, then shook my head. Later. I'd figure out what the hell I had going on inside my weirdo body later.

I kept looking around the small room. When my gaze landed on Cigar, I gave an involuntary start. He'd been mauled—like seriously mauled. What the fuck had done that? The man Bob had chewed on in the warehouse last night hadn't been this bad. I couldn't believe a little groundhog, no matter how vicious, could do something like this. Besides, he was still in the damned cage.

Had Bishop chewed this guy to bits? Ick. As much as I appreciated Cigar being dead, I hoped Bishop stuck to his head-twisting method of killing in the future.

"What happened?" Bishop repeated, looking at me as if he'd thought *my* brains had been leaking out of my head.

I cleared my throat. "They jumped me in the parking lot of the Scientology church, hog tied me, and brought me here to interrogate." Once more I rubbed the bump on my head. "Shit went south."

Bishop grunted. "I'd say. Why are the Scientologists after you?"

I laughed. The idea of Scientologists gunning for me was so damned funny that I had a hard time stopping. Finally, I got a hold of myself and wiped my eyes.

"Scientology has nothing to do with this. They're Fixers. They grabbed me for the bounty. They were trying to get me to give them the bullets or the cash before they turned me over to the tax collectors."

"Fixers." Bishop's lips twisted up into a sneer. "They're a bunch of idiots. Stupidest guns for hire in the entire city. Not that it's any of my business, but how'd you get on the bad side of tax collection?"

I suddenly realized that I'd never told him about the events that started this whole mess. Smoothing my blood-crusted hair back from my face, I decided there would be no harm in letting him know what was going on. I might not know what Bishop was, and he might scare the shit out of me, but I was absolutely confident he wouldn't turn me over to the tax collectors.

"A couple of days ago someone reported me for a really huge salvage that I didn't take, so the tax guys paid the Fixers to collect. They showed up at Bear State Pawnbrokers and roughed the owner up, then went to my home and beat up my foster mother, shot my youngest sister, and kidnapped Nevarra. When I got home and saw what had happened, I went to you for help."

Bishop scowled. "I fucking hate tax collectors."

Me too.

"Have you found your sister?" he asked.

I shook my head. "I'm still working some leads."

He nudged one of the cleaner of the dead guys with his foot. "You might have to take care of this tax problem sooner rather than later."

I didn't have time to do that first, not when Nevarra might be sold and vanish forever.

"What are you doing here?" I'd never met this guy before Thursday. It was kind of strange to just casually run into him two days after I'd hired him to try to track down Nevarra.

He shrugged. "I get paid to find things. Someone's Durft got stolen, and they asked me to track it down."

Where was Bob? Outside waiting? And what the fuck was a Durft? That rabid groundhog?

"Someone hired you to find their...*Durft*?" I repeated, trying to make sense of things. Maybe that head wound was worse than I'd thought.

"Yeah. It's cheaper than buying a new one and spending months trying to get it to accept the new territory and bond to you. Not that Durfts ever really bond."

"Huh?" It wasn't the most intelligent of comments, but I had no idea what the fuck he was talking about.

He rolled his eyes. "Durfts. People buy them from the demons to use as guard animals. They bond better with humans than they do demons, evidently. They're vicious. Demons fucking hate them."

A guard animal brought over from hell. More useful than a Doberman in this new fucked up world, apparently. I glanced over at the mauled Fixer and wondered how much it would cost to get one. Although I wouldn't trust that rabid groundhog around my family, even with the appropriate bonding time and training.

"I tracked Fluffy down, came in to find him munching down on one of your assailants, and put him back in the cage." He shrugged like it had been no big deal to capture the Durft. Judging from the lack of wounds on his person, it probably *had* been no big deal to him.

A smile hovered at the edge of his mouth. "Normally I would have left all this behind, taken the Durft back to his owners, collected my fee and gone home, but I saw you and was curious."

I looked around, retrieving my pistol and noting that the magazine was empty. Great. I'd need to head back home for more bullets, unless...

Searching the room and the messy dead guys yielded me their two empty pistols, the anti-magic gun with five more specialized bullets, two spare loaded magazines that the Fixers hadn't had time to use, my spare magazine, my switchblade, and a hunting knife with a tan camo sheath. I also scored two hundred dollars. I would have gotten two-fifty, but some of the bills had been chewed by the Durft to the point that I wouldn't even be able to tape them together and try to exchange them somewhere. The other money was wet and bloody, but it wouldn't be the first time I'd washed bills in the bathroom sink and hung them up on the shower curtain line to dry.

The whole time, Bishop remained and watched me. It was weird. I'd expected him to take off once his curiosity was sated, but he stayed—even with his payoff in a cage.

I finished cataloging all my goodies, put them in my backpack which I'd found tossed in a corner, then slung the backpack over my shoulder. Bishop followed me out, carrying a strangely subdued Fluffy in the cage. I paused by his truck and watched him load the animal into the bed, noticing that Bob was nowhere to be found. Maybe Bishop had a super nose as well.

"Where's this lead of yours?" Bishop asked me.

"West Hollywood." I went over to the Caddy and peered through the window. The keys weren't anywhere in sight. I hadn't found them when I'd searched the dead guys, so they had to be here somewhere.

"The Durft ate them."

I turned to see Bishop leaning against his truck, arms folded across his chest. It was a drool-worthy scene, which is why it took a few seconds to realize what he'd said.

"The Durft ate what?" Oh hell, no. "The keys? The Durft ate the car keys?"

"Yeah. And no, you can't slice him open to get them. First,

Fluffy would kill you before you managed to kill him. Secondly, I don't get paid if I deliver him dead."

Damn it. I had no idea where I was. It could take me hours to walk back to town. There'd been no signs of another vehicle besides Bishop's truck since I arrived.

That left only one option.

"Give me a lift?" I smiled at him, expecting that the answer would be no or to go fuck myself or something.

He shrugged. "Sure, but I have to drop this guy off first in Bel Air."

It would still be faster than trying to walk to West Hollywood.

"Thanks." I walked around to the passenger side, climbed into the truck and waited for him to get in and start the vehicle up. "Bob's not with you today?"

Duh. It's not like he'd accidentally left the weredog behind or something.

"Not today. He hates Durfts, and they're not fond of him either. It was easier to do this job solo."

We drove the rest of the way in a silence. I was probably the only one who felt it was awkward. As we skirted downtown on the freeway, I got a good view of the battered skyscrapers. Some were pockmarked by blasts, windows blown out, twisted beams of metal and spikes of rebar protruding from the reinforced concrete sides like quills from a partially plucked porcupine. Others looked like a giant belt sander had been taken to the top of them, grinding fifty story buildings down to a lopsided thirty. The fighting had taken its toll on the whole county, but especially downtown LA where demons, angels, and humans had fought for control. I remembered watching the news days after it had all begun. Dragons had swooped around the buildings, and climbed up the high-rises. Their weight and huge talons had sent chunks of concrete plummeting down to the streets as they clawed their way to the better vantage point.

Some effort had been made at clean-up in the last two years. The major streets were quickly bulldozed clear of rubble, which had been hauled off to be dumped in SoFi stadium. Most of the crap remained where it had fallen, though. I guessed budgets didn't allow for extensive repairs. That or no one cared enough to bother. It's not like the owners of the Wilshire were going to get anywhere bitching to the demons, or to the frazzled guy who was governor in pretty much name only. And as for the stadium that was now full of debris…well, we probably weren't going to be watching the Rams play anytime in the near future anyway.

Five billion dollars, and the spiffy, brand new stadium was nothing but a giant landfill.

We turned off the highway and made our way into Bel Air, Bishop's battered vintage truck an eyesore among the Ferraris and Bentleys. Lots of rich people had said "fuck it" and fled when it was clear the demons were here to stay and their rights as US citizens might not mean squat in New Hell, but evidently there were stubborn folk who were arrogant enough to believe their wealth could inoculate them against the shitstorm outside their manicured lawns. They weren't wrong. LA hunkered like a battered beast all around, but these privileged few had no problem fiddling while Rome burned. The wealthy in these neighborhoods just hired big security forces and magical defensive systems along with their lawn care and nannies.

And, apparently, they bought Durfts imported from hell to protect their lifestyle.

Bishop pulled up to a set of lofty, golden metal gates. Trumpet-playing cherubs ornamented the sturdy stone columns the gates were set into. He grunted a few words into the intercom, and the gates swung wide. As if in protest, the truck backfired, belching a puff of black smoke before we drove through.

The house had to have been worth over twelve million a few years ago and was probably still worth close to that now. It was one of those stacked contemporary houses that sprawled out wider than it was tall, all long angles and smoky-glassed windows. Bishop stopped the car, and I gawked as I climbed out. We were up on a hill at the end of a cul-de-sac. Even from the rosemary-and-lavender scented lawn, I could look down at the city.

Ah, how the one-percent lived, even in New Hell.

I left my backpack and weaponry on the seat, knowing that I shouldn't walk up to this house looking like I was ready for a shootout. It wasn't like anyone would steal it while we were gone. There were far more worthy things to lift here than a few guns that needed cleaning and two knives. Plus, I got the feeling that no one robbed Bishop's truck—or Bishop's anything—and lived.

Bishop slammed his door and grabbed the crate from the truck bed. The Durft blinked drowsy eyes at me, snarled, then fell back asleep. I followed Bishop to the front door, keeping a respectful distance between me and the rabid groundhog, just in case it decided to chomp through the cage and come after me.

A man dressed like he should be opening doors in an episode of Downton Abbey answered a bell that chimed out a tune from *The Sound of Music*. Far from being aghast at our appearance, the man's eyes lit up, a genuinely happy grin stretching his thin lips wide. "Fluffy!"

Bishop grunted and held out the cage, but instead of taking it, Jeeves ushered us in, leading us to the back of the house where he informed us we should partake of refreshments while he told Mr. and Mrs. Carlson the happy news.

The back end of the house was one entire mass of

windows, looking out onto an Olympic-sized infinity pool that seemed to drop off the edge of the world into nothingness. In the distance, I could see the ocean even through the faint haze of low-lying cloud cover. We were at the top of the LA world, both literally and figuratively, gods looking at the peons below from our lofty abode.

A couple glided through a set of paneled oak doors. I swear to fucking God I felt like I'd stepped back into a TV Land rerun of Gilligan's Island and was meeting Mr. and Mrs. Howell. The Carlsons were dressed in the sort of casual chic where leisure attire cost more than a waitress's annual salary. The woman's makeup and jewelry were understated. She wore an elegant, simply styled pants suit with a silky shirt and loafers, all in a neutral tan shade. He was dressed to match, although not wearing a jacket. His shirt was more crisp than silky. I noticed he wore no socks with his loafers, no doubt going for that trendy, hip, dot-com entrepreneur vibe. His silver hair was slicked back as if he'd just gotten out of the pool. Hers was in a shiny bob, the curled tips barely brushing her shoulders.

"Fluffy!" The woman knelt down in front of the cage. The Durft inside growled at her, but the growl *did* seem slightly less menacing than when Fluffy growled at everyone else.

The man passed Bishop an envelope. "I should have known you'd come through. You always do. I appreciate it. If Fluffy had injured a neighbor, I would have been devastated."

Bishop grunted and took the envelope, shoving it into his back pocket. The woman rose, giving me a smile. That smile faded when she took in my blood-stained clothing and rat's nest hair.

I was a fucking mess. Bishop, on the other hand, looked fresh as a daisy.

"Oh no! Did Fluffy give you some trouble? Are you injured?" She stepped closer—not close enough for any of my grime to leap off me and reach her, but close enough to better eye the condition of my clothing.

The man glanced over at me, then returned to chatting with Bishop. I guess he figured me to be Bishop's employee, and any damaged I'd suffered during the course of my employment duties were Bishop's problem, not his.

His wife, on the other hand, seemed comically distraught. "Please don't sit on any of the furniture. And maybe you should stand over there, in case you drip blood on the carpet."

"I'm not bleeding anymore." I wasn't. Everything had healed, including that bump on my head. I honored her request though, moving over to a tiled section of the room away from the rug.

I stood there beside Ms. Carlson, neither of us saying anything. It was awkward, and I silently wished Bishop would hurry the fuck up with the small talk so we could get out of here.

"Are you all going into Downtown after this? Or the Valley?" the woman asked.

"West Hollywood. I live in the Valley though." I had no idea why she was asking any of this. Maybe just polite conversation to fill the time until the menfolk were done?

"Would you mind running a quick errand for me?"

"Uh, sure?" I got the idea that this woman wouldn't accept no as an answer.

"Good. It'll save me a trip. I hate leaving Bel Air. We use the private helipad when we fly to our place in Aspen, or to connect with our plane in Vegas. It's just so nasty out there anymore."

I glanced over toward Bishop with some desperation, wishing once more that I could just teleport out of here.

She wrinkled her nose at my shirt, then gestured for me

to follow her. "Come on. Just don't touch anything on the way up."

I glanced once more at Bishop as I followed her from the room. The male half of the Carlson couple was walking him to the glass doors that led to the amazing pool area and talking about stocks or some shit. An employee picked up the cage with Fluffy in it and discreetly removed it from the room.

Mrs. Carlson led me to an elevator. We ascended, then walked into a room with a stunning view of the city. I was told to stand as far away from a white damask couch as possible while the woman disappeared into a closet the size of a gymnasium.

Was this a dressing room? I absolutely couldn't figure out the purpose of this space. Did people lounge around here while Mrs. Carlson hauled outfits in and out of her giant closet? Did they watch as she changed, commenting on her choice of attire for the day? Could someone with a good pair of binoculars in one of those houses about a quarter of a mile away see us? I fidgeted, feeling naked without my gun. Not that I'd be able to counter a sniper shot from one of those houses with my little Glock.

Ms. Carlson returned, her hands laden with silver bags that had Nordstrom emblazoned across the sides. She stopped and held them out to me, remaining as far away as the length of her arms would allow. I took them, because I wasn't sure what else to do.

"You want me to return these?" Was that the errand she'd spoken of? I had no idea where there even was a Nordstrom in the city, *or* in the Valley. My mind whirled, trying to think of some way to politely get out of a task I had no time for or desire to do.

"They're donations. I was going to send one of the staff

out to drop them off, but since you're here, I thought you could do it."

Right. Because there really was no difference between me, a woman she'd never met before, and her paid staff.

She shooed me out of the room and back toward the elevator. "You can drop them off at the women's shelter, or something. I'm sure you know where that is."

No, I didn't. Whatever. These Carlson people were Bishop's problem, not mine. He could be in charge of dropping this shit off.

The elevator door opened, and I practically bolted to Bishop's side, ready to get the fuck out of this place.

Bishop's eyebrows screwed upward as his incredulous glance took in the silver bags in my hand.

"I'm not sure I want to know what's in those bags," he said once we were back in the truck.

"Donations for you to take to the women's shelter," I informed him as I slid into my shoulder harness.

He snorted. "Those donations are going by the side of the road. I don't have any idea where the women's shelter is, and I'm not driving all over town looking for it."

I shrugged and opened up one of the bags, pulling out an armful of neatly folded clothing. There was a cute pair of olive green capris, skinny jeans, tan shorts, and coral leggings.

"I think these would fit Nevarra," I said, holding up the capris. "These leggings too."

I was so keeping this shit. Going through the other bags, I found shirts, dresses, and shoes. One bag had brand new cosmetics in it as well as two pairs of designer sunglasses.

"So what happened with the Durft?" I asked as I opened one of the boxes and pulled out a tube of mascara. "Had the Fixers stolen him from the Carlsons? Were they holding him for ransom? Going to sell him?"

"No. Fluffy gets out occasionally." Bishop shook his head. "The staff 'accidentally' leaves the gates open, and the containment security off, and the Durft is smart enough to bide his time and make a break for it at the appropriate moment. The Carlsons call me, the Fixers, and a few other groups. Whoever brings Fluffy in gets the reward."

So the Fixers had nabbed the Durft *and* managed to snag me too—all in the same day. It would have been quite the payoff if Fluffy and I hadn't unwittingly joined forces to kill them all.

"You tracked Fluffy to the Fixer hangout," I said, as if I was Sherlock Holmes figuring out a perplexing case. "What if the Fixers had been alive when you got there?"

Dumb question. I slid Bishop a sideways glance and saw him grin.

"I would have taken the Durft. I've got a reputation to protect. A bunch of greasy mercs bringing in what I've been sent to retrieve isn't ever going to happen."

That's what I'd thought. "Why didn't Fluffy kill me?" I wondered.

"Because you were unconscious. Durfts have a highly developed sense of territory. Wherever they are, that's their territory. If you're moving and they can see you, they'll try to kill you."

"Even birds?" How the hell did the thing find time to eat if it was attempting to shred insects, blowing leaves, a stray blue jay…

"They're not dumb. They attack what they see as competition. Birds aren't competition. Although if they're on the ground and within claw reach, they're food."

I looked out the window as we passed the expensive lawns and hedges, thinking once about how the uber rich buffered themselves from the war zone just outside their gilded gates.

"Tell me about this lead in West Hollywood," Bishop broke into my thoughts.

"It's the workplace of a guy who takes the pictures and videos for the human trafficking website. At least he did eight years ago, and my source feels certain he's still doing it. If he doesn't know where the kids are being held, then he'll definitely be a maximum of one step away from the people who do."

"It's Saturday," he reminded me.

"I know. If he's not working, I'm going to break in and search his office."

"And if you don't find anything?"

"I don't know," I confessed. I could try to track the man down. Maybe Alfie could help me find his address or something, then I could beat the shit out of him until he told me where my sister was.

It had been eight years though. What if he wasn't working with them any longer? What if he really didn't know where Desiree was or where she kept the kids? If this Jimmie was a dead end, I'd be back to either waiting for Piers to possibly set up an interview with Desiree, or killing my way through the gang members until I found one of them who knew something useful.

"I feel like I'm spinning in circles." I blew out a breath in frustration. "The threads I'm following just seem to lead to more threads. It's been forty-eight hours since Nevarra was taken. I don't have time to untangle everything, I just need to find her."

"Do you have any other leads beyond this photographer and a demon?" Bishop asked.

I thought of the detective, and how it would take the police months if not years to catch these guys—if they ever did. I thought of Fender, who I couldn't seem to easily track down. I thought of Piers who might or might not manage to get me a direct connection to Desiree or one of her minions.

"No. At least, none that are likely to pan out in the next day or two." I slumped back on the seat. "I didn't want the Disciples clued in that I'm looking for Nevarra and am ready to shoot and stab my way through their ranks until I find her, but I'm running out of time."

"Do you think the nuclear approach might be a better option?" he asked.

I shrugged. Most of the Disciples I'd spoken to so far didn't personally know Desiree and weren't involved in that end of their business. The nuclear approach would most likely end up with a dozen gang members dead, me dead, and Nevarra still in their clutches. "No, it wouldn't be a better option, but it would be pretty satisfying."

"And short-lived. They'd band together once they realized what you were doing and kill you before you found your sister."

I know. We fell silent again, me brooding about the odds that Jimmie Pollina was still doing work for the Disciples. If this lead went nowhere, I'd be back to sitting around and waiting for Piers or Juke to come through.

That or reconsidering the nuclear option.

CHAPTER 19

As Bishop drove down the streets of West Hollywood I realized my attire was going to be a problem. This part of Los Angeles hadn't fared as badly as downtown, and most of the high-rises had come through the battles with only a few scars. People still worked here. People still shopped here. They may have accessorized their business casual with hip holsters, but they seemed to be walking the streets without any undue fear of being attacked. Maybe that was because some gang was pulling in enough protection money from the building owners and businesses that they didn't bother roughing anyone up.

My pistol and knives would fit right in. My blood-stained shirt, and my cargo pants with the ripped-up knee and burned hem wouldn't. Walking down the street I'd attract attention, and I doubted I'd be able to waltz through any building security dressed like this even on the weekend.

Looking through the bags once more I realized that Ms. Carlson did not have my ass. These pants and shorts would be perfect for my fourteen-year-old sister, but not for me. In desperation, I pulled out a navy blue knit dress.

There was no backseat in the truck, and I didn't really care if Bishop saw me or not, but the guy at least deserved a warning.

"Don't look," I told him as I yanked my tank top over my head. That would probably guarantee he'd look, which if I was being honest, kinda was my intent.

Shirt off, I pulled the dress over and down my waist, then wiggled it enough over my ass that I could shimmy out of my cargo pants without flashing my underwear to Bishop and every trucker on the freeway.

The dress was tight—really tight. With a muffled curse, I dug around in the bag and found a white cardigan that thankfully had pockets. I put it on trying in vain to get it buttoned over my boobs before giving up. Unbuttoned it was.

The dress was practically painted on me. The cardigan was too small. I would bake walking around with this getup on in Southern California in the middle of summer. Clearly I sucked at the whole disguise thing. I should have just left on the blood-stained and torn clothes, and shot anyone who got in my way.

Bishop snickered.

"Oh, shut the fuck up," I snapped, rooting through the bags in an attempt to find anything else that might fit me and not have me drenched in sweat in under five minutes.

Nothing. My choice was either to go with the might-as-well-be-naked dress, or my blood-stained clothing. We were off the highway and driving through West Hollywood, which didn't leave me any time to change back.

Figuring I'd make the best of a bad situation, I pulled out one of the pairs of designer sunglasses. They had rosy-brown acetate frames and oversized square lenses with Salvatore Ferragamo written in script on the side. I preferred my dime store ones from home, but I wasn't going to turn up my nose at a three-hundred-dollar pair of shades.

I put them on, looked in the mirror and saw a snobby rich girl who'd been out shopping for the day. The only thing that put a dent in the illusion was my shoulder holster with the Glock.

Bishop pulled over to the curb and looked at me. "You want my advice?"

Not really, but I wasn't in a position where I felt I could refuse advise from anyone.

"Sure."

"Stay with the dress. It's better than walking into an office building looking like you're coming from a murder scene," he told me. "And leave your weapons in the truck. These office buildings have scanners at the entrances as part of their security. One pistol means you're being safe. Five means you're looking for trouble."

I didn't want someone to confiscate all my stuff. A metal detector alerting security that I was carrying several guns wouldn't be good. But I didn't want to leave all this with Bishop and have to arrange to get it back at a later date.

"I'll wait here for you," he told me. "Something tells me you'll be running out of there like you're on fire with a dozen armed guards chasing after you. If so, you'll need a getaway vehicle."

I hadn't expected him to offer. Why was he doing this for me? I frowned, wondering if Bishop had been on the clock since he'd seen me lying on the floor with three dead Fixers and a pissed-off Durft. If so, I was absolutely going to protest the double-dipping. No way was I going to pay his hourly rate while he took Fluffy back to the Carlsons.

Although I wouldn't have much of an argument about him charging me for being the getaway vehicle.

I thought for a second, then decided to take him up on his

offer. I might be paying the debt for the rest of my life, but having Bishop at my back made me feel safe.

"Okay." I unloaded the weapons and stashed them under the passenger seat as he watched. The only thing I kept was a multitool stashed in the pocket of my cardigan and a set of lockpicks that I slid into my holster.

"There. How do I look?" I lifted the sunglasses and tried for one of those duck-lip pouts, complete with batting eyelashes.

"Put the Glock in one of the bags and take it with you. That holster looks a bit too professional. You'll raise suspicion, or at least a few wary glances."

I hesitated. "I'm used to having my gun here. If I need to act fast, muscle memory is going to have me reaching for the shoulder holster. The fraction of a second it takes me to dig it out of a shopping bag might get me killed."

He grunted. "Okay. Then you need to keep attention on something else instead of the gun."

He dug around in one of the bags, pulled something out, then leaned forward. Taking my chin between his thumb and forefinger, he popped the lid off a tube of lipstick with his other hand, and carefully applied it to my lips.

I couldn't breathe. He was inches from me, his fingers soft and firm as he held me still. I can't begin to describe how incredibly erotic it was to have a man, to have Bishop, sweeping color on my lips, his blue eyes focused on my mouth.

He leaned back and surveyed his work, putting the cap back on the lipstick and tossing it back into the bag. "Go get 'em, Trouble. Knock 'em dead."

I intended to.

Hopping out of the car, I glanced back to see Bishop watching me. Something about him drew me like a moth to a flame—and I wasn't sure why. He wasn't my type. I got the feeling he was just as dangerous as those demons flying around downtown. I suspected he might be a weredog or a weresomething. He never seemed to get his hands dirty. I got the feeling that if we worked together I'd probably end up doing all of the work—or me and Bob. But still, having him with me made me feel oddly…safe.

I shook off the weird feeling and adjusted my sunglasses. As I headed down the street, I made sure to put some swing in my hips. It was three o'clock on a Saturday. I was hoping that Jimmie was the sort of guy who didn't work weekends. I was hoping nobody in his office were the sort to work weekends.

Plan A was to sneak in, find Jimmie's office, search it for clues, then sneak out before the militia or the police arrived. Plan B was to convince whoever was working there that I was a visitor or client.

Hopefully there would be something informative or at least incriminating in Jimmie's office. I might even try to steal his computer if it was a laptop. What I really hoped to find was some sort of planner where he might have written down the address where they were holding the girls. If I wasn't that lucky, I hoped to find his home address or a schedule that would have photo shoot written across it in big red letters. In reality, I'd take anything—the location of the studio he rented, names and contact information for the people he was working with. Anything.

I stopped in front of a ten-story building that seemed to be made entirely out of glass to check the address Telaney had given me. Just inside the revolving glass doors was a fenced-off area that herded me through a set of metal detectors. I set my multitool and cardigan on the conveyor belt, unstrapped my harness and put it along with my pistol and hidden lock picks in one of the gray bins, then walked through the detector, glad that I'd taken Bishop's advice and left most of my weaponry in the truck.

One of the guards motioned me over to the side and wanded me. As in, with an actual wand that looked like a prop from a Harry Potter set. A purple stone gave a faint glow, and the guard frowned at it.

"What does that mean?" I didn't have any orbs or amulets with me. The white-muzzled gun and spelled paintballs were in Bishop's truck.

"Means this is a piece of shit, and we need to hire a better mage," the guard grumbled. She whacked the wand on her palm a few times, then ran it over me again. The purple stone flickered, lit up, then flickered again.

The guard cursed under her breath, then motioned for me to go on and collect my items as she smacked the wand on the side of her leg. I scooped up my stuff, pausing over near a bench in the lobby so I could put my cardigan and shoulder harness back on. Another set of fencing led me to a bored man sitting in front of a computer. He shoved a good old-fashioned sign-in book at me, so I wrote down an absolutely unimaginative fake name and handed it back. Without asking for ID or even looking at me, he printed off a name badge and waved me toward a bank of elevators.

I contemplated putting the sticker on that announced I was Mary Jones, but decide to shove it in my bag instead and try to pretend I was an employee, working somewhere in this huge building. If pressed I'd pull it out and claim with an airy wave that I wasn't about to put something adhesive on nice clothing.

The hallway with the elevator bank was busier than I'd expected, with some people leaving, as well as a few others coming in. I stood with the crowd, hands held awkwardly at my sides as I stared up at the numbered lights above the elevator doors just like everyone else.

With a ding, the elevator to the right opened and disgorged its occupants. I crowded in with two women bitching about their boss in Spanish, a man holding two coffees, another man with bright yellow pants. We all faced front and listened to an instrumental version of Smells Like Teen Spirit as the elevator climbed upward.

I got out on three, thankful that no one else left on that floor. After a few moments to check for security cameras, I walked toward the big glass double doors with the words Lenasco Communications etched on them. They were locked, the rooms behind the glass dim. On the wall beside the doors, a red light blinked steadily on a keypad. I eyed the card reader on the door, then looked back at the keypad. I'd need to take both out, but I wasn't sure what to do to buy myself as much time as possible before whatever security Lenasco employed came running.

Sometimes it was better to use a hammer than a pick—in this case a lock pick. Going over to the keypad, I sent a surge of electricity through it that blackened a two foot circle on the wall and melted the plastic. Then I did the same to the card reader. The door opened with a solid kick, and I dashed past the receptionist desk, heading left down the hallway.

No alarms were screaming, but that didn't mean something somewhere wasn't going off and alerting a security company or militia that at the very least there had been an electrical malfunction. Time was not on my side. Thankfully the office doors all had nice little nameplates beside them. Halfway down the hall I saw the nametag I'd been looking for. I tried the handle, found the office unlocked, and went on in.

On the wall there were certificates with his name on them as well as the sort of awards companies print out in house and hand out like participation trophies. Jimmie obviously took them seriously because he'd framed them and hung them in neat rows behind his desk. Clearly it was more important for visitors to see how awesome he was than for him to view them as a continuous reminder of his excellence.

Along the side walls were pictures of minor celebrities and a few stills from commercials. An Asian man in a suit posed next to a restored Indian motorcycle. A woman with blonde curls lounged on a lavender papasan chair with her legs curled under her. Three men in chefs' attire stood in front of a table loaded with ornately iced cakes. A group of suspiciously diverse men and women stood next to each other in white coats, a generic laboratory that was probably overlaid onto a green screen behind them.

The rows of frames on the walls were the only thing in the office that was neat. Along one wall were four plastic mail bins full of what looked to be camera parts. Spiral bound booklets were stacked on the desk beside a cup of coffee with mold growing in it. The trash can overflowed with takeout containers and balled up papers. Two tripods leaned against a corner, one with a video camera that looked like it was brand spanking new. I set my bags down and hurried behind the desk. This place was such a mess. It would take me longer than I'd bargained for, which would be a problem if a bunch of armed guys came to check why the security system had melted off the wall.

The spiral bound booklets were screenplays and project details for photoshoots. I quickly leafed through them all, even though I couldn't imagine Jimmie would have a project book for a human sex trafficking photo shoot laying right on top of his desk. Beside the computer was a good, old fashioned paper planner. I looked through it, going back to Thursday, when Nevarra had been taken. They'd want pictures of her, and they'd want them fast so they could get them up on the sale site. There was nothing for Thursday besides an early morning photoshoot in-house and a noon lunch with someone named Lucy. I turned the page.

Bingo. Yesterday, at seven at night, Jimmie had been on a photoshoot. I ripped a sheet of paper from one of the screenplays and wrote the time as well as the address of the studio on it.

Then I tore through the desk, noting that Jimmie had stashed close to twenty granola bars and some packets of Gatorade powder in one of the drawers. Pens. Pencils. Empty notepads. The deep drawer on the left was filled with file folders. Most of them were empty. One held a bunch of paperclipped receipts. Another contained takeout menus. I shoved them to the front to get a better look at the back few folders.

There was something underneath them.

A slim manila folder had three sheets filled with digital proofs. My stomach turned as I looked at the fresh, innocent faces of children, all as carefully posed as the adults in the pictures on Jimmie's office walls. The last sheet showed a blonde boy of around six and three girls—two white and one Asian. They were the exact same photos that had been on the website print out that Detective Juke had shown me.

I was sure that photo shoot on his schedule for last night had been for the "coming soon" kids that included Nevarra. Had he not had time to print a proof sheet for them yet? Or maybe the proof sheet was with Desiree for approval before the files were sent to Thumbs for upload? Either way, this was proof that Jimmie was currently involved in the operation.

Now I just needed to figure out what the fuck I was going to do with this information. Grab Jimmie and beat the living fuck out of him until he told me where the kids were being held or gave me the name and phone number for someone who did? Go to Detective Juke with this and trust the police to bring him in and get the information out of him in an interrogation room?

Or option three?

Sliding the sheet out I stuck it in an empty folder, then replaced the rest where I found them. Then I ran, taking a few seconds to ease the glass doors closed. Hopefully whoever responded to the melted security system would blame an electrical surge and not think someone had gone into the office.

I smacked the button on the elevator and watched the numbers slowly ascend. What if someone was on their way up from the lobby and the elevator door opened to reveal me standing here, a folder in hand and a vandalized office security system behind me?

That would not be good. I ditched the elevator and headed into the stairwell.

Thank God for sneakers and the fact that Lenasco Communications was only on the third floor. I bolted down the steps, only slowing to a walk as I came out into the main lobby. Sweat trickled down between my boobs. I tried to blend, to look as if I was just a weekend warrior finally leaving the office, and the whole time I was hyper aware of the guards, the bored receptionist, the other employees coming and going.

No one stopped me. Once I was clear of the building, that's when I ran.

CHAPTER 20

"How did it go?" Bishop asked as I climbed into his truck. "I'd half expected you to dive in yelling 'go, go' over the sound of machine guns and grenades."

Haha. What a comedian.

I gathered up my weaponry from the floor on the passenger side, never so glad to see anything in my life. There had been this nagging fear in my chest that I'd come back to find Bishop and the truck gone, my clothes, gun, and knives gone with it.

"I managed to get away without an exchange of gunfire. I also got confirmation that Jimmie is definitely still involved in this operation." I pulled the sheet of photos out of the folder. "These are the same pictures that were on the trafficking website. He had a bunch of proofs at the bottom of a desk drawer."

Bishop took the sheet from my hand, his face shuttered as he glanced at it and handed it back. "You're going to the police with this?"

"Maybe. Eventually. I'm not sure." I'd had a lifetime of distrust as far as the police were concerned, and from my discussion with Detective Juke yesterday, I doubted any investigation would move fast enough to save Nevarra.

He started the truck. "Where to? You said your bike was at a friend's house, so should we swing by and pick it up?"

"It's in Silver Lake." I hated to impose on him, but it would be a huge help if we picked up my bike rather than me having to figure out how to get it home from the parking lot of a yoga studio.

Bishop pulled into traffic, and once again, we sat in silence as he navigated the streets toward the freeway. I bit my lip, wondering how I could possibly ask this man for more help after all he'd done for me so far.

Screw it. Embarrassing as it was to ask for help, I'd suffer through it to get Nevarra back safe and sound. Besides, he'd probably just tack it onto what I already owed him.

"As of last night Nevarra's picture wasn't on the trafficking website," I said. "Since Jimmie took the other pictures, there's a good chance he was hired to take hers as well."

Bishop glanced over at me. "Do you know what studio he uses?"

Here goes nothing. "He had a note on his schedule that he was at a studio last night. He might have taken the pictures then." I took a deep breath and plunged onward. "If Bob could come to the studio and pick up Nevarra's scent, we might be able to follow it. Assuming whatever spell they were using to hide her isn't active any longer."

"Those spells are of limited duration. Hiding something or someone long term requires some involved and very specific magic. Most of the time it's easier to just shield the building so no one can detect what's inside than to continue hiding the individual or the object, especially if you're moving it to different locations."

Was that a yes, or a no? I kept my mouth shut, and hoped if I were quiet, Bishop would offer to help.

"There's a good chance they used an amulet to transport her, then took it off at her destination," he mused. "Or they could have just warded the vehicle she was transferred in."

"You think they'd continue to use the amulet or the warding spells when they moved the kids from wherever they were keeping them to the studio and back?" I asked.

He shrugged. "It depends. That much magic would seriously cut into their profits. They might decide it wasn't worth the bother once they had the kids at whatever place they were using. They'd have trusted employees watching the kids, doing the driving, and taking pictures, so there wouldn't be a need to keep warding them. Unless they'd stolen a high-profile celebrity kid and were worried that the parents had spent big money to track them down."

From what I'd heard, these kids were mostly poor, or runaways. Why bother snatching a rich kid when there were so many families in Los Angeles who couldn't afford to scour over four thousand square miles of the county looking for their child?

"So there's a possibility she could be tracked from the studio to wherever they're keeping the kids?"

"Yes, there's a possibility."

I sat for a moment, until it became clear that Bishop wasn't going to make this easy for me. "Can you and Bob try to track her from the studio?"

"Same hourly rates apply," he informed me.

Fuck. Well, at least I didn't have to worry about paying the doctor. That would leave more in my budget for repaying Bishop. "Okay. As long as you'll take payment on time. Or trade."

He smirked. "Still trying to fuck your way out of paying me, Trouble?"

I laughed. "Can't blame a woman for trying. Hell, I'd take a discount in trade at this point."

"Like I said before." He glanced in the rearview mirror, then took the left to merge onto the freeway. Yeah, yeah. If he asked me into his bed, it wouldn't be because I was paying off a debt. I got it.

"So…do we have a deal?"

He nodded. "We do. Let me see if I can get ahold of Bob. Do you have the address where we're going?"

I handed him my notes, feeling rather smug that I'd been right about Bob. Clearly he was a weredog or something, otherwise Bishop wouldn't be dialing him on his cell phone.

I listened in on the conversation, waiting to hear if Bishop was talking to someone at his house who would bring Bob out to meet us—someone like a kennel manager, or a wife, or boyfriend.

"Hey. I've got a job. I'm texting you the address in a few. Meet me there right away." Bishop hung up and stuck the phone in the truck's cup holder, still leaving me to wonder if he'd spoken to Bob in the man's human form or someone else.

The freeway was a mess, and Bishop made illegal use of the shoulders and both entrance and exit ramps to get around the mass of cars, flipping people off if they honked. After two miles we passed by what looked like a giant bonfire in the two left lanes with two lizard looking creatures cooking hotdogs on sticks from the shoulder. The guy ahead of us yelled at them and one of the lizards dropped his hotdog and raced through traffic to dive onto the hood of the man's car. Bishop navigated around as the man swerved, trying to get the lizard person off. When I glanced back, the creature was hanging onto a bent windshield wiper going back and forth on high, washer fluid spraying all over him as well as the glass.

Within half an hour we were in Silver Lake, pulling up in front of the yoga studio where my bike and helmet still sat in the parking lot next to a shiny white Bentley. I hopped out, lowered the tailgate, then wheeled my bike over.

After watching me struggle with the thing for a few minutes, Bishop sighed. "Get in the truck bed," he instructed.

I had no idea what he was going to do, but I wasn't about to argue. Grabbing the top of the bed, I stepped on the bumper and hopped to swing myself up. Bishop grunted, picked my bike up, and slid it up to me as if it weighed no more than a ten speed Huffy. The dude had a weredog friend that he could telepathically communicate with, he could twist a man's head around like the cap on a bottle of ketchup, and he picked up a four-hundred-and-fifty-pound bike as if it were nothing. Bishop was one scary guy. And I was glad he was on my side right now.

I carefully laid the bike on its side and secured it with some rope, then vaulted out of the bed. We got in. Bishop texted the address to Bob, and off we drove.

It was another half an hour before we pulled up in front of the studio.

Both the city and the Valley were filled with little studios for rent—some geared toward audio recording, and others for video. Yes, there were huge Hollywood studios with massive sets and millions of dollars in equipment, but many of the film, music, and audio productions were produced in little rent-by-the-hour studios such as the one we were parked in front of.

Camera, Lights, Action was in a strip mall with a gyro joint on one side and a liquor store on the other. Judging from the faded lettering on the concrete, the studio was occupying what used to be a bail bond place. Bail bonds businesses generally didn't go under, so I was assuming the former occupants had experienced enough success that they'd been able to move out of the strip mall and to a higher rent spot, probably closer to a detention center or courthouse.

Bob sat outside the liquor store, a brown paper bag by his side. I peeked into it as we walked up and saw the top of a pint.

"Seriously?" Bishop picked up the bag and pulled out a bottle of Bacardi Gold. Bob did the dog equivalent of a shrug. Grumbling something under his breath, Bishop walked back to his truck and put the bag with the pint inside.

"Do you drink it straight, or mix it with soda?" I asked Bob. "Are you whipping up a batch of dark-and-stormys later tonight?"

Bob bared his teeth at me, then turned to watch as Bishop came back from his truck. We walked into the studio, which looked to be little more than a ten-by-ten room with a green sheet stapled to the wall and a few lights on tripods. A woman loudly chewing gum sat on a metal chair behind a card table. She eyed us, pushed her glasses up her nose with her middle finger, then looked down at the spiral notebook on the card table.

"Name?"

Bob began sniffing around the room and Bishop wandered toward the back, leaving me to deal with the woman who may or may not have been passive aggressively giving me the finger.

"Jimmie Pollina? I mean, *I'm* not Jimmie Pollina, but he was here last night. He had the studio from six until nine."

The woman ignored me, scowling at Bob as he sniffed around the fabric green screen. "Your dog better not take a piss in here."

"He won't," I assured her. "I'm wondering if you could give me any details on who Jimmie Pollina was working with last night? Names, or companies, or if anyone else was here when he was?"

She watched Bob for a few more seconds, then gave the weredog the middle finger as she pushed her glasses up once more. "I can't give you any information about other clients. Did you all have a reservation? If not, there's an extra fifty dollar fee for on-the-spot rental of the studio. And a two hundred dollar fee if the dog pees or takes a shit anywhere."

I might not get any information out of this woman, but I needed to stall her long enough for Bob to do his sniff test. It would suck if we got kicked out before he managed to get enough of Nevarra's scent to track her.

"How much is an hour rental?" I asked the woman, knowing full well that it would be more than I'd be willing to pay.

"One hundred an hour. Six hundred for the full day."

Yeah. No.

"Do we get the studio completely to ourselves, or is there always an employee present while we're here?"

She shot Bob another suspicious glance and adjusted her glasses once more, letting the middle finger linger. "Someone always has to be here. It's a liability thing. Otherwise you can say it wasn't your dog that peed on the green screen, or that the crack in the drywall happened after you left and was probably just from the building settling."

Okay, so Jimmie would have had an audience. Clearly he wouldn't have been doing kiddie porn at this studio, but maybe if the employees were slipped some cash, they wouldn't say anything about reluctant children being photographed.

"Is there someone else who hangs out when the studio is in use, or just you?"

"Are you joking? You think the owner would actually come here and watch amateurs film used car commercials and Taco Tuesday ads? It's me. It's always me." This time she turned the glare my way. At least I didn't earn the middle finger.

"What if someone wants to make questionable videos? Or take pictures of kids that are upset, or scared, or drugged?"

Now I got the middle finger. "I'm not renting to any weirdos. You wanna film your mangy dog attacking drugged kids, or take porno pics, then you gotta do it elsewhere."

Bishop came up to me before I could even attempt to reply to that.

"She hasn't been here. There's no suspiciously blank spots in the scent that would hint at magic either."

Damn it, she *had* to have been here. How else would Jimmie have gotten pictures of her for the website? I couldn't imagine Desiree would wait more than a day to get a photo up for a new kid. None of the other pictures looked like they were candid shots. They were all professionally done with good lighting and props, with makeup and costuming, with Photoshopped backgrounds. Nevarra wasn't on the proof sheet I'd stolen from Jimmie's office—the one with pictures I'd seen already up on the website. He had to have taken Nevarra's picture last night—or maybe he was taking it tonight? But if that were the case, why wasn't there anything on his schedule?

There had to be another studio he was using—one that he wasn't writing in his planner. But just in case...

"I need to know what Jimmie Pollina was scheduled to do last night." I sent Bishop what I hoped was a significant glance, then looked back at the employee.

"Well, tough luck, tootsie, because I ain't telling you that." I got the middle finger again, followed by arms folded across her chest.

"Do it," I told Bishop.

His eyebrows went up. "Do what?"

I waved a hand at the woman. "That hypnotizing thing you do."

The woman jumped up so fast she knocked the metal folding chair to the ground. "What? You *what*?"

Bishop's eyebrows remained elevated and he slowly shook his head. "I don't know what you're talking about."

Oh for fuck's sake. "The compulsion thingie you do to get people to tell you things. Just like you did with the guy in the warehouse right before you twisted his head around backward."

The woman shrieked, pushed past me, and ran out the door.

"Well now it's too late," I complained. It wasn't too late to look at the scheduling notebook she'd left behind, though. I'd need to hurry because she was probably dialing 911 as she ran to hide in the gyro place. Not that we needed to hurry *that* much, since the police would probably take two hours to respond at the quickest.

Last night. Six o'clock. Jimmie Pollina—photos for a juice cleanse ad campaign. That was it.

I shut the notebook in disgust. "Did Bob smell any kids at all? *Any*?" Maybe juice cleanse was the covert name for the human trafficking operation's business.

"None. Bunch of men and women. Gyros. Sawdust. Oranges and pineapples. The woman who just ran out chews cinnamon gum. One of the people was wearing some sort of spicy aftershave that made him think of his grandfather."

The weredog's grandfather wore aftershave. Huh. I wondered what he looked like? Actually, I wondered what Bob looked like when he wasn't a dog. Would I ever get to see him as a human? And would I recognize him if I did? Probably not.

All that was keeping me from thinking about the fact that I was back at an absolute dead end. It had been a long shot thinking Bob could pick up Nevarra's scent from here and track it back, but I'd pinned my hope on that long shot and now I had nothing.

Some guy named Thumbs. Someone named Desiree who was probably a demon and who might or might not contact me in reference to a job. Jimmie who was definitely taking pictures of the kids for Desiree, but might not even know where they were holding the kids.

Wait. I looked up at Bishop, wondering if his services would extend beyond using Bob to track. I mean, he had mesmerized that guy at the warehouse for answers. He might be trying to deny it now, but I knew what he'd done. And I really wanted him to do it again.

"If I go back to Lenasco Communications on Monday morning I can wait for Jimmie and grab him." I figured I'd throw that out first since it was the least objectionable of what I was proposing.

Bishop stared at me. "So you grab him and what? Drag him out of the office and down the street? Haul him away on a bike that you can't start? Hog tie him and strap him to the back while you walk the bike all the way to Sun Valley? That's got to be the worst plan you've come up with to date, and you've come up with some real doozies."

I winced. "By me, I actually meant we. *We* grab him and put him in your truck." I added quickly because it was clear from the scowl on Bishop's face he wasn't going along with this plan.

"Then do what? Beat the answers out of him? Kill him afterward so he doesn't report us to the police or call and warn the Disciples and Desiree that you're after them?"

Pretty much, yeah. "We might not have to beat the answers out of him. You can mesmerize him like you did with the guy in the warehouse. He'll tell us everything he knows about Desiree and where they keep the kids and other stuff. Then we can kill him. Oh—and I promised a friend I'd send him a picture of Jimmie's balls and dick after I cut them off."

Bishop rolled his eyes. "What a great plan. Sign me up, Trouble, because I'm eager to get started on this new caper of yours."

I scowled. "I'm not going to lose sleep over offing a guy who made kiddie porn and worked with human traffickers." One who I suspected had raped Telaney when she was fourteen.

Bishop just stared at me. The moments ticked by and I fidgeted, uncomfortable with his non-response.

"So? How about it?"

"It's Saturday. We won't have a chance to grab this Jimmie until Monday. That's a long time to wait."

I threw up my hands in frustration. "There's one guy I can go to who might be able to find me Jimmie's home address. Otherwise Monday morning is the earliest I can find him. Besides that, I'm waiting for a possible job interview with Desiree. The only action I can take in the meantime is trying to find more Disciples to interrogate and kill."

"*You're* going to get yourself killed with the last two." Bishop let out a sigh. "Look, why don't you go home, work on your bike, and check on your youngest sister. I'll track down this Jimmie, then swing by and get you as soon as I find him."

I was going to owe this guy so much money. But he was right. With my bike broken, I'd need him to drive me to Alfie's and back, and end up paying for his time anyway. I might as well let him do the digging around while I got my ride up and running. If he couldn't find Jimmie, then I'd go back to hunting down Disciples.

"Okay. Thank you for helping me." I turned to look over at the weredog. "Thank you too, Bob."

I wasn't sure why I was thanking them. I was paying them what was going to be an obscene amount of money, and hadn't gotten anything for it outside of a couple of names and a few cases of chili and toilet paper. Still, it never hurt to be polite.

Bob waved a paw at me then headed out the door. I followed him, and waited in Bishop's truck as he carried Bob's bottle of rum over to whatever form of transportation the weredog was using. We were silent on the drive home. Bishop helped me unload my bike, wheeling it up beside Bea's car. I thanked him again and watched him drive off, once more feeling bereft as his truck turned the corner.

I liked him. He was grumpy and growly and laughed at me. Most of the time it seemed like he just stood back and let Bob and me do all the work. He was scary, and I got the feeling the compulsion and the unusual strength were just the tip of the iceberg when it came to his abilities. But something about him drew me in. I felt weirdly safe when he was around, I felt…happy.

CHAPTER 21

The electricity was off, but I smelled roast pork the moment I walked through the door. I popped into the kitchen and saw a pot of barbeque that had been warmed up on the little butane cookstove, a basket of rolls and a bowl of potato salad on the table. Dinner. But where we would normally all gather around the table to eat together, tonight would probably be just Bea and me.

I'd called out when I came in and assumed Bea was in the bedroom with Sadie. When I entered, Sadie was by herself, sitting up in bed with a smile on her pink-cheeked face. There was a fresh bag on the IV stand, and a basket next to the bed held rolls of gauze and bottles of ointments and water.

"How's it going, peanut? See any more elephants and angels?"

She shook her head. "Nope. My fever is gone, and I'm hungry."

That was a good sign. I sat in the chair beside the bed and gently lifted the sheet to look at her leg. Thick white bandages covered her entire calf, making it look twice the size of the other leg. I couldn't tell if some of that was swelling or just overzealous application of gauze and cotton pads.

"It hurts," Sadie admitted. "If I hold very still, it's not too bad. Aunt Bea said a doctor was here to see me and that she doesn't think it's broken. I can't remember the doctor, so I guess I was pretty sick."

"You were." I reached over and gently tugged a lock of her silky brown hair. "When you were ranting about elephants in the room and an angel visiting you, we got worried." It was amazing what IV antibiotics, fluids, and painkillers could do. I could hardly believe in less than twenty-four hours she was sitting up and wanting food.

Her brown eyes turned serious. "Did you find Nevarra?"

I thought about lying, but she'd known something was wrong even when she'd been racked with fever. "Not yet. I'll find her. You just worry about getting better."

Sadie shifted on the bed, wincing. "They took her, didn't they? I remember hearing the back door and a bunch of noise while I was under the kitchen sink. I couldn't get out and sat there until you came. That's when I knew Nevarra was gone. She would have come and helped me if they hadn't found and taken her."

"They did take her." I took her hand in mine. "I'm looking for her, and other people are as well. We'll find her. *I'll* find her."

She smiled. "I know you will. You can do anything, Eden."

If only that were true. "What are you hungry for? Bea's got barbeque, rolls, and potato salad on the table, but I can make something else if you want."

"Maybe just a roll." She shot me a mischievous grin. "Unless you've got candy."

I remembered the chocolate bar in the fridge and grinned back before I headed into the kitchen. Bea came through the back door just as I'd put a roll and the chocolate bar on a plate. She had three eggs in one hand and a gorgeous dark red tomato in the other.

"I've got something for Sadie," I told her. "I'll be back in just a sec, and we'll have dinner together."

Sadie cried over the message attached to the chocolate bar, then broke it in half, saying she was saving that for Nevarra. I left her in the throes of a sugar high, and changed my clothes before returning to the kitchen. Over dinner, I told Bea about the day, unloading all the frustrations and fear that I never wanted anyone else to see. Like Sadie, she expressed faith in my ability to find Nevarra, then shooed me away, saying she'd do the dishes tonight.

Sadie was asleep with some chocolate smeared across the corner of her mouth when I checked on her, so I headed outside to work on my bike and think. Next door, a woman in a flowered dress sat in her driveway on a plastic chair, a shotgun across her lap. She nodded at me then picked up a plastic tumbler of iced tea and took a sip. I nodded back.

The late evening sun was warm on my shoulders as I got the toolbox, a tarp, and a couple of rags from the tiny garage that served to hold a mower and miscellaneous outdoor equipment rather than a vehicle. By the time I'd wheeled my bike to the front left side of our driveway our neighbor had company. Javier stood beside her. They fell silent, the boy watching as I tried to start my bike, because sometimes the motorcycle repair fairies swoop in while you're eating dinner.

The motorcycle repair fairies obviously hated me because the bike still wouldn't start.

Javier wandered across the neighbor's weed-choked, dirt lawn and stood over me as I pulled off the seat and stared down at the battery. Connections looked good, but just in case I tightened them and tried it once more.

Nada. It just wasn't turning over, which in my very inexpert opinion meant fuel or air intake. Although all the battery juice in the world wouldn't do shit if the spark plugs were fouled.

"Won't start?"

The kid had brilliant deductive powers. He also had a fairly large pistol jammed deep through the waistband of his pants. I thought about asking him if he was happy to see me, but the kid was fourteen.

"Don't shoot your dick off," I said instead as I rummaged in the toolbox for a twelve-millimeter socket.

"Safety's on."

Maybe so, but he still shifted the gun to the side. Great. Now he'd just shoot his leg off and bleed out. For a teenage boy, that was probably preferable to losing his love sausage.

"Hopefully it didn't flick to off when you moved it around in your pants. Get a damned holster, Javier." I fiddled with the idle screw as a sort of Hail Mary. When that didn't work, I started taking shit off, setting parts aside in neat rows on the tarp I'd laid down. Had the throttle cable disconnected or broke? Because that would be an easy fix. I followed the line, then watched the lever wiggle as I engaged the throttle.

Javier snorted, but did a quick check of the pistol safety before squatting down to stare at the side of the bike with the expert gaze every teenager had when it came to anything in the world.

"Give me a hand here, would you?" I was going to have to pull the gas tank, and while I'd done it before, it was really a two-person job—especially since I'd just filled the bike up yesterday.

Javier stood, eyed the tank, then put a hand on the top as if he were blessing it. I rolled my eyes. "Let me get the bracket off first and lift the tank, then you can hold it while I unhook shit. Don't drop it. It's full and heavy, and I don't want to crack the tank or ding my paint."

He nodded, his eyes riveted on my hands as I pulled the bracket, setting the nuts and bolts carefully aside on the tarp. Grabbing one of the rags, I balled it up and slid it under the tank so the hose from the fuel filter could drain on it, then I eased the tank up. Javier reached out and supported it while I removed the rubber bumpers that had long ago come unstuck from the frame, and set them aside.

The boy seemed to be having no problem at all balancing the tank, so I went ahead and removed the hoses and tach cable, turning the fuel cock to off before pulling the hose from the fuel filter. A trickle of gas spilled from it down onto the rag, filling the air with the sharp odor of flammable liquid. Javier's nose wrinkled, but his hands remained steady.

"Go ahead and lift the tank off and set it gently on the tarp away from the other parts."

He hesitated. "Isn't the gas going to spill everywhere?"

I pointed to the fuel cock. "No, because I turned that off. Otherwise we'd have about four gallons of gas all over our pants, the driveway, the yard…"

He grinned at me. "I've never worked on a bike before. This is a-fucking-mazing."

I pointed to the tarp with my screwdriver. "Well, put the a-fucking-mazing gas tank over there, so I can try to fix this thing."

He moved the tank as if he were handling a nuclear bomb, but I noticed no strain at all in the ropy muscles of his arms. Strong kid. Sassy, smartass kid, but strong and skilled. He'd done a good job on the door, the windows, and the cabinets. Carpentry knowledge would serve him well in life, as would mechanical knowledge.

Drew had taught me the basics of working on a motorcycle, and the rest I'd learned on my own through trial and error and YouTube videos when we'd had a computer and internet.

"What now?" Javier asked as I unscrewed the cap on the air box.

"We replace the air filter, just because. Then I'm going to replace the fuel filter. I ran it pretty low, and with these old bikes, there's crud floating around in the bottom of the tank. If the filter's clogged, it won't get enough gas to start."

"And if that's not the problem?" He leaned forward, looking at the air filter as I pulled it out.

The real question here was diagnostics. The engine on this bike was a-fucking-mazing, as Javier would say. The carburetor system? Not so much. Do I replace the fuel filter, button it all up, and see if it starts? Or do I go ahead and rebuild the shitty carburetor that had been giving me fits? I'd put it off because I'd needed my bike, but I also needed it to be reliable. Stranding me in Silver Lake wasn't reliable.

"Run in the garage. Grab an air filter and a fuel filter for me. They're on the shelf toward the back," I told Javier.

He'd figure it out.

I always grabbed parts for my bike as well as Bea's car whenever I could.

Air filter. Fuel filter. Spark plugs, although I'd replaced them and the wires early last year. I'd already checked the throttle cable, but I needed to check the fuel line to the carburetor and see if it was pinched or blocked. If it was a switch or a sensor, then I was pretty much screwed since I had no idea how to do anything other than just replace those, and it was kinda late to run to an auto parts store. My gut was telling me the problem was a stuck carburetor float. I really needed to pull and rebuild the carburetors. I had a set of gaskets. I had a manual to walk me through it. It was just a matter of time. I couldn't be hitching rides all over LA right now, and spreading the guts of my bike across the dining room table to clean and reassemble would take me an entire day.

I didn't have an entire day.

Javier brought back the correct items, although he could hardly screw it up since they were neatly labeled in boxes. Then he sat and watched as I cleaned contacts, checked cables and hoses, and replaced filters.

"Sadie…she gonna be okay?" Javier asked as he handed me a six-millimeter socket.

"Yes." I felt more confident saying that now than I had in the last two days. Sadie would live. She'd be okay. She might have a long painful recovery learning to walk again, and I had no idea if she'd regain full mobility, but she'd be okay.

"How about Nevarra?" Javier yanked a blade of grass from our barren lawn and began to twist it into a knot. "They took her, didn't they? That's what Mom said."

Nevarra. My stomach knotted into a hard ball at the thought of what she might be going through right now, what she'd go through if I couldn't find her.

"They did take her. I'll find her. I won't give up until I find her, no matter how long it takes."

That panic that had been simmering below the surface since the studio flared to the surface once more. Didn't those cop shows always say the first forty-eight hours was the critical window in finding someone or solving a crime? That first forty-eight had come and gone. Just realizing that made my stomach churn. I was getting desperate.

The time for subtlety and care was over. I needed to go back to my guns-a-blazing approach. I'd hit every Disciple location, kill every one of their gang members until I found one who knew something. I'd slaughter my way through the county until I brought Nevarra home again.

Neither of us said anything as I put the bike back together. The neighbor went inside then resumed her watch with a fresh glass of iced tea. A man carrying a rifle walked down the middle of the street, his eyes vigilant as he scanned his surroundings. I recognized him as one of the locals and figured that he'd drawn the short straw for neighborhood patrol this evening.

Javier helped me attach the gas tank. I made sure everything was connected and that the fuel cock was in the on position, then I sent up a quick prayer and tried to start the bike. It took a few tries and ran a bit rough even after I'd adjusted the idle screw, but it would have to do for now.

Hopefully the thing wouldn't leave me stranded again. I just needed to get through the next week or so, and then I'd tear it apart and see if I could get it running at a hundred percent—well, as close to one hundred percent as a bike manufactured before I was even born could be.

I let the bike run, adjusting and tinkering until I figured it was as good as it was going to get. Javier finally got bored and wandered off. The sun slipped low on the horizon, at the edge of the barren stretch of fenced in land across the street that constituted the landfill transfer station. Just as I was putting the toolbox and tarp back in the garage, my phone rang. With grease and oil covered hands, I fished it out of my pants pocket and eyed the number. I didn't recognize it but answered anyway. It could be for me. It could be for the former owner of this phone. Either way, I'd rather bullshit through a few awkward moments then let it go to voice mail and potentially miss important information.

"Yeah?" It wasn't the politest greeting in the world, but I really didn't give a shit.

"Andrea? Get your ass over to the airport. Century Boulevard and Postal Road—the old US Customs building where they used to store cargo awaiting inspection. Just pull in off Century, park out front, and walk on in. They want you there at nine. You've got one chance to impress the bitch. And you owe me a blow job."

I recognized the deep snarly voice as Piers. Why the fuck did I kinda like this guy? He was a shot caller of a notoriously violent gang. And he worked out of a fucking In-N-Out.

Okay, the last wasn't a deal breaker—not in the least. The other should have been, but for some reason I felt a moderate amount of respect for the guy. And I got that the blow job demand was meant to be funny. He'd absolutely take me up on it if I agreed, but he wouldn't be pissed if I told him to fuck off.

"I'm not sucking your dick, Piers. If you're lucky you might get a hand-shake—your actual hand, that is. That's not slang for me jerking you off."

He sighed, and I couldn't help but smile at the disappointment the noise conveyed. "How about if I buy you dinner? Do I at *least* get a hand job then?"

What the hell was wrong with me? Earlier I was lusting after a scary guy with unknown and clearly dangerous abilities, and now I was considering a hit-and-quit with a gang member.

"Sure. Better be good food though. As much as I like In-N-Out burgers, that's not gonna cut it."

He laughed. "Princess. I'll call you in a few days. Don't screw up this interview."

The call disconnected. I ran for the house, unbuttoning my shirt as I tore down the hallway.

"What is it?" Bea's startled voice called from Sadie's room.

I didn't want to get her hopes up. For all I knew I was going to get myself killed in a shootout with a bunch of gang members and a woman who was probably a demon. Nevarra might not even be there. Nobody might be there except the "bitch" who was interviewing me for a job.

But if I wanted to keep a bunch of kids and possibly other

people and supplies in a secure spot until they were sold, the old Customs and Border Protection warehouse would be the perfect spot to do so.

It seemed kind of silly to change out of greasy oil-stained clothes when I was probably going to get blood on them. It wasn't like this was a real interview, and even if it had been I got the impression that looking a little on the scruffy side would be to my advantage. So instead of putting on clean clothes, I rebuttoned my shirt, loaded an extra magazine for my pistol, and strapped on the bracers with the thin set of knives. Just to be on the safe side I grabbed the anti-magic gun I'd salvaged from the Fixers. I hated using a gun I hadn't had time to clean and inspect, but it was the only thing I had that would work against magic. If Desiree was truly a demon, I wanted to go in there prepared.

"Eden?" Bea poked her head into my bedroom, and I realized I been too preoccupied to answer her.

"I got a lead on Nevarra," I told her, trying to decide if I should take a few throwing knives or not. I wasn't all that accurate with them, but what the hell. Might as well go in with everything I had.

"That photographer?"

Bea eyed my weaponry. I didn't look like I was going to meet a photographer. I looked like I was about to role-play a *Call of Duty* game.

"No. I managed to get a job interview either with the woman who runs the trafficking operation for the Disciples, or one of her flunkies." I eyed my switchblade, then stuck it in a pocket of my cargo pants. "I've been beating the bushes for days now. This is as close as I'm going to be able to get to them, so I'm taking my chances and going in hot."

Bea's eyes widened. "Not alone?"

Who the heck would I take with me? I did everything alone. That's how I ran. That's how I'd always run, even when I'd been with Drew. Still, my mind immediately detoured to Bishop. If everything went to hell, that's the guy I wanted at my back.

But Bishop cost money, and I'd already run myself way into debt with him.

"Eden, you're not immortal. I don't want someone dumping your body on my lawn because you thought you could run into a den of gangsters with guns blazing like a Wild West shootout. You take backup, you hear me? I don't care if it's a friend of yours, a neighbor, or that good-looking man with the big dog, you take backup."

"I think Bob is a shifter," I told her. "Bishop might be one too."

She shrugged. "I don't care *what* that man is. He looks like he'd be handy in a fight, and I think you should take all the help you can get."

Bishop *wasn't* handy in a fight. He stood around and let Bob and me do all the work. Although, I got the feeling he'd jump into action if either of us looked like we couldn't handle something.

I shoved a couple more knives into various pockets on my cargo pants, thinking that Bea was right. I did need backup. The goal here was to bring Nevarra home, and I couldn't do that if I got killed.

"I'll ask Bishop," I told her, wincing at how quickly I was racking up an astronomical debt to this man. I'd pay it off eventually. Hopefully, he'd be patient about it. That or take giant cans of chili in trade.

CHAPTER 22

For some reason Suerte seemed less intimidating tonight than it had the first time I'd been there. As soon as I went through the door I noticed a smaller but more multicultural group of customers were at the bar. A Black guy brooded into his beer. Two Filipino women were drinking wine and laughing over something on the one's cell phone. A Latino guy dozed against the wall, a half-eaten burger on a plate in front of him. The only white guy in the place was that head on a pike by the bathroom door.

There was a head on a pike. I took back my earlier thoughts about Suerte being less scary.

HB came out of the back room and followed my gaze. "I told Bishop to take that thing down before it starts to stink. But nooooo, he suddenly needs to make a statement or something."

I took a few steps closer, and realized that in spite of the battered and bloody condition of the head, I recognized this guy. King, the racist asshole who'd attacked me the first time I was here.

"Where's the bearded guy's head?"

HB grinned. "Cody? He got smart, and shut his yap. This one? Not so smart. I've got no idea what got into Bishop the other night, but it's about time. I couldn't stand having those assholes in the place. Half our customers wouldn't come in when they were here."

Had what I'd said given Bishop the incentive to finally act? I'd been hoping he'd just kick them out and ban them from the place, not decapitate one and stick his head on a spike.

"His eyes are gone." And noticing that nearly made me upchuck my dinner.

HB shrugged. "Bishop was in a mood. I think he was trying to bowl with the guy's head. Didn't work since it wasn't exactly round."

Okay. Now I was even more scared of the guy. Who better to have as backup when I was going to possibly have to fight a bunch of armed Disciples and a demon?

I tore my gaze from the head and went over to sit at the bar. "Is he here?"

"Nope." HB shoveled some ice in a glass, filled it with tea, then slid it over to me. "He had a job. Haven't seen him since early this morning."

He was still out looking for Jimmie. For some reason I'd assumed he'd make Bob or other people do that while he came back to the bar. He must have decided to track down the photographer himself, and I didn't have any way of reaching him.

"Can you get a message to him?"

HB's eyes narrowed and she leaned over the bar. "Another job? When you most likely haven't paid him for that tracking he and Bob did a few days back?"

Or what he'd done for me this afternoon, which she clearly didn't know about. At least she hadn't implied I'd paid him with sex.

"It's part of the same job. Can you ask him to meet me at nine tonight? Here's the address. It's the old US Customs warehouse by the airport."

She looked at the address and frowned. "You think they'll have the kids there?"

I nodded. "I'm supposed to meet some of the Disciples there—ones that are involved in the child sex trafficking operation."

One of her thin eyebrows shot up toward her hairline. "And if your sister's not there?"

I didn't want to think about that. "Then someone should be able to tell me where they're keeping the kids."

This was my beat-the-crap-out-of-everyone-until-I-found-out-what-I-needed plan, the one Bishop thought was going to be the death of me. These guys I was meeting with tonight were one step closer to the operation than Jimmie. If Desiree was there, then I'd have the one person who would definitely know where Nevarra was.

If I managed to get her to talk, and if she didn't kill me, that is.

"So you need backup, and possibly a tracker to follow the scent if no one talks?"

I nodded. "If Bishop doesn't come…I understand. You're right. I haven't paid him yet. I will. I just need to get Nevarra back, then I'll give him every spare dollar I make until we're square. I promise."

"Like I haven't heard that before." She looked over at the head on the flag pole, then muttered a soft curse.

"So, you want him to meet you here?" She tapped the paper with the address.

"Yeah. I need him to meet me in the parking lot. If the kids are there, I need to have them safe before bullets start flying or before someone can grab them as a hostage. If they're not there, I need to decide who needs to stay alive—who's most likely to have the information I need."

"I'll try to reach him. How's your other sister? The one that got shot?"

Had I told her about Sadie? I'd always been a private person, and it felt weird to have all these solicitous strangers dropping off casseroles, replacing our front door, and asking how Sadie was doing.

"Much better. I don't want to jinx anything, but I think she's out of the woods now as far as infection and fever goes. Once her leg has some time to heal, the doctor will be able to evaluate if she's had any permanent damage or not."

HB made a tsk noise and shook her head. "It always hits me hard when the kids get hurt. I'm really sorry about your sisters."

"Thank you." I glanced at the clock on the wall, feeling absolutely awkward about this conversation. "I really need to run…but thanks."

I gave the head another quick glance as I left then got on my bike and drove south out of the Valley, navigating the maze of freeways as I headed for the airport.

It was full on dark by the time I eased down the back road that led to the rental car lots, the airplane cargo areas, and the Customs warehouse. The parking lot out front was lit up. Half a dozen cars were parked in front of the building. The open trailer portion of a tractor-trailer sat empty over to the side.

We might no longer be part of the United States, but LAX was still in use. American travelers would go through Customs in Denver, or Dallas, or Phoenix, but the billions of dollars of product that came via plane and boat still needed to pause here in what was now a part of New Hell. The demons and various civil servants would take their slice of the pie along with a few bribes before sending everything eastward.

The warehouse wouldn't be empty. There'd be a huge open space for pallets, as well as offices and locked areas for shipments that were more valuable or susceptible to tampering. If the kids were here, I'd be willing to bet they'd be locked in one of the offices, or some sort of back room.

I parked my bike across the street in front of the rental car lot and waited. At five minutes to nine I started to get nervous. What if Bishop didn't come? Maybe he didn't get the message. Maybe I'd reached my credit limit with him.

I glanced at my watch once more and started my bike. It was nine o'clock. I couldn't wait any longer. I was going to have to face these guys on my own—possibly face down a demon on my own. The prospect scared the shit out of me, but I didn't have a choice. This was my best chance at finding Nevarra, and I wasn't going to let a bunch of armed guards and a demon deter me.

Parking my bike up front next to a souped-up Subaru, I walked up and knocked on the locked front door.

One of those fish-eye lens cameras swiveled so I waved at it. A few moments later a gray metal door on the far wall swung open and a beefy man with a pistol on each hip and a rifle over his shoulder sauntered across the four feet of foyer to unlock the glass entrance doors.

"You that Andrea chick?" The man looked like a professional heavyweight wrestler, but his voice was surprisingly high pitched and soft. I figured it wouldn't be in my best interests to comment on that, so I didn't.

"Yeah. I'm Andrea Delgado." I hoped that was the correct last name. Keeping aliases straight was proving to be challenging.

It must have been correct because the guy ushered me in, locking the glass door behind me.

The foyer was sparse with worn beige Berber carpet. The only light came from the parking lot through the big glass entrance doors. To my left was a small receptionist area—separated from the foyer with what I was sure was bullet-proof glass. The walls were an indiscriminate neutral color, the only ornamentation a framed picture of President Donald Trump seated behind a desk in the oval office, smiling as if he were posing for an Olan Mills photographer. Someone had drawn black devil horns on the glass so they appeared to be sprouting from the president's head. I wasn't sure if that was a parting shot from the US Government employees before they left, or something the new occupants had added.

Soprano guy spoke into a radio clipped to the neckline of his shirt. Something buzzed. The steel door behind him clicked. Reaching back, he swung it open and ushered me in.

Two steps in and I stopped, hearing the steel door close behind me. The room was a mantrap—a tiny windowless room with only one way in and only one way out. Another fisheye camera eyed me from a corner. A plastic mail bin sat against one wall.

"Weapons in there," Soprano squeaked, waving a meaty hand at the mail bin.

Things were not going to go according to plan if I had to walk into this warehouse virtually naked. "You're fucking kidding me. I'm one woman weighing all of one-forty. You could probably cave my forehead in with a single punch. I'm no threat to you guys."

"If you're no threat to us, then you're not gonna be right for this job." He looked me over. "I'm pretty sure you could draw that pistol and fire a few rounds before I managed to cave your forehead in with my fist. Some boss might have given you his thumbs-up, but you're not one of us. We don't know you. Weapons go in the bin, or you don't go inside."

Damn it. "I don't know you either, and I'm not going to walk into a warehouse owned by a gang known for violence unarmed. I'm a woman, for fuck's sake. You've got two pistols and a rifle, and I'm sure anyone else in there has the same. I've got one damned gun. *One*," I lied.

"One gun and enough knives to open up a cutlery store." He chuckled. "Tell you what—you leave the pistol in the bin, and I'll let you keep the knives."

I sighed dramatically, unbuckled my shoulder harness and set my gun in the bin. There. Hopefully he wouldn't search me because I had the little 43 in a pocket of my cargo pants, and the white-muzzled anti-magic gun in my waistband against the small of my back. Plus, he was right, I did have enough knives on me to open a cutlery store.

Something in my stance must have changed Soprano's mind because he started patting me down. The other two guns, my bracers, my knives, my multi-tool, my lockpicks, my electronic password thingie, my stolen cell phone, even the ring with my bike and my house key on it joined my Glock 17 in the bin. I have to say that Soprano was professional about the search. No groping, no fingers trying to go where fingers shouldn't go without express consent. It almost made me sad that I was going to end up killing him tonight.

"Damn, woman. That's a lot of shit to be packing to an interview."

I shrugged. "A girl never knows what she's going to need when she goes out. And this might be a job interview, but if I'm going to go out to a warehouse surrounded by nothing but rental car lots and runways, I'm going to be prepared."

He nodded, then surveyed the contents of the bin, pulling out one of my knives and handing it to me. It was a stubby Boker with a push-blade that measured less than two inches.

Fuck. My. Life.

I took it, wishing I had a wrist bracer on so at least I could have it at hand. I did the next best thing and shoved it in the tiny little pocket at the top of my cargo pants. The top two inches of the handle stuck out of the pocket, which would hopefully be enough for me to grab the knife and get it out fast. One good thing was that with a quick push of my thumb on the switch I could extend the blade. The bad thing was, as I mentioned, it was two fucking inches.

Size matters, but two inches was better than nothing, at least in this instance.

Soprano spoke into his mic again and the far door unlocked with a buzz. He ushered me through, and I walked into the main warehouse. Much like the one Bob, Bishop, and I had broken into a few days ago, tall rows of heavy-duty steel shelving were stacked with pallets of cellophane-wrapped goods and wooden crates. They were all marked and dated, and I noticed as we passed by that some had been logged in over a year ago.

Huh. Clearly a few people weren't paying their bribe money.

Two forklifts stood idle alongside the front wall—both of them with forks tall enough to access the top shelves. In front of them was a line of pallet jacks for moving the crates off-shelf. A few desks were clustered by one of the middle rows, complete with computers, an assortment of handheld scanners, and old-fashioned clipboards. A man lounged at one of the desks, his feet on an open drawer. He rocked the chair back and forth, creating a rhythmic squeaky noise that was almost drowned out by the fierce whir of the warehouse air-conditioning system.

Two men so far.

Soprano led me to the left of the warehouse, not so far ahead that he couldn't keep one eye on what I might be doing behind his back. Smart guy because as little as the blade was on that Boker, I could have jabbed a kidney or sliced an inner thigh with a few quick motions.

I heard the beep-beep of equipment backing up and glanced over to see a forklift whipping down a parallel aisle halfway through the warehouse.

Three men.

A line of offices stood to the left front of the warehouse, both with open doors and huge glass windows. Previous management must have liked to survey their domain, making sure the employees weren't goofing off like the guy who was currently out there rocking his chair. No one was in the offices, and obviously the kids were not being kept there.

Soprano made a right, hesitating to keep me in his peripheral vision as I turned after him.

"I thought this job was going to be personal security for kids. Something about me being a woman would be less threatening?"

There was another man prying the top of a crate off with a crowbar. Four. And if I couldn't get my hands on someone's gun right off the bat, I was definitely grabbing that crowbar.

Soprano grunted. "Piers. Man's always thinking with his dick. Like the kids aren't gonna be just as scared with a grease-covered, gun-toting woman who looks like she's ready to knife them. You aren't the white-van-and-lollypops looking type, but we do need an extra hand, and clearly Piers thinks he's gonna get laid if we give you a job, so there you go."

"So, you keep the kids here?" At his sharp glance, I quickly backtracked. "Look, I live in the Valley. This is a hell of a haul. I'll do it if the money's right, but I'd take less if I didn't have to drive halfway to Mexico every day to work."

"The kids are here for now, but Desiree likes to move them around, so a new batch might be elsewhere. You wanna bitch to her about the distance, go ahead and be my guest."

We walked all the way to the back of the warehouse where there was a series of loading dock doors and a line of windowless rooms—each of them probably no more than a hundred square feet. It would be an awfully small place to keep a bunch of kids, especially if you had to squeeze in a portable toilet. I was assuming that's what they did. I couldn't see these guys walking children back and forth to the employee restrooms to go potty.

Another man came around the corner, this one hauling a pallet jack with a crate full of boxed shoes wrapped in clear plastic. One of the handheld scanners was clipped to one side of his belt, a pistol in a holster was clipped to the other. Five.

"She here yet?" Soprano asked the man.

The other guy shook his head and eyed the diamond-encrusted Rolex on his wrist. Clearly this job had its perks.

"She's supposed to be here, but…yanno."

The other guy looped around and down the next aisle and Soprano turned to me. "Gonna have to wait. Which sucks because that means I need to babysit you, and I got shit to do."

A new idea sprang to mind—one in which I hopefully wouldn't have to fight the might-be-a-demon Desiree.

"So, lock me in with the kids until she gets here." One of these guys *had* to have a key in case of an emergency with their very valuable human product. "You can go back to work, and get to see firsthand if having a female guard is less traumatic than a male one for them."

He clearly didn't want to hang with me because it took him all of half a second to make the decision. "Okay."

Soprano pulled a set of keys out his pocket that would make a school janitor proud. I followed him over to the middle door and watched as he sorted through the wad of keys on the ring. For once he wasn't looking at me, so I turned slightly as if I were looking at the contents of a pallet, then slid my knife from the pocket, holding it by the side of my thigh as I turned back to face the door. I was right-handed, but held the knife out with my left hand, sacrificing muscle memory for the extra few seconds of surprise it would buy me to stab Soprano without having to jab across my body.

"Fucking keys," he snarled. "You think we could spring for some magic shit, or at least a handprint recognition system or something. But no, I gotta lug around forty fucking keys, trying to remember which one goes to what."

He tried a few keys, then cursed some more. I couldn't hear a sound from inside the room. Either the sound-proofing was out of this world, the kids were gagged, or Soprano was getting ready to trap me into an empty room. The last scenario didn't really bother me, because I planned on stabbing him before I stepped so much as a pinky toe over the threshold.

He finally found the right key, twisted the knob, and pushed as I slowly extended the blade and held it tight against my thigh. The pungent aroma of sweat and urine hit my nose. Through the open crack of the door I saw sleeping bags, a few toys, and a little blond boy whose frightened eyes met mine.

They were here. The kids were here. Nevarra was here. I'd finally found her and the only thing standing between us and freedom was five guards.

I took a step forward, and plunged the knife into Soprano's lower back. Just in case I'd missed his kidney, I threw myself to the right, letting my weight and momentum drag the knife deeply through the muscles of his back and side.

He howled, let go of the door, and spun to face me, one hand trying to stem the blood and the other hand groping for his pistol. The keys fell from his bloodied hand, as the door swung shut. I saw a rush of motion as the children rushed to grab the door, but they were too late. It clicked, and from the rattling of the handle, it must have locked automatically.

Switching the knife to my right hand, I jumped forward and slashed at his wrist. He backed up flinching at the blade and frantically trying to pull his pistol out of the holster with bloodied fingers. I kept slicing, carving thin lines into the man's chest and arms. He was scrambling backward, nearly tripping in his attempts to get away.

As he pulled his pistol, I dove for him, letting him grab my wrist. While he was raising the gun, and trying to keep me from stabbing him, I slapped my other hand on his chest and let loose with my magical stun gun powers.

The man jerked as the voltage shot through him, but still managed to get off a wild shot. The loud AC in the warehouse might have muffled his screaming, but it didn't cover up the sound of a pistol firing. The noise echoed, and I knew I was about to have a serious fight on my hands.

Letting go of Soprano, I grabbed his gun, then swooped up the bloodied keys and dashed down the nearest aisle.

There was some serious déjà vu going on as I squeezed between the crates, pocketed my knife and keys, and gave the pistol a quick check. Soprano's pistol was a Smith and Wesson 1911 E series Rail 45ACP. Damn, this was a seriously expensive gun. Not that I'd trade either of my Glocks for it, but it would do nicely as a side piece if I got out of this thing alive.

But this wasn't the time to be swooning over a weapon.

I held very still, making sure my feet were up on the pallets and that I was hidden by the crates. After counting to thirty, I peeked out and saw the crowbar guy come around the aisle. He shouted into his mic as he saw me and started shooting. Scrambling backward amid a hail of flying splinters from the wooden crate, I jumped out into the next aisle and ran.

These guys were a whole lot savvier than the men who'd been in the other warehouse. I'd hit an intersection, nearly get my head shot off, then switch directions, too busy trying to evade them to get a decent line of sight to shoot myself. After a few turns, I realized they were coordinating this whole thing with their mics, herding me into an ever-smaller space in the warehouse so they could converge and take me out. I thought of going up by climbing the racks, but these guys were moving too fast. I'd be open and exposed.

Hiding in the crates wasn't an option. I'd be trapped while

they closed in, so I kept running and turning, trying to move fast enough to break out of this trap.

I was out of options. This was going to turn into a Butch Cassidy and the Sundance Kid scenario, and my only choice would be to try and shoot my way out of it. Four of them and one of me. This would have been a really good time for back-up to appear. Bishop. Bob. Hell, I'd be happy to see anyone on my side right now, but that clearly wasn't going to happen.

I picked my spot—between a wooden crate and a pallet full of three-foot-tall concrete garden gnomes—and put my finger on the trigger. Desk-guy was unlucky enough to slink around the corner first. I aimed for center mass, but wasn't used to this pistol and ended up shooting high, luckily nailing him in the head. Blood sprayed like a paint can had exploded in aisle four, and he dropped to the ground.

Shots rang out in response. Ducking back in between the crate and the gnomes, I cringed and covered my head, protecting myself from the flying bits of wood and concrete. Maybe they'd run out of bullets. Maybe I could dive into the aisle and take them all out in a blaze of glory. Maybe a shelving unit would collapse and kill them all, but miraculously spare me. Maybe…

What was that screaming? And why did none of the gunshots seem to be coming my way?

Taking the opportunity, I dove into the aisle and rolled, aiming in the general direction the shots had been coming from. Two men were dead in a pool of blood on the opposite end of the aisle from the guy I'd shot. As I watched, one man ran past the aisle, screaming loud enough that I heard him over the air conditioner. Right behind him and gaining fast was a mountain lion.

A fucking mountain lion.

I stared, open-mouthed, as I processed the fact that there

was a giant cougar in the old US Customs warehouse, chasing down and killing the gang members who worked here.

What. The. Fuck.

Had it been shipped in, and gone into a frenzy from all the shooting, breaking out of its cage? Because I couldn't see how a mountain lion could have wandered from the hills all the way to the airport, and managed to get through multiple locked steel doors.

I wasn't going to waste time thinking about it. I needed to unlock the room where the kids were being held, get Nevarra, and get out of here before the mountain lion finished with his appetizers and decided I might make a good main course.

Keeping the safety off and the gun in my hand, I dug out Soprano's keys, and snuck my way over to the door. Cursing the dead guy just ten feet from me, I tried key after key. The gunshots had ended, but I kept trying to keep an eye on my surroundings as I worked my way through the keyring.

Finally, one of them worked. I pushed the door, and nearly had a heart attack when a small hand grabbed around the edge and yanked it open. Looking down, I saw the little kid I'd managed to catch a glimpse of right before I'd stabbed Soprano.

The little kid gripping the door shot past me. Suddenly I was nearly knocked off my feet by a stampede of children racing through the warehouse to freedom.

Oh, shit. Mountain Lion.

"There's a cougar loose," I shouted after them.

They vanished like little mice and I stood there, holding the door open. Where was Nevarra? She hadn't been one of the kids who'd ran out. Was she hurt? Was she tied up inside the room? I let the door shut, then grabbed Soprano by the legs, hauling him over and using him to prop the door open. Then I went inside.

Ten by ten was bigger than my bedroom at home, but it wasn't big enough for eight kids. The room stank. The blankets and sleeping bags were scattered around on the floor. A bucket in the corner reeked of urine. The cool air pouring down through a vent in the ceiling did nothing to combat the stale air. It was horrible. It reminded me of a puppy mill I'd once seen where the filthy dogs had been kept in tiny wire cages, cleaned up only when they were sold.

But beyond the bucket and the blankets, the room was empty.

Where was Nevarra?

I yanked the keys out of the door and tried the other rooms. The warehouse by this point was silent aside from the hum of the HVAC system. Hopefully the cougar wasn't eating the kids. Had they gotten out somehow? I assumed the place had fire doors that would allow rapid evacuation. I didn't like the idea of eight little kids racing around the streets where they'd get picked up again. Hopefully they'd stay in one place and I could...what? I rode a fucking motorcycle here. I couldn't drive eight kids home on a bike. Maybe I'd call the police.

Yes, that's what I'd do. Get Nevarra. Get all my stuff out of the mantrap room. Call the police to come help the kids. Warn them there was a mountain lion loose in the warehouse. Take Nevarra home. There. That was my plan.

Except there was no Nevarra.

I'd checked all five rooms and was starting to panic. Was there another place they were holding children? Multiple batches they'd separated and were selling maybe on different sites? I tried to remember the faces of the kids that had run out of the room, to think if any of them I recognized from the proofs I'd taken from Jimmie's desk drawer, or that I'd seen on the website. I thought a few of them had matched, but they'd run out so quick I couldn't be sure.

Where was Nevarra?

Holding back tears, I jogged up to the offices and started going through the desk drawers. Maybe there was paperwork somewhere that would tell me where they were holding her.

Calm down.

I tried to slow my breathing and think logically. There had to be another location somewhere. Damn it all, why hadn't I kept one of these guys alive to question? Although that wasn't completely my fault. I hadn't expected a mountain lion to burst in on the scene and start killing them off.

Speaking of which…

"Looking for this?"

I whipped around and saw a woman with golden-blonde hair and the eyes of a reptile. In one hand she held the mangled body of the cougar. With a flick of her wrist, she tossed the animal into the corner where it landed with a pained cry.

Desiree. I looked at her eyes with their weird pupils and wished I had to face the mountain lion instead.

"I'll admit that I'm impressed. This wasn't quite what I had in mind when I set up the interview, but I'll go with it." She took a step toward me and I backed up, realizing that I was trapped. I'd need to go through her to get out of the office.

"Points for taking out all of the staff here. Points for creative use of this creature, although you need better control over your beasts. Damn thing tried to bite my throat out."

Too bad it hadn't.

"And judging from your energy signature, you're also the

one who killed off a bunch of Disciples in a warehouse and at an auto parts store. All in one week. You've been a busy girl."

Energy signature? Did she mean my magic? I'd electrocuted someone at both locations. Did that sort of thing leave some sort of magical trace behind that could be linked to me? Fuck, that would have been good to know before I started frying gang members.

"I'm taking points away for almost letting the product escape though. That's the whole point of the job. Keep the brats alive, uninjured, and contained until we can unload them on their buyers." She made a tsk sound. "If you can't manage to do that while you're shooting and stabbing men, then you're of no use to me."

"Where's Nevarra?" I put my shoulders back and decided to stand my ground, no matter how scared I was. "Where's my sister?"

She blinked and tilted her head, staring at me in a way that was creepily inhuman. "Your sister?"

"The Fixers took her from my house and sold her to the Disciples—to you. She's not here. She's not with the other kids."

Who was I kidding? This woman wouldn't tell me what had happened to her or where she was. She probably didn't even know the kids' real names.

Desiree did an undulation motion with her head, then smiled. "Oh, the little Black girl. Around thirteen or fourteen? Pretty? The one I got two days ago?"

"Yes. My sister. Her name's Nevarra." My heart raced, I felt a trickle of hope that I feared was false.

Desiree's smile widened, showing a line of teeth that looked like they'd been filed into points. "Ah, her. Sorry. She was perfect for one of my clients. I sold her outside the auction. She fetched a very high price. You know, I'm not sure I want you guarding the brats, but I think I might be able to use you on a freelance basis for some jobs that require a woman's touch. What's your rate?"

Sold. She'd been sold right away. She could be halfway across the country by now. She could be dead by now. I was too late.

Maybe I was too late, but I still needed to know. Even if she was dead, I needed to know.

"Who?" I choked back a sob. "Who did you sell her to? I'll pay you. I'll work for you. I'll do anything, just tell me who you sold her to and where to find her."

Desiree's eyes morphed into something more human. She stared at me for a moment, as if she were trying to weigh whether to tell me or not.

"I already got paid for that girl," she mused. "There is no shortage of clients, but this guy does like to throw his money around. Every three months he buys a new one. Every three months, right on time. You'll work for me, be loyal to me? You'll be mine if I tell you his name?"

I had the feeling I was selling my soul, damning myself for all eternity. "Yes, but I need his name, and where I can find him and Nevarra. There's no deal unless I bring her home alive."

Desiree laughed, revealing those sharpened teeth once more. "William Matthew Cumberland. Santa Monica. 488 Mesa Road. We have a deal. Now come over here. I'm going to mark you as mine."

"The fuck you are."

I looked up to see Bishop standing in the doorway of the office. He looked furious, like he was about to rip the threshold apart with his bare hands and bring the ceiling down on us all. His knuckles whitened as he gripped the doorway, then he let go and stepped forward.

Desiree bared her teeth at him and hissed. "You don't belong here."

He snorted. "And *you* do?"

She jutted her chin out. "This warehouse belongs to the Disciples. One of my businesses is loosely affiliated with them. Thus, I belong here."

He blinked at her and laughed. *"You're* Desiree? You're working for the *Disciples?"*

Desiree hissed again. "They work for *me.*"

"That's not what I heard." Bishop looked the woman over then shook his head. "You're kidding me. You? And *Desiree?* Who the fuck names themselves Desiree?"

She sneered. "Bishop is worse."

He shrugged. "Not like I picked it. You actually sat down and decided that it would be awesome if you called yourself by a stripper name."

Desiree snarled. "It's not a stripper name. It's a sexy name. It's powerful. I like it."

Bishop rolled his eyes. "Whatever." He pointed at the cougar then at me. "That's mine. That's mine."

Desiree also pointed at me. "She is *not* yours. She's mine."

Bishop snarled, his blue eyes suddenly glowing gold. "She's mine."

I was starting to get a complex here. Were they fighting over me like I was a steak? It seemed as if there was something else going on here. I had no idea what that was, but I got the impression it would be wise if I just kept my mouth shut and let them work it out.

"Fine," she snapped. "For now, anyway."

"Twenty-four hours," Bishop told her.

Her eyes narrowed. "One."

"Twelve."

"Two. I've got a business to run."

"I don't like your business."

The demon snorted. "I don't give a fuck what you like.

You've got two hours. After that, we're even, and all bets are off."

Bishop folded his arms across his chest. "Two. And I strongly suggest you focus your efforts on a business that doesn't involve kidnapping and selling children."

Desiree's eyes went back to looking like a crocodile's. The air crackled, and for a second I wondered if the warehouse *was* about to come down around our ears.

Then she let out a sigh and flicked a bit of lint off her sleeve. "You're a fucking dick, Bishop."

"Yep."

"It's gonna get you killed one day. You're seriously outnumbered, you know."

"Yep."

Desiree stared at him a few seconds then smiled. It shocked the hell out of me because the smile actually seemed genuine, as if she and Bishop had been doing this sort of dance for centuries and had come to a weird level of respect.

"See ya around then." She strolled past him.

I watched through the window as she walked to the front of the warehouse and out the same way I'd come in.

"What the fuck just happened?" I sputtered.

"You really do get yourself into the damndest situations, Trouble," Bishop said, ignoring my question. "You've got two hours to get your sister. The demon won't move on you, won't warn the buyer, won't send anyone to interfere. I suggest you get going."

"I made a deal." The ramifications of what I'd done hit me. "I sold her my soul, or something like that. She gave me the guy's name and address because I promised to work for her."

"Yeah? Well, that deal's off, and next time be a bit more careful what you offer."

What was going on here? Desiree was a demon. Bishop

knew her. There were at least five dead guys and a fucking mountain lion in this warehouse, and Nevarra still in danger.

The mountain lion.

"He's hurt." I pointed toward the big cat crumpled up against the wall. The thing had saved my life, and I hoped there was a veterinarian nearby that could do the same for the cougar.

"She," Bishop corrected me.

She. I'd been too busy looking at the thing's sharp, bloody fangs to notice whether it had balls or not.

Bishop walked over to the mountain lion, sighing as he knelt down beside it. "Dumb ass. What do you think you're doing coming here by yourself?"

The animal's eyes blinked open, looking up at Bishop, then over at me. Bishop turned his head to follow her gaze.

"Yeah, I know. But you still should have waited for me. You're lucky she didn't kill you."

Was she...the mountain lion...a shifter like I suspected Bob was? A werecougar? Whatever the fuck that was?

"You didn't see a bunch of kids running through the parking lot on your way in, did you?" I asked Bishop.

He looked over at me. "They're locked in that first office. One of the kids was trying to smash through the glass window with a stapler."

I liked these kids already—liked them enough that I didn't want them trapped in an office in a warehouse with five dead bodies until I managed to make a 911 call and the police eventually showed up. Two hours. Would that be enough time to rescue Nevarra, steal a minivan, and drive eight kids to safety?

Bishop chuckled. "I'll take care of my mountain lion, *and* I'll take care of the kids. You go find your sister."

I really *did* owe this guy. With a hurried thanks, I ran past him and quickly searched the dead guys—even the one who'd been majorly chewed on. I took everything that would fit in my pockets. Keys. Wallets. Weapons. Then I went back to the mantrap room where the doors stood wide open and collected my gear.

Weighed down like a video game character who couldn't help but pick up and take every single item she came across, I got on my bike and drove north, heading for Santa Monica.

CHAPTER 24

I drove like a bat out of hell, only slowing down as I pulled off the 405. The sun had set hours ago, and the moon was ascending, spreading a silvery glow over the ribbon of black asphalt. Desiree had said three months—she'd said the fucker who bought Nevarra purchased a new kid every three months like clockwork. Nevarra had been with him less than forty-eight hours. She was still alive; I knew it. Nevarra was smart. She'd watch, learn, play the innocent, and all the while she'd be formulating a plan to escape. She wouldn't do anything that would jeopardize her health or safety. She wouldn't go off half-cocked and ruin her chances of escaping.

She was alive.

I was going to get her, and I was going to kill everyone who stood in my way. And if this William Matthew Cumberland wasn't there, if he miraculously managed to get away from me, I'd hunt him down. I'd make him pay. I'd make sure no other child ended up in his hands.

But what if everything went wrong? I pulled the bike over to the side of the road. Bishop and the possible werecougar had heard the name and address of the guy who had Nevarra, but I couldn't count on them to do anything about it. I didn't want to dump all this on Bea. Maybe I could leave a message on Detective Juke's phone, just in case I got killed. Bags had vouched for her. It might take the police freaking forever to catch this guy, but as a worst-case scenario, I got the feeling she'd at least try to see justice done. I pulled my stolen phone out, dialed the number, then cursed when the "no service" notice flashed on the screen.

Of all the times for the owner to get the line switched to a new phone, it had to be tonight. Fuck. Shoving the phone back in my pocket, I pulled my bike back into traffic and drove on.

It was all on me. I was going in alone. Nevarra's life depended on me. I couldn't die—at least I couldn't die until I'd gotten her to safety.

I parked five blocks away from the house and walked, feeling completely exposed on the empty sidewalks. This was a nice neighborhood—not one-percenter Carlson nice, but still upper class. Every house was hidden behind solid stucco fencing and verdant, manicured hedges. Only garages were visible from the street—garages and a few gates with security boxes blinking at their sides.

A car drove by, slowing as it passed me. I could practically feel the driver's eyes on me. A woman in ripped, filthy cargo pants and a tank top, covered in guns and knives, didn't exactly fit the profile for a resident out for a late-night walk.

These neighborhoods wouldn't be relying on the police for protection; they'd be forking out to a local militia. I'd be willing to bet that driver was on the phone right now, and that in twenty minutes tops there would be someone pulling up beside me to ask who I was and what I was doing here.

The clock was ticking. Bishop had bought me two hours, and I'd eaten up almost an hour of that getting here. I paused in front of the address Desiree had given me. Eyed the garage and the gate, and made a decision.

The car turned a corner. I pulled the anti-magic gun from my pocket and shot a bullet at the gate. Blue paint splattered across the handle and the latch and dripped down. Three regular gunshots took out the light, the camera mounted to the garage, and the security device on the gate.

I kicked it open and went through, ducking down behind a bush as I took in the scene.

Lights were on upstairs in the house and toward the back —probably where the kitchen was. There was also a porch light that spilled a gentle golden glow across the lawn. Boxy devices up along the roofline were most likely additional cameras and probably motion-control lighting. A faint beeping noise announced that the security system was offline. If the driver hadn't called their militia, then this alarm would absolutely bring them.

I was willing to bet a pedophile wouldn't have actual guards to witness his activities, pass judgement, and possibly blackmail him. There'd be a perimeter alarm, that I already triggered, multiple locks on all doors and windows, cameras, and possibly magic. Durft? No. The neighbors were too close and a Durft would bring unwanted attention and bring the association complaining.

With time running out, I made a decision and ran for the house. On the way, I knocked over a ceramic bird feeder, grabbed the base, and hurtled it through the largest of the front windows. I was sure people two blocks away could hear the shattering of glass and the shriek of a second alarm. The floodlights illuminated the lawn and me as I dove through the broken window—and crashed into an invisible force field.

My shoulder went numb from the contact.

I slid to the ground, groping for the anti-magic gun. The

blue paintball splattered across the magic barrier, then abruptly dripped to the ground as the magic fizzled. Just to check I stuck my hand through the broken window, then climbed through, tearing a gash in my pants on my way in.

With my 43 in one hand and the anti-magic gun in the other, I cleared the first floor, checking in pantries and cabinets as well as behind bookshelves for any secret areas. Was the guy home? What other security shit would he have? I needed to be careful, but I had no time to be careful.

Upstairs I found three bedrooms, two full baths, several closets, and no hint of either Nevarra or the home's owner. One bedroom looked as if someone actually occupied it, but the only sketchy thing I found was a large assortment of tweed jackets with suede elbow patches and collars.

The noise of the alarms was driving me crazy. I couldn't think with all that racket going on. I also couldn't hear if someone was approaching, or even if someone was screaming for help. Heading back downstairs, I shot the alarm panel beside the door until it shut up. That left the more manageable noise of the perimeter alarm.

Think. Where would he have hidden her? I refused to believe that the demon had lied, so where was she? With more care, I went back to the kitchen, checking the fridge and the cabinets once more. Fruit Loops. Juice boxes. A bag of gummies next to a box of chocolate chip cookies. Maybe the guy had a sweet tooth, but I couldn't imagine a grown man with a house like this drinking a juice box.

Tears of frustration stung my eyes as I made my way back to the foyer, once more checking in the coat closet built into the space below the stairs. Who the fuck needed this many coats in Southern California? And snow boots? I kicked them aside, frowning as something on the floor caught the hallway light. It was a tiny barrette in the shape of a heart, covered in little rhinestones.

Shoving the anti-magic gun in my waistband, I yanked the coats out of the closet, throwing them on the floor. There, behind the boots and shoes, was a narrow set of wooden stairs leading downward.

A *basement*? I'd lived my whole life here in Los Angeles, and I'd never seen a house with a basement before.

There was a light switch against the back wall of the closet next to the steps. I clicked it on and off a few times, but got nothing. Pulling my cell phone out of my pocket, I turned the flashlight app on, and held it with my left hand, high and slightly behind my head. This was going to suck. I'd be illuminated and an easy shot for anyone down in the basement, but stumbling down these stairs in the dark wouldn't be any better. Ducking under the closet pole, I put one foot on the top step and hesitated.

Thirteen steps down. Cement floor. Block wall about eight feet across from where the stairs ended. From the house layout, the basement should extend approximately twenty feet to both my left and my right, and another twenty feet behind me. That was a lot of space to cover—and a lot of time I didn't want to be an easy target.

Clicking the light off, I eased the closet door shut behind me, plunging the world into darkness. Slowly I eased down the stairs, alert to sounds or any movement in the dark. Thirteen steps later, I crouched on the cement floor. No windows. I couldn't see a damned thing. Carefully I raised the cell phone up and to the left, clicking the light on for a quick second before clicking it off.

The brief flash of light showed me the back of the basement had been made into a room—a child's room with plush carpets, pink furniture, and pictures of kittens on the wall. In the middle of all this crouched a man with a pistol.

I'd already clicked the light off and had begun to roll as I heard the sound of three shots in rapid succession. The muzzle flare gave me a good indication of his location, but I was too afraid to return fire in case Nevarra was there behind him. With the echo of the shots ringing in my ears, I took advantage and moved at a diagonal toward where I'd last seen the man. My foot hit the edge of the carpet, and I sprang forward, hoping the guy hadn't moved. In the unfamiliar and dark basement, I must have misjudged because instead of slamming into a body, I hit what felt like a bookcase, toppling it over and knocking the contents to the floor with a crash.

Shots rang out again and I rolled, feeling something burn along the back of my calf. Clicking the cell phone light on once more, I slid it across the floor. The light strobed around the basement, giving me a split-second glimpse of the man before the phone hit a fallen book and flipped over, leaving us once more in darkness.

I grabbed something hard and round from the ground and pitched it, hearing a grunt of pain as the projectile hit my target. The man fired again, one quick shot then a click.

Empty.

I jumped to my feet, grabbing the phone on my way up. The beam of light arced up from the ground, illuminating the man fumbling with the pistol. I kicked him in the face and dropped down on top of him, my knees pinning his arms to the ground.

"Where is she?" I asked, pointing the muzzle of my gun in his face.

He tried to hit me with his pistol, but could only manage to smack it against my ass. "The safe is upstairs. Take everything in it, just don't shoot me."

With the light from my cell phone I could finally see the guy clearly. He was in his late forties, or early fifties, with either gray or blond hair and a softness around his jawline and chin that told me he wasn't likely to be throwing me off with any badass MMA moves. A glossy coating of sweat covered his forehead and made dark patches in the armpits of his shirt. His thin lips trembled, then pressed tightly together as his gaze nervously darted to my pistol.

"I don't want money. I want the girl. Where is she?" I repeated.

"There is no girl. I've got money. Just take the mon—"

I placed the muzzle of my pistol against his forehead, propped the phone against a fallen shelf, then shifted my weight until I heard the gun drop from his hand.

"This is the last time I'm gonna ask: where is she?"

He licked his lips, eyes darting to the left of me, then to the right. "You kill me, and you'll never find her."

I shrugged. "You tell me, and we'll leave. I'll take the girl, and we'll walk right out of here. You don't tell me, then I'll kill you and bring in a dog to track her by her scent."

He glanced to the left again, a small involuntary movement that I might have missed if I hadn't been watching him so closely.

"If I tell you where she is, you'll let me go? Alive? Unharmed? And not come after me?"

I fucking hated making deals with this slime, but time was running out. "I'll let you go, but only if she's alive."

Again, there was that telltale glimpse to the left. I could take my chances. I could shoot the guy, and hope that Nevarra was over to the left under the bed, or behind the dresser, or in a secret room somewhere, but I didn't want to risk that this asshole was eyeing a weapon he was going to make a grab for and not stupidly clueing me in to my sister's whereabouts.

"Swear it. Swear on all the souls you Own that if I tell you where she is, that you and she will leave here and not come back, that you won't kill or harm me now or in the future."

What the hell was that about? This dude didn't strike me as particularly religious, but whatever. I'd play along.

"I swear on whoever the fuck my mother was that if you tell me where Nevarra is, and I find her alive, I won't kill you. Or hurt you. Now or in the future."

"I don't give a rat's ass about your mother. Swear on the souls you Own," he demanded.

This guy was fucking nuts. "Souls I own? Like slaves? I don't own any people. I don't even have a pet fish."

"Swear on the souls you Own, or she'll die before you find her," he babbled. "Do it or I won't tell you, no matter how much you torture me."

This man was truly nuts. "Okay, okay. Don't get your dick in a knot. I swear on the souls I Own that I won't hurt you or kill you now or in the future if you tell me where Nevarra is, and if I find her alive and well. There. Does that cover it? Do I need to pinky promise, too?"

"Let me up." He squirmed. "Let me up, so I can show you."

This wasn't my first rodeo. I kept my weight on the guy's arms as I scooped up his empty pistol and shoved it into my rear waistband. Then using my knees for leverage, I rose to my feet, keeping my gun trained on him the entire time.

He scrambled up, then backed over to where the dresser stood against the wall. Reaching around to the side, he pushed a button and the entire front of the dresser unlocked.

"Stop," I ordered, not sure if he'd swing the door open and grab a weapon. "Sit here, right here. And don't move."

Keeping my eye on the man, I edged forward and swung open the false front of the dresser. A girl was inside, bound and gagged. She was wearing a frilly white dress, her hair smoothed into a series of neat braids with white bows at the ends. Frightened eyes met mine, and then filled with tears.

"Nevarra. Oh God, Nevarra." I reached in and tried to

untie the gag, only to realize I couldn't manage to free her while I was watching her captor.

Pulling a knife from my pocket, I pushed the blade out and began to saw at the fabric tying her hands. I caught a movement out of the corner of my eye and spun around too late. Something hard hit my arm, knocking me to the side. The knife fell from my hand, and the shot I instinctively fired going into the back of the staircase.

The man kicked me and hit me again with the bookshelf, whacking the gun from my hand. I reached for it, only to see him kick the gun away.

I scooted backward as the man kept coming, trying to evade both the blows from the shelf and the kicks from his feet, and not succeeding with either. I kicked back, rolled, tried to grab the man's ankle or anything I could use to defend myself. The wood cracked and splintered, but he kept coming at me. Desperate, I grabbed at the shelf and pulled. My hands slid, but I held on long enough to yank the man off balance. A quick kick had him stumbling back and giving me a second to scramble to my feet and yank another pistol from my pants pocket.

A shot rang out before I could rack the slide, and everything seemed to move forward in slow motion.

The man and I stared at each other in confusion. I glanced down, half expecting to see blood spreading across my chest.

Then I looked back up just as the man dropped to his knees.

Two more shots and he fell facedown to the floor. Behind him stood Nevarra holding my Glock. Her hands trembled, and she slowly lowered the pistol, setting it to the side before she rushed toward me and fell into my arms.

I wrapped my arms around her, rocking her a bit as she sobbed, still keeping watch on the dead guy, just in case. The last few days had been weird as fuck. I honestly wouldn't have been surprised if the man jumped up and came at me like an extra from a zombie film.

He didn't move. The light from my cell phone dimmed, and I realized if I wanted the pair of us to get out of here safely, we needed to get going.

I pulled away and held Nevarra's shoulders as I looked down at her. Her wrists were bloody, and part of her gag was still tangled up in one of her braids. She didn't seem badly wounded, but I knew that the worst of her injuries wouldn't be physical.

"We need to go." I smoothed a hand along her braids, plucking out the fabric of the gag from her hair and tossing it to the floor. "My bike is down the street. There's a good chance whatever militia covers this area is coming, along with whatever security guys this asshole may have privately hired."

We were probably about to have a pack of demons descending on us as well. Or perhaps just Desiree, which might be worse than a pack of demons.

She nodded, then stepped out of my arms to cross the basement and flick a switch on the far wall. Light flooded the room. I picked up the Glock then gave the dead guy a parting kick in the head before leading Nevarra up the stairs.

"I wish I could change first, but the only clothes here are his and these stupid dresses," she whispered.

"You can change as soon as we're home," I promised her. "Then you can burn the dress in the backyard."

"That would feel good."

I led her through the kitchen and carefully unlocked the back door. The floodlights were still on, their white brilliance harsh in the night. This guy's neighbors must hate him. Even with the fences and the hedges, they'd be treated to a flash of light every time a cat hit the motion control sensors.

"Here." I handed Nevarra the Glock 43 and pulled Soprano's Sig out of another pocket. We walked through the yard without incident, pausing at the gate beside the garage. I went high, and Nevarra went low as we swung the gate open and scanned the street. It was empty and eerily quiet. The gate closed behind us with a soft sound, shutting out most of the light. We held in position, eyes adjusting to the relative darkness of the moonlit night. A weird sensation crawled up my back, making the hair on my neck quiver with uneasy expectation. Something was wrong. It was too quiet, too still.

"Where's your bike?" Nevarra whispered.

"Five blocks." I caught her eyeroll and bit back a smile. "It's not like I could roll on up to this guy's front door with my beat-to-crap bike unnoticed. Hell, I'm surprised the militia aren't breathing down our necks right now just from me walking down the sidewalk."

"We running or walking?" Nevarra glanced down the street and shivered.

"Walking. Fast walking." Two armed women running down a residential street in the middle of the night would draw notice. Two armed women fast walking down a residential street probably wouldn't be much better, but I was going to pretend otherwise.

We moved to the sidewalk and headed toward where I'd parked my bike. I let Nevarra get half a step ahead so I could guard our rear. Halfway down the block Nevarra stopped so abruptly that I nearly ran into her.

"To the left. By the carport," she whispered.

I looked in that direction and saw nothing. "Keep walking. Slowly," I whispered back.

We took two steps, and I saw a flash of orange a few feet from where Nevarra had indicated. Eyes. It reminded me of catching an animal's gaze in the beam of a flashlight, only these twin orange lights glowed with their own illumination. The orange blinked in and out of sight, only to appear eight feet away.

"It's not fireflies," Nevarra murmured. "And unless it moves hella fast, it's more than one animal."

Fireflies were rare in Southern California, but I'd seen the occasional one down by the river. But these lights weren't pairs of shockingly coordinated insects, they were eyes. I couldn't see this neighborhood being home to rats, and the lights seemed to be at a height that belied that theory—unless these were rats the size of large dogs. Opossums? That was more likely. Could be the animals were climbing up a hedge or wall, or standing on top of a trash can in the shadows.

"Possums," I told Nevarra, even though the fear skittering along my spine told me otherwise.

More eyes came to light to the left of us, and to the right, bouncing slightly as whatever the fuck these things were followed us.

"Slow," I warned Nevarra, feeling very much like prey. The bike was three more blocks ahead. I could see it parked by the curb, the helmet still on the seat. We just needed to get there. I was sure we could outrun whatever was following us —if my bike started.

Please start, I prayed as the hedges swayed and rustled with movement.

A click of nails on pavement had me spinning around, but no one, and no thing, was behind me. The bike was two blocks away, then one, then fifty feet. I resisted the urge to break into a run.

"Put on the helmet quickly, get on, then cover me while I start the bike," I whispered.

Nevarra nodded, swiping a hand down the frilly white dress before clasping the gun with both hands.

We were ten feet away when the air shimmered and a figure appeared. I pushed Nevarra behind me, grabbing the white muzzled gun with my left hand and pointing it and the Sig at a tall woman with golden-blonde hair and reptile eyes.

Desiree's eyebrows rose. She tilted her head and eyed the anti-magic gun. "Smart girl. Of course, you'd need to hit me for either of those toys to work."

"Not hard to hit someone at ten feet away." I wasn't worried about my aim, I was frantically trying to remember how many of the spelled paint ball bullets I'd shot and whether there were any remaining in the gun. If there weren't, we were totally screwed.

"I'm supposed to have two hours," I reminded the demon. "We've still got at least ten minutes."

She shrugged. "Demons lie. And I wanted to see if you managed to collect your sister or not. That way I know whether the contract between us is binding or not."

"Contract?" Nevarra squeaked. "Eden—"

"There is no contract," I blurted out, hoping Desiree didn't catch that my sister had called me Eden, not Andrea. "Bishop called in a favor."

She leaned against my bike. "That favor bought you the hours, it didn't get you out of the contract. I offered. You accepted. An Owned soul or a bound demon cannot enter into a contract, but you're neither of those things." She pushed away from the bike and took a step toward us. "Demons aren't the only ones that lie. You don't belong to Bishop--which means you now belong to me."

Like fuck I did.

I steadied my aim with the anti-magic gun. "You're two shots away from dead, bitch. Then I won't belong to either of you."

Desiree stopped, eyed my weapons, and chuckled. "True. And as you pointed out earlier, you still have a few minutes left on the clock—time enough for you to scurry to the safety of your home. But you still owe me, little one. You have your sister back, and that would never have happened without my telling you where she was and who had her. Even if the contract is in dispute, the fact that you owe me a favor is not."

Fuck these demons. Were they all like this? It was like verbally sparring with a goddamned lawyer.

I took a deep breath and slowly let it out. There was no good way out of this, and the more we stalled, the more sand ran out of the hourglass. I could shoot her and be done with it, but I had a feeling those dozens of glowing eyes behind me would tear Nevarra and me apart before Desiree's body hit the ground. I didn't spend the last two days trying to find my sister only to have her die because I refused to pay the piper.

I was so going to regret this. "There is no contract between us for my soul or anything else. If you let the whole contract thing go, then I will accept that I owe you a favor."

She smiled, the jagged teeth brilliantly white. I had no idea what toothpaste the woman used, but it was really doing the job.

"Done."

The word had barely left her lips before she was gone, vanished into a shimmer of air before us. I held my breath and looked around, still feeling the presence of *things* behind and beside us. She'd gone, but she hadn't taken her minions with her.

"Hurry." I kept both guns out and ready as Nevarra put on the helmet and climbed on the back of the bike. Then she covered me with the Glock as I tried to start the fucking thing. Three tries and a lot of swearing, and the bike finally roared to life. Nevarra wrapped one arm around me, still covering us as I pulled away from the curb.

I picked up speed as we turned onto a main road, then

opened up the throttle on the highway. Once we hit Burbank, I pulled over to the shoulder and hopped off the bike, motioning for Nevarra to do the same.

She pulled the helmet off and shot me a puzzled look. "What are you doing?"

"This." I pulled the anti-magic gun from my waistband and shot my bike. A splat of blue spread across the gas tank, making my ride look even more like cheap trash. I had no idea what the radius of effect was on these magic bullets, but hopefully this would negate any sort of demon tracker Desiree most likely put on my bike. She didn't know my real name. The cell phone number I'd been using now went back to the original owner. If she couldn't track me home, there was a good chance she couldn't find me to collect on that favor.

Not that I believed any of that, but the longer I could delay her finding me, the longer I'd have to pay off Bishop and get us the hell out of here—hopefully somewhere Desiree couldn't ever sniff me out. There were roughly seven billion humans in the world, and over two million still living in the greater Los Angeles area. If she didn't have a homing device on me, her chances of finding me were slim.

Hopefully.

"Okaaaay." Nevarra eyed the dripping splotch of blue, put her helmet back on, and climbed onto the bike.

By the time I pulled in the driveway it was nearly dawn, thanks to whatever decided to pile a lovely arrangement of mangled construction equipment on the northbound lane of the freeway. Somewhere in LA there was a demon who really did not like the highway system.

I'd waved to Dave Rickard, patrolling the streets with his shotgun as I'd pulled into the neighborhood. Three houses down, Linda sat in a lawn chair perched in the back of her pickup truck, drinking coffee, a pistol in her lap. The neighborhood had our back, and as I nodded to Linda, I vowed to have theirs as well. They'd helped us when we needed it, and that was a debt that wouldn't go unpaid.

A light came on in the kitchen as I helped a sleepy Nevarra off the bike. The back door opened, and Bea's head appeared.

"Oh!" Moving faster than I'd ever seen, Bea was down the steps, across the backyard, and through the gate. With a flood of tears, she grabbed Nevarra and held her tight. I stood and watched as they both cried all over each other. Then Bea reached out with one hand and pulled me in.

"My girls are all home," Bea announced with a watery voice. "Tonight, I can sleep knowing all three of you are safe here at home."

Safe. For now. Sadie was healing. Nevarra would heal as well. Bea would go back to work, and we'd slowly start saving again so we could leave this hellhole and start a life somewhere else.

Who am I kidding?

So *they* could leave this hellhole and start somewhere else. I still had a price on my head with the tax collectors. I probably had a price on my head with the Disciples. I owed Bishop. I owed a fucking demon. Trying to make money when I had Fixers out to get me, when no legitimate pawnshop would fence my salvage, was going to be damned near impossible. But even if I managed to make things right with the taxing authority, I'd be little more than dead weight to my family. I couldn't leave until I paid off Bishop, and even then, I'd constantly be worried that Desiree would find me and use my family to force me into some sort of hellish servitude to her.

I owed a demon a favor. And I got the feeling that "favor" was going to be a whole lot more than I'd bargained for.

Dave Rickard and Linda were making sure we could all

sleep without worry. Nevarra was home. I'd bunk down for the night on the floor of the girls' room with her on one side and Sadie on the other. I'd read them stories from the Gilgamesh book, do their hair, watch them share Sadie's get-well chocolate.

Tomorrow I might be back in hell, but for tonight... tonight I'd relax and enjoy the closest I'd ever come to heaven.

* * *

Keep reading for an excerpt from Sinners on Sunset, California Demon Series, Book 2

SINNERS ON SUNSET

CHAPTER 1

Jagged metal sliced the back of my shirt as I slid under the gate and into the yard. A high-pitched scream was quickly followed by the sound of gunfire—from behind me as well as to my left. Thankfully the woman in a bikini on her back deck looked to be aiming more at the rooftop next door than at me and the fuckers chasing me had the aim of Kindergarteners.

But even Kindergarteners occasionally get lucky. Rolling away from the fence I felt dirt spray up beside me, then the sharp stab of pain in my side.

I sprang to my feet, threw my backpack over one shoulder, and ran. It never crossed my mind to ditch the thing. I needed every bit of salvage I could find, so I wasn't about to lose a morning's work to some assholes who thought I was poaching on their territory.

Admittedly, my license had been suspended, so technically I *was* always poaching at this time. But Karen and Chad were dicks. They would most likely have shot me even if I'd been in good standing and within legal rights to salvage anywhere in the greater Los Angeles area.

"Get off my lawn," the woman screamed, shooting the downspout off her neighbor's gutter.

"I'm trying," I shouted back, pressing a hand to my side and running for the opposite fence. Wow, her yard was big. It hadn't seemed this big when I'd first stood up, but weird spatial distortions apparently happened when you were shot and going into shock.

"Stay out of Sherman Oaks!"

I glanced back and saw Karen waving her revolver wildly. The woman had no sense of muzzle or trigger safety. It was a wonder she hadn't shot her husband. Not that Chad knew what he was doing with that semi-automatic .338 he'd outfitted to look like a fucking machine gun. It was bad enough they dressed like suburban yuppies, the least they could do is learn how to safely use a weapon.

That's what happened when Vulture licenses went to anyone with the money to buy one. They were supposed to be restricted to a certain number per area, but money talked, and Karen and Chad clearly had more money than sense.

I finally reached the end of the yard and jumped, catching the top of the chain link and nearly passing out as I pulled myself over the top. Blood decorated both sides of the fence as I slid down the other side and held on a few seconds to catch my breath. Neither Chad nor Karen were in any shape to climb, or even run, more than half a block, and the homeowner had stopped shooting now that I was out of her yard. It felt as if I were out of immediate danger, but I didn't want to linger, so gritting my teeth, I slowly jogged across a few more unfenced yards and got a few blocks away before pausing under the shelter of an overpass to evaluate my injuries.

I couldn't really see much of the bullet wound on my side, but it hurt like hell. It was low and enough on the side of my waist that I didn't think the bullet had hit anything vital.

Yanking a bandana out of my backpack, I wadded it up and pressed it to the wound. Then I took off my belt and used it to hold the makeshift bandage in place.

Fuckers. I wasn't surprised that Karen and Chad came after me, but the odds that they'd actually hit me with one of their poorly aimed shots had been slim. With the amount of bullets they'd been shooting, they were bound to hit something occasionally. It sucked that their luck hit on the one day they were shooting at me. I'd need to clean this wound up, put some sterile gauze on it, and maybe throw down some of the antibiotics I'd bought for Sadie. I didn't need a raging infection right now.

Despite getting shot, the haul had been worth the risk. The dead guy must have been flush from some big drug deal because I'd scored at least seven hundred in cash. I'd also grabbed both his guns along with a fully loaded second magazine for one of them. I'd been about to grab the gaudy-ass gold chain sporting a ruby-eyed dragon pendant he'd been wearing, but the arrival of Chad and Karen had prematurely ended my scavenging.

Cash. Guns. A handful of bullets and a spare mag. Normally that wouldn't have been that great of a haul, but the cash had me nearly giddy with excitement. Cash meant I didn't have to risk going to a pawn shop and hoping the broker would deal with me under the table and not turn me in for a bounty. The surveillance at Bags' place was no longer 24x7, but I knew the taxing authority was auditing his books regularly, and I didn't want to put him in danger by running stuff through his store right now.

I needed my license reinstated, but to do that I'd need to get that crooked cop to revise her report that pegged me for salvaging a haul I didn't take and put me in the crosshairs of the demons who ran the tax office. That wasn't likely to happen without pointing a gun at her head, and I wasn't sure

I wanted the entire LAPD after me for threatening and assaulting one of their own.

Not that I *could* threaten or assault her. I didn't even know the cop's name or where she could be found. Finding that out was quickly moving up my priority list—just as soon as I threw some cash at Bishop. It had been over two weeks since I'd brought Nevarra home. I wasn't sure what Bishop's expectations were as far as a payment plan or even exactly what I owed him, but I wasn't willing to test his patience by letting too much time go by without some effort at repayment.

Smoothing my shirt back down, I turned to leave and barely missed getting punched in the face. As I dodged a second punch, another assailant grabbed me and slammed me against the bridge abutment. Pain bloomed through me and I gasped.

"Don't kill her," the initial guy said.

"More worried about her killing me," the other replied, pinning my arms against the concrete.

I kicked out, nailing the one guy's shin, then squirmed in an attempt to get free.

He swore. "Little help here? Grab her gun."

The other guy hesitated.

"Five thousand, Jeff," the guy who held me said. "Five fucking grand. Ten if we get her to tell us where the loot is."

That motivated Jeff who tried to grab my pistol from the shoulder holster. I twisted, blocking him with my shoulder as I kicked my attacker once more. He stepped closer, trying to pin my legs with his own, which put him close enough for me to head butt him as hard as I could.

The guy yelped and jumped back, his grip loosening enough for me to get an arm free. I spun, punching Jeff in the nose. Then I kept turning, bringing my elbow up and slamming the other guy in the face with it.

They both stepped back. I pulled my pistol at the exact same time they pulled theirs.

"Drop—"

I fired, not waiting for the guy to finish his sentence. I'd been aiming for his shoulder, but missed and hit the bicep of his gun-arm instead.

He screamed, the pistol falling from his hand. I hopped to the side and swung my gun around, hearing a gunshot and feeling the spray of concrete chips less than a foot from my head. I unloaded in a wide pattern, hoping at least one of my shots hit something vital. Small groupings were impressive as hell on a target at a range, but I'd learned long ago that in an adrenaline-filled situation, shooting a broad pattern was what got the job done.

Four in Jeff. Pivot and duck, then put three more in the other guy, who'd picked up the pistol with his non-dominant hand and was seconds away from plugging me. I ran over to Jeff, kicking his gun away before doing the same to the other guy. Then I spun in a slow circle, looking for other assailants and walking backward to park my rear against the bridge abutment and catch my breath.

Thank the Lord for a twelve round magazine that had been illegal in California up until the demons came. With the traffic noise and the pain from my gunshot wound, I hadn't even heard these until they were attacking me. I'd been lucky. If the one guy had knocked me out, or if Jeff had been able to get my pistol free, this might have ended very differently.

No one else came for me, but I wasn't taking any chances, so I switched out my magazine for a full one, kept my pistol in hand, and tried to decide if I should linger and see if these guys had anything worth stealing, or get the hell out of here.

Five grand. My hands shook as what the two had said sunk in. The typical bounty on someone was anywhere from five hundred to a thousand, depending on what they'd done and what sort of risk a mercenary might have to take to bring them in.

Somehow I'd gone from an easy job to one requiring a large bounty. No doubt that had something to do with the fact that I'd been leaving a trail of bodies in my wake for the last month. A bounty that big mean I was going to have a whole lot more people gunning for me. Five grand would bring out the big guns, the experienced and highly-skilled mercenaries who didn't bother with the little jobs. And if that wasn't bad enough, I was evidently worth ten grand if someone could bring me in along with the loot.

My life just got a fucking whole lot more dangerous. I'd need to be looking over my shoulder every second. Bea and the girls would be in even more danger, from mercenaries trying to pump them for information to those who would use my family as leverage to get me to come in on my own.

This needed to stop. It wasn't just about getting my license reinstated anymore. I needed to get my name cleared. I needed to get this bounty off my head. There was only one person I could think of that might be able to help me, and luckily I had a meeting with her this afternoon.

Quickly rooting through the dead men's pockets, I grabbed what little cash and bullets they had, leaving their guns behind. Then I settled my backpack on my shoulders, made my way to my bike, and headed east to the mountains. I had a bit of time before my meeting and I didn't like the idea of walking around with this much cash on me. The quicker I got it into Bishop's hands, the better.

Bishop's bar, Suerte, was up in the hills, on a winding road that held only a few widely spaced houses and the occasional gas station. I wasn't too surprised to see a few vehicles in the parking lot as I pulled in. It was a little before noon, but I got the feeling they had a few regulars who popped in for lunch, as well as a few who made it a habit to hang out in the bar all day, or night, long. Parking my bike beside Bishop's old truck, I checked to make sure my bandage hadn't slipped and I wasn't bleeding all down my side before heading in. Blood-soaked wasn't a good look for me. It wasn't a good look for anyone. Normally I wouldn't care, but I had a bit of a thing for Bishop and found myself oddly concerned about my appearance whenever I expected to see him.

I'd learned early on that Suerte wasn't always a welcoming place, so I hesitated once I was over the threshold to survey the patrons. A guy wearing a cowboy hat and looking to be a leathery eighty sat at the corner of the bar watching the news and drinking a beer. Four middle-aged women chatted at a table covered with coffee cups and half-eaten sandwiches. HB was behind the bar. I took a few steps toward her then hesitated as I saw there was another patron off to the side. He seemed to be mid-forties with his long wiry dark beard shot through with streaks of iron gray.

Fuck. Our eyes met and for a few long seconds he held my gaze. With an exaggerated yawn, Dale turned his back on me and focused his attention on one of the TV screens.

Dale had been at Suerte the first night I'd come here looking to ask for Bishop's help to find my kidnapped sister. He and his buddy had attacked me. It didn't look like he was aiming to repeat the events of that night, but a person couldn't be too careful.

Keeping a careful side-eye on Dale, I finished my walk to the bar. HB was her usual platinum blonde perfection except for a faint scar running from her jaw down her neck and across her chest. It hadn't been there when I'd last seen her at the bar, but given the way the scar was indented and puckered, it looked like it had been a very serious wound—one that shouldn't have healed to this extent in a couple of weeks.

It was one more thing that gave me reason to put HB in the not-a-human category.

The woman looked up at me, smiled, then took a few careful steps over to fill a glass with ice and tea. She moved like she was still recovering from a bad accident.

"Are you okay?" I asked as she sat the tea down in front of me.

"I will be in a few more weeks." She shrugged. "At least I'm up and walking. Broke six ribs, and fractured my pelvis as well as two vertebrae. That shit takes a while to heal."

If you were human, that shit took a good sight more than three or four weeks to heal. HB, obviously, wasn't human.

Demons walked among us. Dragons occasionally flew overhead. Weird creatures were now the norm in Los Angeles, and that included shifters—although from what the news reports said, there had always been shifters, living right beside us for eons, pretending to be human. I was convinced Bob was a shifter—a weredog or werewolf or something. Bishop either wasn't human or he was a human like me with magical abilities. Clearly HB was *something* as well if she was up and walking around two weeks after being crushed like an aluminum can and sliced from jaw to sternum.

I thought back on that night in the Customs warehouse, when a mountain lion had saved my life, when Bishop had spoken to that mountain lion as if she were an old valued friend. Desiree had nearly killed the mountain lion, but Bishop had picked the animal up and taken it to safety—*her* to safety. Bishop had known the mountain lion, known it was a she. He and HB were close. All this supernatural shit might be new to me, but I wasn't an idiot. Even I could tell that two plus two equaled HB being a cougar shifter.

"I never had a chance to say thank you. For everything. For that night," I finished awkwardly, not positive about my identification of HB as the mountain lion, or her willingness to admit to being "other".

She shrugged. "Bishop's not the only one whose got a soft spot when it comes to kids. I'm just glad you got your sister back. Is she doing okay?"

"She's fine."

Hopefully she *would* be fine, eventually. Nevarra was the queen of bottling it all up and refusing to show any pain—physical or emotional. I couldn't exactly cast stones on that front, so I let her deal with it however she wanted. It bothered me that she hadn't burned that lacy, frilly white dress the moment she'd changed out of it, though. It was still balled up in a corner of the girls' room, in plain view, where she had to see it every time she was in there. Why would she want that constant reminder? Was she harboring some guilt, some silly belief that what she'd gone through was her fault? Or did she need that dress to keep her anger stoked up, because if the anger faded, that's when the fear and sorrow crept in?

Knowing Nevarra, it was probably some combination of the two.

"Eden?" HB's nose twitched. "You're bleeding."

Damn it. I hiked up my tattered, bloody tank top and saw that she was right. Blood had soaked through the second bandana and was dripping down my hip, leaving a dark wet stain along the side of my olive-colored cargo pants. I grabbed a fist full of bar napkins and undid the belt. Letting the blood-soaked bandanas drop to the floor, I pressed the napkins to the wound. None of the patrons in the bar seemed bothered about my bleeding all over the establishment, but I wasn't sure how Bishop, or HB would feel about it.

"Sorry about the mess." I held the napkins in place and bent down to pick up the bandanas, swiping the floor with them. Instead of wiping up the blood, I ended up just smearing more across the shiny oak planks.

I stood and my eyes met Bishops'. He'd moved with unnatural silence, somehow managing to appear before me from wherever he'd previously been in mere seconds. I didn't know if the guy was just superfast or teleported, but I added either option to my growing list of things that made Bishop scary.

"How in the hell did you get shot?" he demanded. "Or did you manage to do that yourself?"

I bristled at the thought that I was such a noob I'd manage to put a bullet through my own side. "Some competing Vultures thought I was poaching. One of them got lucky and hit me."

I didn't bother telling him that the two mercenaries who'd attacked me directly afterword hadn't helped the situation any.

Bishop's hand shot forward to grab my wrist. He pulled my hand with the wad of bloody napkins away and knelt down to inspect the wound.

"It's not that bad," I protested. It wouldn't be that bad if I stopped fighting, running, and driving long enough for the thing to clot.

He grunted. The noise carried a lot of disbelief with it. Whether that disbelief was over my being idiot enough to get shot, being idiot enough to try to staunch the wound with a handful of napkins, or being idiot enough to claim the wound wasn't that bad, I didn't know.

"Want me to bandage it up?" HB offered, as if she were volunteering to run the trash out to the dumpster and not perform serious first-aid on a gunshot wound.

"I'll do it." Bishop jerked a thumb toward a door behind the bar. "Office. Now."

I wasn't going to decline an offer for medical attention,

especially when the alternative was probably losing another pint of blood before the wound clotted up, so I grabbed my backpack and followed Bishop into the office.

He shut the door and I quickly looked around. The room was small, or rather it looked small with everything that was crammed into it. An L-shaped oak desk took up most of the space, and a couch took up the rest. The desk was stacked with papers and three-ring binders, an office chair barely visible behind them. The couch was a dark leather, worn to a shiny gold in spots. Someone had put a tasseled teal silk pillow at one end. Wood paneling covered every wall and the ceiling was done in a white popcorn finish. Outside of the decorative pillow, I felt as if I'd stepped back into a gritty 1970's cop movie. Yep. I was pretty sure I'd seen this exact same office on a Starsky and Hutch rerun a few years ago.

I sat my backpack down on the couch and pulled up my shirt, turning to Bishop so he could get another good view of the carnage.

He stared at my side. I stared at him. I got the strange feeling he was waiting for something to happen.

"Well, go ahead." He waved a hand at my waist.

"Go ahead and what?" I gaped at him.

"Fix it. No one can see in here." He waved at my waist again. I kept staring so he made an exasperated noise and turned around so his back faced me. "There. Is that better?"

Was I supposed to get naked? Dance the cha cha? What the fuck did he want me to do? "I thought you were going to bandage me up?" I tentatively asked. "Or maybe heal me."

Someone had healed me when I'd had my knee shot out a few weeks ago. The Fixers who'd grabbed me had been dead, so the only living beings in the room were me, Bishop, and Fluffy the Durft. I'd been out cold, and even if I'd been conscious I had no ability to speed-heal injuries. I doubted the rabid groundhog from hell was able to magically heal, even if he'd wanted to. That left Bishop.

He muttered something that sounded like "Fucking masochists" and spun around.

I'm not sure what I expected, but it wasn't him taking a stapler off his desk and coming at me with intent.

"Whoa, whoa!" I backed up. "Bandages. Or stitches. Needle and thread, buddy, not a stapler."

"Do I look like I have a sewing kit handy?" He clicked the stapler at me and I held up both hands, prepared to defend myself.

I took another step back. "HB offered to help. I'd rather she bandage the wound then you puncture the crap out of me with a desk stapler."

"HB doesn't have a sewing kit or bandages either." He put the stapler back. "It's not like we need ever to doctor up wounds around here."

Probably not. I imagined shifters healed quickly, especially if HB was any indication. She'd been a mangled mess on that warehouse floor, and here she was walking around two weeks later. Limping and scarred, yes, but still she'd healed far faster than any human I'd ever seen.

"How about this?"

I looked up to see Bishop holding a roll of duct tape and shuddered thinking how painful that was going to be to remove after the wound started to heal.

"How about just some more napkins? I'll clean it up with water, and use my belt again to hold them in place."

"Suit yourself." Bishop tossed the duct tape on the couch and went out of the office. While he was gone I had a chance to look around and basically snoop. The three ring binders were filled with papers that held a solid wall of text in a language I'd never seen before —single-spaced, double-sided. Not a chart or graph to be seen. The other papers were bills, a survey for some property up in the mountains, a flyer with special sale items from a liquor distributor. I saw a name on one bunch of papers that caught my eye, and pulled it out from the stack.

Something about a formal request to dissolve a pack, and re-establish under new leadership. Off in the margins in blue ink was "Need to take some action on this one!" The comment was signed HB.

I stuffed it back in the pile as Bishop came through the door. He kindly didn't mention my snooping. I took the bowl of water and clean rag from his hand and cleared a space for it on his desk. Then I took my shirt off.

It sounded sexier than it was. I was filthy, covered in both dried and fresh blood, and I didn't even have a pretty bra on. Sports bras covered more than most bathing suit tops, and didn't really do the whole lift-and-separate thing. Basically I was a mashed uni-boob with a smudge of dirt across the front of my chest.

Ignoring the dirt, I got to work on carefully cleaning the wound while Bishop opened a little first aid box and rooted around in it.

"Thought you didn't have one of those." I winced as I pressed the wet cloth to the still oozing wound.

"I didn't think we had one either. HB said she picked it up on a Costco run a few months back." He grumbled something under his breath. "I hate sending her to Costco for anything. She always comes back with eight hundred dollars' worth of jumbo-sized crap."

"You don't know you need eight hundred dollars' worth of jumbo-sized crap until you see it there on the shelf," I countered.

Costco was still open and in business. The only real difference between the mega store now versus two years ago was that the guards at the door eyeing your membership card were armed. I was pretty sure you wouldn't get shot trying to steal a ten-pound pork loin and a six- gallon jug of barbeque sauce anywhere outside of LA.

I missed Costco. Bea had let our membership lapse two years ago when the demons came. We'd tightened back on a lot of things since then. It seemed silly to pay for a membership to place when you couldn't afford to buy stuff in mega-sized containers.

"I get that we need the crate of paper towels and two crates of toilet paper, but an entire case of pumpkin spice coffee pods? And a four pack of sonic toothbrushes? And this thing?" He waved at the first aid kit .

I was glad she'd bought the first aid kit, especially when my only other alternatives were duct tape or a desk stapler.

"You've got pumpkin spice coffee pods?" I said with a grin. "Sold. I'll be here every morning from September first until spring."

He pulled out a box of Band-Aids from the first aid kit. "Good. Because if we don't get rid of that shit, I'm going to sit HB in a chair and make her drink it all herself in one go."

I took the box, selected a few, and started to open them.

"Here." Bishop knelt down beside me, taking the edge of the rag and blotting around the wound. With one hand he held the ragged edges together. I handed him the Band-Aid, and he secured it on the lower edge, snugging it tight on the top so the wound remained closed. Then he continued with a second and a third bandage.

I repressed a shiver at his touch. Looking down at the top of his head, I wondered how soft that wavy sun-streaked blond hair was. Having him kneeling down beside me made my mind detour to all sorts of fantasies. I could strip off my pants, sweep all those papers and binders off his desk, sit up on the edge and lean back while he drove himself into me.

Or better yet, he could kneel down and get busy with that sexy mouth.

"There." Bishop had finished with the Band-Aids and put a thick square of gauze over them. He looked up at me, and I saw the golden sparks in his ocean-blue eyes. For a second we were frozen in time, our gazes locked.

Then I sucked in a breath, turned my head, and picked up a roll of gauze. As I wrapped it around my waist, I wondered at this attraction I had for him. He was strong. Confident. Dangerous. When I'd said he wasn't my type, I'd meant his looks. His personality most definitely was my type—in spades. Which meant *I* probably wasn't his type at all.

He and HB were close. I could feel a bond between them that came with a long affectionate relationship. Were they partners? Lovers? Just really good friends? I couldn't believe that two such gorgeous people *wouldn't* have fallen into bed at one point or another. It was really going to suck if I continued to be desperately in lust for Bishop only to find out he was committed to a woman I admired, respected, and might even consider a friend.

What had he said when I'd offered sex in trade for his help in finding Nevarra? Had it been *if* I was ever in his bed it wouldn't be because I owed him? Or was it *when*? Either one hinted at a future possibility.

Yeah. I was totally grasping at the slightest bit of hope here.

I held the gauze while Bishop cut the end and taped it in place. The wound still hurt, but it was down to a dull ache now, muffled by layers of gauze and bandages. He'd done a good job. This should keep it from bleeding again unless I had to sprint a few blocks, jump over a fence, or fight off a pair of bounty hunters.

Not bad for a gunshot wound. I'd been lucky it was so

minor, even if I'd been unlucky enough to catch one of Karen's poorly aimed bullets.

He stood, his hand lingering for a moment on my waist. "Hope you've got another shirt. That one's trashed."

My laundry basket at home was filled with trashed clothes. When I got a few seconds in my day, I washed the blood out of them, hung them up to dry, then turned them over to Bea for repair. Some were usually beyond repair, but most were wearable again if I didn't mind having big Frankenstein-looking patches on my clothes.

"I've been carrying a spare in my backpack." I turned away from Bishop, feeling a sudden chill. He radiated heat, like someone who was in the throes of a high fever, or like someone who'd just come out of working at a kiln. He wasn't sweaty, just warm. It was the end of summer, which in LA meant it was still upwards of one hundred degrees on the regular. You wouldn't think standing next to a Bishop furnace would be comfortable, but it was.

The spare shirt I'd packed was a little snug, and the layers of gauze wrapped around my waist plus the bandages didn't do my silhouette any favors. It's not like I was going on a date though. I doubted Detective Juke would care if I looked a little thick around the middle.

"I've got something for you," I told Bishop as I pulled a wad of blood-stained cash out of my backpack. I counted my stash for the last few days. Nine hundred in total—seven just from the salvage this morning. I hated to hand the majority of it over to Bishop, but Bea had told me that we were good with food at home. She was back to work now that Sadie was healing, while Nevarra took care of her sister with some unusually eager help from Javier down the street.

If I paid the debts off, then we could start to save again. I hated being in debt to anyone, and I especially loathed owing Bishop money. Not because he was any sort of hard-ass when it came to me paying him. It was the fact that my pulse raced like a thoroughbred at the track every time he touched me that made me not want to be in debt to him.

I wanted to fuck him, and he'd made it clear that wouldn't happen while this obligation stood between us. It might not happen even after I'd paid up, but I was still going to give it my best shot.

And if he and HB were involved…well, I'd need to take an icy shower, dig that vibrator out of the dresser drawer, and never see this man again.

Actually, I should probably find that vibrator sooner rather than later.

I peeled a hundred in twenties off the stack, shoved it in my pants pocket, then handed the rest over. Bishop took the money, recounted it, then pulled a receipt book out of the mess on his desk. I took the receipt with some reluctance, not comfortable with this business-like formality. I wanted trust, and a receipt for what I'd paid, a declining balance on the ledger books, wasn't trust in my mind.

"Thanks for the doctoring," I told him as I stuffed the receipt and my ruined shirt into the backpack. "I almost brought you a necklace, but got chased off before I could take it off the dead guy."

"A necklace?" Bishop shot me an incredulous look. "You were going to give me a necklace?"

"Not to wear or anything. It was insanely ugly." I shrugged. "Could have been worth something at one of those places that buys crap jewelry and melts it down. Although with my luck it was probably electroplated and not even real gold."

Bishop grunted. "Do me a favor, and don't bring me ugly necklaces."

"Got it. I'll only bring you the pretty ones, not gaudy chains with big-ass dragon pendants." With a name like

Bishop, he was probably into rugged-looking crosses. Or maybe those leather and bead surfer necklaces.

If I'd been able to grab the necklace, I might have taken it to the Gray Dogs first. They were good about paying a finder's fee for salvage that was gang-related. Although I doubted ruby-eyed dragon pendants were a symbol a gang named the Gray Dogs would choose. Still, maybe one of them was a friend of the deceased and would want his hideous necklace to remember him by. A finder's fee would have been more than I'd would have gotten anywhere else.

But all that was moot anyway, since the ugly necklace was probably gracing the stocky neck of either Karen or Chad right now. I'd gotten what was important—the cash. And I'd managed to get away from both the salvage and the following attack with only a minor gunshot wound and some bruises.

Once more I thought about the two guys who'd tried to grab me under the bridge. Yes, I'd gotten away, but next time I might not.

And with five thousand dollars in bounty on my head, there would definitely be a next time.

* * *

Preorder Sinners on Sunset now!

Cornucopia

Unholy Pleasures

City of Lust

* * *

<u>Imp World Novels</u>

No Man's Land

Stolen Souls

Three Wishes

Northern Lights

Far From Center

Penance

* * *

<u>Northern Wolves</u>

Juneau to Kenai

Rogue

Winter Fae

Bad Seed

* * *

<u>The Templar Series</u>

Dead Rising

Last Breath

Bare Bones

Famine's Feast

Royal Blood

Dark Crossroads

* * *

<u>Accidental Witches Series</u>

Brimstone and Broomsticks

Warmongers and Wands

Death and Divination

Hell and Hexes

Minions and Magic

 Fiends and Familiars

Devils and the Dead (2021)

* * *

<u>White Lightning Series</u>

Wooden Nickels

Bum's Rush

Clip Joint

Jake Walk

Trouble Boys

Packing Heat (TBD)

ACKNOWLEDGMENTS

Sending a big shout-out to Melissa Marr who read my very clunky first draft, saw the diamond in the rough. Her suggestions made this book really shine!

Thank you to my friends and family who were my sounding boards and helped me connect with resources as I did my research.

I really appreciate the help of Adam Richardson from the Writer's Detective Bureau who gave me a cop's view on how the police might work in a dystopian LA.

Also, big thanks to my copyeditors Kimberly Cannon and Jennifer Cosham whose eagle eyes catch the typos and keep my comma problem in line, and to Damonza for once again providing me with an amazing cover design.

ABOUT THE AUTHOR

Debra lives in a little house in the woods of Maryland with her sons and two slobbery bloodhounds. On a good day, she jogs and horseback rides, hopefully managing to keep the horse between herself and the ground. Her only known super power is 'Identify Roadkill'.

For more information:
www.debradunbar.com